"BUCKINGHAM PALACE IS
NOT AMUSED."
LIZ SMITH, *NEW YORK DAILY NEWS*

"A 'KISS AND TELL' VERSION OF LIFE WITH
PRINCE CHARLES, THE BOOK HAS RAISED A
STORM OF CONTROVERSY IN ENGLAND."
COLUMBUS CITIZEN-JOURNAL

"ONE FEELS GUILTY READING THESE
REVELATIONS."
CHRISTIAN SCIENCE MONITOR

"HAS CAUSED A STIR ON BOTH SIDES
OF THE ATLANTIC."
CLEVELAND PLAIN DEALER

"NOW FOR THE FIRST TIME, SOMEONE CLOSE
TO BUCKINGHAM PALACE REVEALS WHAT
GOES ON UPSTAIRS AT THE PALACE."
BOSTON HERALD

"EXCITING, REVEALING . . . BANNED IN
BRITAIN."
WASHINGTON POST

ROYAL SERVICE

MY TWELVE YEARS AS VALET TO PRINCE CHARLES

STEPHEN P. BARRY

AVON
PUBLISHERS OF BARD, CAMELOT, DISCUS AND FLARE BOOKS

AVON BOOKS
A division of
The Hearst Corporation
1790 Broadway
New York, New York 10019

Picture Editor: Vincent Virga

Cover photographs courtesy of Colour Library International USA Ltd.

Published by arrangement with Macmillan Publishing Co., Inc.
Library of Congress Catalog Card Number: 82-22844
ISBN: 0-380-67397-5

The Macmillan Publishing Co., Inc., edition contains the following Library of Congress Cataloging in Publication Data:

  Barry, Stephen P., 1948–
Royal service.
1. Charles, Prince of Wales, 1948–
2. Great Britain—Princes and princesses—Biography.
3. Barry, Stephen P., 1948– . 4. Valets—Great
Britain—Biography. I. Title.
DA591.A33B37 1983   941.085′092′4[B]   82-22844

First Avon Printing, January, 1984

Printed in the U. S. A.

K-R 10 9 8 7 6 5 4

Contents

ROYAL SERVICE

$\mathcal{E}$VERY TIME I met people both in England and around the world as I traveled with Prince Charles, during my years of service at Buckingham Palace, one of the first questions invariably was, "What are they *really* like?" And I must admit, even in 1983, Prince Charles and the British Royal family still retain a unique mystique. But, despite the eyes of the world always on them, they are still very private people.

When it was announced that I was leaving the Palace after twelve years of Royal service with the Prince of Wales, I received many letters and telephone calls from the media asking for interviews and making offers for stories about my life with Prince Charles. This used to amuse him a lot. "What's today's latest offer, Stephen?" he'd ask, and when I showed him the letter, he would gasp, "As much as that," in an amazed tone. One day he turned to me and grinned. "How much do you suppose they'd pay me if I wrote about my twelve years with *you?!!*"

Working for the Prince was a marvelous experience as you will see when you read on.

1

The Wedding

WHEN I WENT into Prince Charles' bedroom to wake him on the morning of July 29, 1981, I found there was no need. For the first time I could remember in twelve years of calling Prince Charles, he was already lying there wide awake.

I went to run his bath and as usual I turned on the radio. Already the prewedding program had begun.

The Prince was excited, yet he wasn't nervous at all. The buildup had been enormous, but as the future King of England he had been preparing for this moment all his life. Outside in the Mall we could hear the sound of the curious crowds and see them waving banners. The slightest motion of a curtain in the windows of the Palace was all that was needed for everyone out there to cheer and shout.

Prince Charles bathed, dressed in a pair of cords and a shirt, and ate breakfast leisurely, and at 9:30 managed to find time to say good-bye to Paul Officer, his longtime policeman companion who was leaving. In his rooms the atmosphere was one of complete calm. He could not have been more relaxed.

By 10:20 I had him dressed in his naval uniform and ready for the carriage ride to St. Paul's and his bride. He turned from the mirror and said, "It's been a long time, but at last. . . . Thank you for all you've done, Stephen."

"Thank *you*, sir," I said.

It was nearly time to leave.

"Is everything ready for Broadlands?" he wanted to know. The newlyweds were to spend the first two days of their honeymoon at the home of Lord Mountbatten, who had been Charles' godfather and almost a grandfather to him.

"Everything's under control," I told him.

"Good." He was quiet for a moment and then said, "How are you getting to St. Paul's?"

"I'll follow you, sir," I said.

He laughed. "Let's hope we don't both get lost."

I walked downstairs with the Prince and then out to the crowded Grand Entrance of the Palace. (This entrance isn't visible from the Mall.) Prince Andrew was already waiting in the hall, and the Queen and Prince Philip were about to leave for St. Paul's. All the staff who were not going to the cathedral filled the entrance, waiting to wave everyone off. They clapped when the Prince came down the stairs, then cheered as his carriage drove away.

I then ran through the Bow Room, the main room

leading to the garden, and jumped into a waiting car
at the garden entrance steps. As we drove off on the
shorter route along the embankment to St. Paul's, all
the way I could hear the crowds cheering and clap-
ping as the procession went by.

The Master of the Household was in the car with
me. I remembered all those years ago when his prede-
cessor had employed me—such a long time ago.
"Well, it's finally happened, Stephen," he said. "We
can only hope they'll be very happy."

All I could think was who would have guessed the
previous summer at Cowes that today we would sit in
St. Paul's Cathedral, watching the Prince marry Lady
Diana, so short a time after they met.

I took my seat in the cathedral before the Prince had
arrived as there was nothing for me to do at this
point. Lady Diana, of course, had her hairdresser and
makeup girl waiting, but the Royal men do not, as it is
sometimes believed, wear any makeup on state occasions. In fact they don't need to as they all seem to
have perfect skins. The Prince will not even put on
any makeup for a photographic session, and I can remember how amazed he was at the way Princess
Anne looked at her wedding. "She's far too made
up," he said when he saw her.

There can be few people in Britain (or for that matter in much of the rest of the world) who did not see
the Prince's wedding ceremony on TV, but actually
being there was something extraordinarily special.
St. Paul's was bathed in light, magnificent flowers
abounded everywhere, and gorgeous music soared to
the cathedral dome. Everyone craned his neck to rec-

ognize everyone else, which somehow made it like the sort of wedding any large family might have.

The ride back to the Palace in the procession after the service with the rest of the guests was an unbelievable experience. From the car where I sat with the Prince's Household I could see a sea of faces. Smiling, happy faces. The sun was shining fitfully, brightening waving flags. We could hear cheers, an incredible noise, and were aware that the crowd was trying to identify who we were. They didn't seem disappointed that we weren't anyone in particular. That day I think the people would have cheered anything.

The car dropped us at the Privy Purse entrance to the Palace, and we went to the forecourt for a very privileged view of the balcony scene. As we shared the sight of the Prince kissing the Princess with the handicapped people whom the Prince had requested be looked after in the courtyard, I was deeply aware of watching a slice of history.

The wedding breakfast back at the Palace was a family affair. None of the Household went, but we had our own special lunches in the Palace.

Then the Prince and his new Princess came upstairs to change before they set off in the Royal coach for Waterloo and the start of their honeymoon. Briefly they each went their own ways—she to change in her own little suite with her mother to help her, while I was waiting to assist the Prince in his own bachelor rooms.

"Did you see the service properly?" he asked as I put his naval uniform back on a hanger.

"I had a splendid view. It was absolutely *wonderful*," I said. "Did you enjoy Kiri Te Kanawa?"

"I could only hear her," he said. "I was signing the register at the time."

I'd put out his favorite gray pin-striped suit and a fresh shirt, and he changed quickly, talking all the time he was dressing. "I'm so pleased it went so well," he said. "Did you think it went well?"

What a question! Outside the people were still calling for him and the Princess.

He then went to his study to pack up the papers he wanted to take with him. Even on honeymoon his Royal work would not cease.

He peeped through the curtains. "There was a man out there who had painted his head like a Union Jack," he said. "Incredible!" He was genuinely full of wonder at the people's response. "Are they never going home?" he said, amazed. "I can't believe it." He turned away from the window. "Are you coming to see me off?"

"Yes, sir," I told him. "I'll be down in the quadrangle with everyone else."

"I didn't mean that," he said. "Come to the station."

Times had changed! This time he ran down the corridor—he runs everywhere—to collect the Princess from her rooms, while I rushed downstairs with his briefcase to the Rolls. Again, Sir John Miller, the Crown Equerry, and I followed them through the cheering crowds to Waterloo Station where the Royal couple were setting off for Broadlands.

The atmosphere at Waterloo was very informal. The Princess impulsively kissed several people, and just before they got on the train, the Prince said,

"Thanks for everything, Stephen. I'll see you on Saturday at the airport."

"I'll be there, sir," I said.

That Saturday I was to join up with them again for the honeymoon. The Prince had graciously asked his old team to accompany him. The group included John Maclean, his policeman; his Equerry, John Winter; me; and the Princess' maid and newly acquired policeman, Graham Smith. It was a special thank-you to us all for the extra work over the past months.

I drove back to the Palace through the streets where people were slowly drifting away, streets which were still colorful with bright papers, Union Jacks—the debris of an all-out London celebration. Street sweepers were cleaning, and when we arrived at the Palace, one of the footmen came up to me.

"There's something for you in the kitchen," he said.

I had no idea what it was but went to find out.

There was a small bottle of champagne. It was from the Prince.

❧ 2 ❧

The Job
by Royal Appointment

THE PRINCE OF WALES was in his sitting room at Windsor Castle—a room right above the Queen's in the Queen's Tower, and I was waiting nervously for a footman to announce me. It was July 1970. James MacDonald, the late King George's valet, was with me, and together we walked into the Prince's cluttered sitting room where he seemed to be working on some papers.

"This is Stephen Barry, Your Royal Highness," James said.

I bowed, and the Prince looked at me with his bright blue eyes. He said, "You're going to have a go at being my valet, are you?"

"I'd like to, sir," I replied.

He just nodded. "I hope you'll be happy, and I hope I don't drive you mad."

I was still nervous, but I managed to say, "I'm very honored and I'm sure you won't. Thank you very much for appointing me."

It was practically the first proper conversation I had ever had with the Prince. In the three years that I had been a footman in the Queen's service, I had hardly seen him. He had been at school in Gordonstoun, and later at Trinity College in Cambridge. He always came to Windsor for Christmas, and sometimes he managed to get over to Sandringham in February when he could get away from Trinity.

I had been in Royal service since September 1966. I had come to the conclusion that I wanted a change. I thought I would like to become a valet because it seemed to me that valets had very pleasant lives, dashing off here, there, and everywhere with their masters.

The Duke of Edinburgh's valet, Joe Pearce, was a friend of mine, and I had decided to have a word with him. I knew that James MacDonald was retiring, and it was rumored that the Prince, who was leaving the University, was going to employ his own valet for the first time. James had been looking after him part-time, and it was assumed that before James left he was going to find someone to train to look after Prince Charles.

Becoming the Prince's valet was a particularly sought-after job. Most Royal staff would give their eyeteeth to work for him. Everyone at the Palace loved the Prince and had done so since he was a small child. No one had a bad word to say for him, a unique occurrence in the kind of enclosed world in which we worked.

Even staff who had worked at the Palace in previous years and left long before had guessed that the Prince would now be needing someone and had written in, asking to be considered for the post. Many people who leave Royal service later feel they have made a mistake and wish they could come back. One is so protected working for the Royals that it can be difficult to function on one's feet outside. And to return to that protected environment and work for Prince Charles, as well, was extremely tempting to Royal servants—past and present.

I landed the job because it just so happened that I was in the right place at the right time and because I was twenty-one, the same age as the Prince. I had let MacDonald know that I was keen for the job, and one day in early 1970 he said to me, "I need someone to help me with Prince Charles. He's away a lot, but there'll be enough for you to do."

He did not have the last word on the selection for the post of valet, but he had let my interest be known to the Prince's Private Secretary, Squadron Leader David Checketts. The Squadron Leader sent for me to make sure I was serious. I assured him I was and then he asked the Master of the Household if it would be all right for me to be released on a temporary basis to see if I were good enough. The Master said he would be delighted to give me the opportunity, and that was more or less that.

That brief conversation with Prince Charles was the nearest I had to a formal interview for the job. I wasn't a stranger to him as I had been around the Palace for so long. He would have remembered me from the days when I had been the Nursery Footman when his two younger brothers, Prince Andrew and Prince Edward, had been small. I had always found him very pleasant, and I was also fascinated to know what really made him tick. Now I had the opportunity to find out.

The Prince called me Stephen from the start. The Royals always call their policemen, pages, chauffeurs, and older servants by their surnames. Footmen and valets are called by Christian names. No one, of course, would dream of calling the Royal family by *their* Christian names.

Every Royal male has two valets, a senior and a junior one, so I wasn't left to swim alone in the deep water. I had James MacDonald to guide me and teach me what had to be done, and my personal circumstances began to improve immediately. I had gone several steps up the ladder. I still stayed in my very pleasant rooms at Buckingham Palace. I never changed quarters in any of the other Royal houses. As it happened, my room at Windsor was not far from the Prince's—just down the stairs and along the corridor. When he rang his bell, I could be there as quickly as it was possible to run up a few stairs.

At the Palace my rooms were quite a distance from his, but it did not matter because the Palace itself is really more of an office than a home. We work there, and in the evening when the day's work is done the staff go back to their own apartments and rooms. If I wanted to have people in for drinks, it was much easier living in what I call the staff area rather than be embarrassed by bumping into the Royals in their corridors.

Most evenings are off-duty when in residence at Buckingham Palace; one can go out or have friends in—just like living anywhere. When the Royal family are staying at Windsor, Balmoral, or Sandringham, their staff are on full-time duty, so then it is more sensible to live fairly close to their principal Royal.

At Buckingham Palace the Prince's rooms were on the front of the building and overlooked the Mall. I'd acquired two sunny rooms with a shared kitchen and bathroom at the back, with a view over the gardens, and I didn't want to give them up. In any case I soon realized that we spent so little time at the Palace that there was no great point in moving myself. I merely had to be around when the Prince was in residence. There was no real reason to be close at hand, because more often than not he was in the city on engagements during the week and away on the weekends.

Of course, I was enormously proud to get the job. There was quite a lot of envy. People said, "Why did *you* get it?" but the old brigade at the Palace thought I had a good chance of making a success. And the pleasantest thing was that I immediately went from being a number to becoming a face and a name. It was very exciting.

I didn't start working with the Prince straight away as he went off to Canada with the Queen for two weeks. They were visiting the Northwest Territories and I, back in London, was learning the basics of the job.

Before he had gone, the Prince had said to me,

"When we go up to Balmoral, would you like to come shooting, as my loader?"

I liked the sound of this and said, "Yes, sir."

"Right," he said. "I'll tell the office to make sure you go on a course at Purdey's [the gunmakers] so you know what you're doing. We don't want you killing anyone."

He knew I had no experience with shotguns or any other kind of gun for that matter, and it was only sensible that the chap standing behind him for the day, holding his gun, knew how not to let the thing go off. The course was a simple one designed to show how lethal a shotgun can be and to teach basic shooting. I'd never be as good a shot as the Prince, but I finished up able to hold my own with him.

In that fortnight I learned my way around his rooms and his possessions. And when he came back from Canada, two more weeks went by while I became more and more used to working for him, until he called me in and said, "We're going down to Cowes tonight."

I was a bit surprised—I thought James would have gone with him, but I was pleased. This was my first time working for him totally on my own.

We were joining the Royal yacht, *Britannia*, and he had decided to drive himself down. There I was in the back of his brand new Aston Martin (which is his pride and joy) while one of his policemen, Paul Officer, took the passenger seat. The Prince loves to drive, and he drives very well with tremendous consideration and caution. Still it was a funny feeling to be sitting in the back of his car thinking, "Gosh! The

Prince of Wales is driving *me!*'' It took a while to sink in.

He always plays music when he is driving and that night we sailed down the M3 to Cowes listening to Handel's *Messiah*. He had said, turning briefly to look at me, ''Do you mind this sort of music?''

''Not in the least,'' I said, hardly in a position to tap him on the shoulder after five minutes and say, ''I don't like that, thanks. I'd rather listen to the Beatles.''

I had packed his clothes for Cowes, under James' supervision, excitedly since this was my first trip, but I felt more at home when we arrived at the *Britannia* late that night. I knew everyone aboard as I'd been on the yacht for nine weeks when I went to Australia with the Queen as a footman in April that year. My accommodation had changed though. Instead of being in a cabin below decks with the footmen and other staff, I was suddenly up on the same deck as the Prince. Very comfortable it was, too.

Life generally became more comfortable. I was kept on my footman's salary for three months while I was on trial, and then I was given the proper valet's salary of £98. My living standard rose. I was taken out of my uniform—pumps and tailcoat went forever—and put into suits, which the Prince paid for.

Cowes was a very easy introduction to becoming a valet. He just used to go sailing all day long, for the short time we were there, and about the only piece of clothing that was of any importance was his raincoat. I was just around, taking advantage of the chance to start the slow process of getting to know him.

While he was sailing, those of us who worked for

him would take a motorboat and go ashore. At this
stage I was very cautious about getting back well before he joined the yacht. He'd say he would be back
about five, so I was careful to be ready and waiting at
four. Gradually I got to know his timings. I learned
how to be there just before I was required so that in
between times I could get on with my own life.

Cowes only lasts three or four days for the Royals
and then the yacht sails off on its usual routine up to
Southampton where the Queen gets aboard with the
younger children. Prince Philip was on board already,
of course. He is a Commodore at Cowes and very
much in charge, but the Queen never goes to Cowes.
She is not at all interested in sailing. We would pick
her up along with the little Princes and then set off for
their Scottish holiday, stopping daily on the way,
cruising the Western Isles.

I remember my first trip to Scotland on the yacht.
We sailed to Milford Haven where the Queen was to
open a huge new petrol storage plant. Then on to the
Western Isles where the *Britannia* would anchor. It
was my first experience of the endless Royal picnics
that they so enjoy, however inclement the weather.
Picnics to a Royal are as banquets to the rest of us. We
would finally leave the ship at Aberdeen and join a
fleet of cars to Balmoral.

After three years as a footman, it was strange to go
back to Scotland as the Prince's valet with my only responsibility to him. I was absolutely my own boss.
The only person I had to think about was the Prince.

My lessons at Purdey's paid off. I went out with the
guns, acting as the Prince's loader. For this he bought
me a shooting suit with tweed plus fours and the

jacket in the Balmoral tartan. And there I was out on the grouse moors with Royals, dogs, beaters, ghillies—Scottish gamekeepers—all around, and birds falling out of the sky.

But I discovered there was **rather** more to being the loader than just swopping guns and putting in cartridges. I had to keep up with him on a shoot. My God, I was stiff after the first few days! Muscles I didn't know I owned were hurting. He always seemed to land up at the top of a hill while I was struggling behind. "Can you keep up?" he asked after the first couple of days, half-mocking, half-concerned. The ghillies were fortunately very kind, and they'd say to me, "Go that way, it's quicker and less painful." The Prince goes straight up mountains like a goat—not easy for those who aren't so fit.

What was a pleasure on that Balmoral holiday was seeing my employers totally relaxed. I found myself sitting down with the Prince on the grouse moor with perhaps Prince Philip, talking about how the day was going. The Queen, whom one always imagines in tiaras and ballgowns, would be wearing an old-friend Burberry macintosh, a headscarf, muddy rubber boots, and be wrapped up against the rarely kind Scottish weather.

I never stayed at Balmoral for the entire holiday. I would try to take my own when the Prince was holidaying himself so that the important work routines would not be disturbed. I had five weeks a year off, but often that stretched to much longer. If he were going away for weeks and I wasn't needed, he'd say, "I won't be wanting you, Stephen. Why don't you go off somewhere yourself?'' And I would take myself off to France for a few days.

That first Balmoral holiday as his valet, though, I was almost reluctant to leave as I was so fascinated with everything that was going on. Being a valet was definitely better than being a footman.

◈ 3 ◈

Going to Work at Buckingham Palace

*I*WAS EIGHTEEN YEARS OLD in 1966 when I first went to work at Buckingham Palace. Prince Charles was also eighteen and away at school in Gordonstoun. Prince Andrew and Prince Edward were six and two respectively, and Princess Anne a horse-mad sixteen-year-old.

I had left school at sixteen with no real idea of what I wanted to do and found myself selling advertising space for the Rank Organization. It wasn't a bad job, but I felt strongly that I didn't want to work in an office for the rest of my life.

Royalty had always fascinated me from the time my parents had taken me to watch the Trooping the Colour when I was seven years old. The pageantry, the precision and emotion of the occasion had really excited me. I'd stood on pavements many times since watching processions go by, and on a sheer impulse I telephoned the Palace—the number was in the phone book—to ask about available jobs. I wanted to be a part of the pomp and circumstance of monarchy, and working for the institution seemed like the best way.

The Personnel Office at the Palace advised me to write to the Sergeant Footman. I did and posted my letter off without many expectations.

Back came a formal little note in a few days' time asking me to present myself to him for an interview. I was living in Hammersmith with my widowed mother, and I hadn't told her what I was up to because I didn't want to build up my own hopes by even talking about it. But there was an envelope with the Royal crest stamped on the back lying on our doormat. My mother was intrigued, to say the least.

I didn't really think I had a chance of getting a post. I was under the impression that the jobs were handed down through relations and families, but though there are families who have been Royal servants for generations, many, like me, are natural Royalists who work for the monarchy for the same romantic reasons that I did.

When I went for the interview I wished I could have gone into the Palace through the imposing iron gates on the Mall, but the staff entrance and the office where I had been directed are on the side, near the Royal Mews. The office itself is quite ordinary, but when I was taken along what is called the Masters corridor, I was transported into a wonderful world. I

22

was walking on the thickest carpet I had ever seen, the walls were lined with pictures, gilt glinting from the frames, and the impression was of amazing peace. Outside was traffic and noise, but the Palace has this wonderful tranquil silence. I felt I was in a gentleman's club at that moment, but I was to find out later that the Palace is, in spite of the hush, a very busy place. It is huge, but easy to navigate as it is built on a rectangle.

People do get lost sometimes, but not as often as they do at Windsor Castle. At Windsor, people have been known to be lost for hours, particularly in the days when the Royal family held State visits there. I was always finding some poor official or dignitary from a far-flung land, wandering around, totally lost and attempting to tell me in his best English where he thought he ought to be.

At the first interview the Sergeant Footman took me to see the Master of the Queen's Household, but nobody seemed to ask me anything much. They were judging me entirely on appearance. The point which concerned them the most was if I were tall enough to be a footman. Footmen have to be tall, and more important in those days, they had to be paired with another footman of exactly the same height.

The Sergeant Footman went off and came back with another footman, dressed in his tailcoat, black trousers, and wing collar. "Stand back to back," the Sergeant instructed us both.

We did as we were told. He peered at us and said, "That'll do. You match." The other footman who was to be my "pair" for the next three years was then

23

dismissed, and I was taken to see the Master of the Household, Sir Mark Millbank.

He didn't say anything to me but just listened to what the Sergeant Footman had to say about my background and nodded. "You'll be hearing from us," he said.

A couple of weeks elapsed, and then I received the letter telling me the job was mine at £28 a month, all found. In September 1966, clutching my luggage, I went to live in Buckingham Palace. My first room was on the front, overlooking the Mall, and the first thing I did after I arrived was to be measured by the Palace tailor for my livery. Then I was taken down to one of the basement rooms where all the State livery with its gold trimmings is kept. These incredibly ornate costumes are kept for years in stock. The expense of refitting each page and footman with new livery would be astronomical. The Sergeant Footman found me one that fit. It was a scarlet coat with gold trimmings, red velvet breeches, and black leather pumps. And very uncomfortable they were, too. Years before, he said, I would have had to wear a wig or powdered my hair when wearing the State livery, but happily they didn't do that anymore.

The everyday livery was much less exotic. I had to wear a black tailcoat or, on special occasions, a scarlet tailcoat. We wore this about the Palace or when standing on the back of Royal carriages, delivering and collecting Ambassadors when they came to present their credentials to the Queen.

Carriages are great fun. We got ourselves dressed up in our scarlet tailcoats and off we went, round to the Mews where the carriages waited. We were not supposed to talk once we were standing in place on the footplate, but people in the streets would grin and wave at us while we looked straight ahead and pretended we hadn't noticed. We were all young, and sometimes I'm afraid we giggled.

After dropping the Ambassador off at the Palace, we'd hang around in the courtyard until it was time to take him back to his Embassy after presenting his credentials. There would usually be a reception going on at his place, and we'd be given a glass of champagne or two—they always sent out a tray of drinks for the coachman and footmen.

Happily the horses knew their way home.

You had to learn to keep your balance while standing outside on the carriage, particularly, of course, for the State openings of Parliament when we wore full livery with a huge tricorn hat and a sword. It was a marvelous feeling to be helping in the ceremony. In the early days, I was usually on the back of Princess Anne's carriage or Princess Margaret's, looking straight ahead as they waved to the crowds.

Being part of all that tradition was the best thing about the job. I remember my first night at the Palace. Before getting into bed, I stood staring down the Mall and thinking, "How exciting. I'm on the inside looking out."

Of course, I longed to see the Queen, but it didn't happen for a while. I was being shown around by another footman while I learned the ropes, and we were by the garden entrance one day, where the Royal family usually comes in and out of the Palace. This door leads on to Constitution Hill, near big black gates where spectators can see Royal cars disappear. The

Royals like using this entrance because it is private and opens on to the gardens.

In came the Queen that day, returning from an official lunch, and I was struck by her tremendous presence. There is something about her that says loud and clear that she is someone of importance.

I watched her arrive, trying not to stare, and she stopped and spoke to her Lady-in-Waiting. Then her Page showed her into a lift, and she disappeared to her own apartments on the first floor.

She had come down to London from Balmoral breaking her holiday for the Commonwealth Prime Ministers' Conference. I never knew why but the Sergeant Footman decided I could go back to Scotland with her and her personal Household. I'd only been at the Palace for five minutes so I always consider I really started to work properly at Balmoral.

We traveled up to Scotland on the Royal train. Each member of the Royal family always uses his or her own carriage. The one the Prince uses was once Winston Churchill's. The staff live in a first-class compartment, with a sleeper, of course. There wasn't anything for me to do—the Queen had her own footman with her—and we trundled north in a very comfortable fashion. The Queen had an engagement at Peterborough, so we stopped there and then carried on overnight to Scotland. I sat enjoying the views. I'd never been to Scotland before. When we arrived I found I had to look after a member of the Queen's Household. I was assigned to Lord Plunket, a delightful man who was a great friend of the Queen and acted as her Equerry. Sadly he died in 1975.

I was trained to look after him—acting rather more

as a valet than a footman, as I had to care for his clothes. I liked him very much. He had a marvelous sense of humor and great elegance. I remember him coming back from stalking one day, very cold, very wet, and collapsing into a chair, exhausted.

"Oh, Stephen," he said. "They call this pleasure?"

He like many others had fallen into the trap of doing what the Royals like to do—regardless of whether they enjoy it themselves.

It seemed to me that very first time that Balmoral was a a very grand place. Having come from an ordinary suburban home, to walk through endless corridors and into large rooms seemed very splendid, though by Royal standards it isn't at all, I realized later.

The house is the Royal family's Scottish summer home. They use it for ten weeks of the year and it is quite beautiful. Very cold outside, but comfortable and warm in the house. Most of the furnishings, and even the gold and white wallpaper with "V Rex" embossed on it, were left over from Queen Victoria's days. I doubt if the house has changed much since then.

I stayed in Scotland for six weeks and then came back to Buckingham Palace with a lot more confidence. I was beginning to know my way around the Palace, and I felt I'd mastered Balmoral, and I was getting to know the other staff and the members of the Household. Back in London I was still partly assigned to Lord Plunket when he was attending the Queen, but for the rest of the time being a footman at the Palace is rather like being a messenger in an office or a page in a hotel. There's a lot of time spent sitting around waiting for something to do. I took boxes and letters around to different members of the Household but rarely got out. If a letter had to be delivered somewhere in London, the Sergeant Footman would use one of the outdoor messengers for the job.

The Queen's Footmen—she has two of them—were exempt from that sort of thing. Their basic job was to look after Her Majesty's corgis and do any running around that's necessary. If the Queen needed a letter posted, they'd bring it to one of us humbler footmen to deal with. The pecking order was very precise.

Since I started working at the Palace a great deal has changed. More and more of the rooms have been taken over as offices as the business of monarchy becomes more complex. The type of staff employed has changed, too. Today it would be more difficult for someone like me, with no training, to get a Palace post. The staff now come mostly from college and catering schools. Or they have been in hotel work and are already trained or qualified.

In my day it was different. You could start as young as fourteen as a servant's hall boy, and probably wouldn't see anyone but the footmen and the pages for the first two years. You would be trained by waiting on them.

After, the progression was to looking after the Queen's Household as a junior footman. Perhaps here I should explain exactly who the Queen's Household are.

At the head is the Lord Chamberlain, Lord Maclean, but the day-to-day running is in the hands of the Master of the Household (who is in charge of all Royal residences). He also employs all staff. He is rather like the managing director of a large corporation and is always high born. At the time of writing, the Master is Admiral Sir Peter Ashmore, an ex-naval man.

Other members of the Household are very often friends of the Queen or her family, people she has known all her life who have been brought in to act as ladies-in-waiting or courtiers, like her Equerry. There are four full-time ladies-in-waiting and a lot of extras. And two equerries—one who acts as Deputy Master.

She has a private secretary, and two assistant private secretaries. Today these tend to come from a civil service background.

Another section of her Household are the Privy Purse—a group of people, headed by the Keeper of the Privy Purse—who guide her in financial matters.

The head of the Press office is a member of the Household, as are several members of the Lord Chamberlain's office.

Another section, which she takes a great personal interest in, is the Royal Mews, headed by the Crown Equerry—Sir John Miller.

The Master would sit down to lunch every day with other members of the Household and be attended by the junior footmen—like me—who were really practicing. But today things have changed. People are rarely waited on in the Palace. For years now, at her express wish, the Queen has had her food served on a hot plate and then she helps herself. When she has finished eating, she rings for her coffee and the tray is taken away.

Everyone now follows the same system of "serve yourself" food—including the Prince, who before his marriage was inclined to eat alone, catching up on TV shows that he had missed. He has his own video, and one of my jobs was to record anything he particularly wanted to see that was shown when he had an engagement.

At Balmoral or Sandringham the routine is different, because at these homes there is almost always a house party in progress and proper meals are served with silver, linen, and butlers—exactly as one would imagine royalty had their meals served.

Almost immediately after I started work I was transferred to helping in the Royal nursery. My job was to look after Nanny—the lovely Mabel Anderson—and the two little Princes. I didn't have to do anything personal for the children—Mabel had her nurserymaid for all the minor things—but I did try to help keep Andrew amused.

It was no easy task. He was a very energetic child—indeed, one might say a boisterous child. It didn't take him long to absolutely exhaust his Nanny who was no longer that young. He was into everything. Always trying to follow us downstairs where he wasn't allowed, tugging at the footmen's tailcoats, climbing to reach anything that had been put out of his reach. He had a very strong personality and he was extremely good-looking even then.

"He's going to be one of the best of the Royals," Mabel Anderson always said. And she should know. She was Nanny to all the Queen's children.

She adored him, and he could get away with almost anything. He was inclined to give the grown-ups a thump occasionally, generally when Nanny wasn't looking.

Years later when Prince Charles saw his brother

give me a friendly whack across the shoulders in the corridors of the Palace one day, he said reprovingly, "Andrew, don't hit Stephen."

"But Charles," said Andrew. "I've always hit Stephen."

It was true. He had.

It was just as well that Edward was a quiet child. Two Andrews would have been too much for one nursery.

In those days we called the children by their Christian names. The Queen liked us to do this in an effort to keep them as natural as possible. I called them Andrew and Edward until they were fourteen and before going to Gordonstoun School. After that they became Prince Andrew and Prince Edward. Then the situation changed again when they reached eighteen. The Lord Chamberlain's office sent out a note saying, "Her Majesty the Queen wishes that Prince Andrew on reaching his eighteenth birthday, should be addressed as His Royal Highness."

I had to learn to graduate from saying Andrew to Prince Andrew and then to Your Royal Highness. A strange feeling when one has watched them as little children crawling on the nursery floor.

But Palace staff are trained to take such changes in their stride.

My job in the nursery went on for two years and the surroundings themselves were very cozy. The nursery itself is a big room with high ceilings and long windows, but there were lots of toys about with small-scale furniture for the children to use. Much of this had been handed down from Charles' and Anne's days. Each child had his own bedroom. Now the nursery quarters are out of use. The playroom has been turned into a sitting room. The night nursery, which Prince Edward used as a baby, is now his bedroom, with grown-up furniture, of course.

On Mabel Anderson's day off, the Queen would come in the evening and babysit with the two children. She'd arrive in the nursery, settle herself down in Mabel's chair to watch TV or to read, and wait quietly until Mabel came back. Her own page and footman would attend her, bringing her dinner, and if the children woke she'd go and soothe them back to sleep.

I always felt she enjoyed those evenings. Buckingham Palace is very much the "office" for the Queen, her work load there is enormous, which means she saw very little of the children. Their family times together were at Balmoral, Windsor, or Sandringham, which the Royals regard as their real homes.

I had an easy start working in the nursery. It was very good grounding for me. I was getting to know the Royal Household, and they were getting to know me. Prince Charles was in and out of the nursery all the time when he was home—always at mealtimes. He particularly liked to have nursery breakfast there, and he was very fond of Mabel Anderson, a tall Scottish lady, just a year older than the Queen.

She, in fact, is one of the very few people I have ever seen him give a kiss. Mabel was always given one, and he was a welcome sight in her life. She had brought him up from a baby and probably knows him better than anyone.

When Prince Andrew and Prince Edward were small he liked to play with them, and they adored him. He enjoyed the big brother role because the Duke was away so much when they were tiny that they rarely saw their father. The Queen would be busy downstairs being Queen, so he was the only one of the family whom they saw in the mornings. He still tries to retain his big brother status even though Andrew is now taller than he is. He and Princess Anne never got on that well—she was always impatient with him.

"Oh, come *on*, Charles," you'd hear her shouting at him. She was always complaining that he was slow in those days.

When I got to know the Prince well, I realized he likes anything that he calls "cozy" and the nursery is nearer to being cozy than anywhere else in the Palace. It even has an open fire—and there are only two left in the building that actually work. One is in the Queen's sitting room, the other one in the nursery.

The turnover of staff is quite rapid at the Palace. The pay is not very high and many young people apply for jobs only because they are intrigued to see what goes on. A lot quickly lose interest and go. But it is a good place to start if you come to London as a young person. All food, hot water, light, and clothing are provided, and no one could have a better address!

The fast turnover means that the ambitious ones in Royal service can get promoted quite quickly. My chance came when the Queen went to Malta in 1967 for a State visit. She always takes some members of the Household and her own staff to look after her on an overseas tour, plus a footman. And the Household take a footman to look after them. This time I was experienced enough to be chosen.

My job on that trip was to attend the Queen's Equerry, Major Howard. It was my first experience of traveling overseas, and as it was quite a small party of people I got to know the Duke's valet. Perhaps this gave me the ambition to become a valet myself. He seemed to have such a pleasant life. I'd never had any conversations with the Royals' valets before because they were higher in the pecking order. I still had to be careful because I didn't quite understand the structure of the staff.

Though the Malta trip in itself was very short and not very interesting, being away I got to know people much better; it did widen my horizons.

I had become friendly with a chap named Joe Pearce who was valet to the Duke of Edinburgh, and in 1968, after two years' experience, I was chosen to go with the Duke on a six-week trip to Australia. He was to appear at an engineering conference in Sydney, but we took our time over the trip. We went in an Andover of the Queen's Flight, stopping everywhere on the way. There were only six of us: the Duke; James Orr, his Private Secretary, whom I looked after; the Duke's policeman, Michael Trestrail—who went on to be head of Palace security; a girl called Ann McCormick who was one of the Duke's secretaries; Joe; and I.

I'd always been a bit afraid of the Duke, as he has a reputation for being somewhat irascible, but in fact he turned out to be very nice. When there are only six of you working together and living most of the time on a small airplane, it is impossible not to get to know people. He seemed to like me, and he couldn't have been pleasanter.

34

We had a stopover at Jeddah, and we were sitting around the airport drinking thick, sweet Turkish coffee. I began to feel rather poorly, and by the time we got back on the plane I was very poorly indeed and disappeared to be ill for the first, and I hope the only, time on an aircraft.

The Duke gave me a sharp look as I reappeared, no doubt pale green.

"All right?" he asked in his brisk way.

I nodded shakily.

"You'll learn from experience not to drink that muck," he said.

On the way back he gave us a thank-you meal in Pakistan. For the first time we all sat down and dined together at a hotel in Karachi, and I couldn't believe it. There I was, twenty years old and dining with the Duke of Edinburgh. I was beside myself! But, of course, when I look back I realize it was all very good grounding. Maybe the Royals had been told that I could be a useful member of their personal staff, and being taken on the trip was a sort of test. People who can't relax properly with the Royal family are not efficient. It's necessary to learn to become unobtrusive and stay in the background and not keep bumping into them. And if you do bump into them, you quietly melt away.

However kind and friendly they are, in the end they are Royal.

❧ 4 ❧

Royal Plumage

*T*HE PRINCE and I were both a little shy with each other when I started work for him. He'd never had a valet before—and I'd never been one. I didn't have to dress him or anything like that. He didn't want a semistranger in his room watching him put his clothes on, so I just laid things out on a chair, and he got on with it from there. "Thanks, I can manage, Stephen," he'd say. It was really only on special occasions when he had to wear complicated things like decorations, uniforms, that I would dress him. But for the first few weeks my main task was to find my way around his wardrobe.

By the time I left his service he had acquired forty-four uniforms. We counted them once. He was dressing in his Welsh Guards frock coat, and knowing how perturbed I used to get about uniforms—worrying about having all the bits and pieces in the right places (if you didn't the regiment concerned was mortally offended)—he said, "How many uniforms have I got, Stephen?"

I was tugging him into his frock coat at the time. Uniforms are always just that tiny bit too tight.

"I don't know, sir," I said. "We'd better count them."

That afternoon we did. One of the wardrobe rooms is totally set aside for ceremonial clothing. There is a dummy in there that used to belong to George V. It is used to help portrait artists paint various robes and also to check out a uniform before the Prince wears it. The only problem is that his legs are longer than George V's, but the jackets fit perfectly.

After the count he said, "Have I really got that many uniforms?" surprised at the number.

"Yes, sir, you have," I said with feeling.

He laughed. "You do have to work hard, don't you?"

To roughly list them there are three different Navy uniforms and two RAF ones. He is also Colonel of six different regiments, all of which have three uniforms each—mess dress, khaki, and No. 1's.

There is also a selection of tropical whites, his Gordon Highlanders kilt, and all sorts of other paraphernalia. He has three sets of robes for the Order of the Garter for England, the Order of the Thistle for Scotland, and the Order of the Bath. The Prince is a Great Master of the Order of the Bath.

Then there are his Parliamentary robes and several boxes of robes all connected with universities and dif-

ferent degrees, as well as several colored robes which
go with honorary degrees received from abroad. And
one day, when he becomes King, he will be Com-
mander-in-Chief of all the Armed Forces, as well.

I had to learn about these and which decorations
went with them. It was useful knowledge while I was
working for him, but I really can't see it coming in
handy in the future.

He said to me one morning not long before he married, "I took the key to the wardrobe room last night,
so don't worry if you find the doors open. I just
wanted to show Lady Diana the amount of uniforms I
have."

It was a subtle way of showing her the unexpected
responsibilities he has.

But uniforms can hang in the wardrobe for months
at a time without being worn, and it is easy to forget if
something needs repair. The linen room downstairs
at the Palace would make any running repairs that
were necessary and tighten up buttons and sew on
braid for me.

Nor did I have to clean his shoes. An orderly from
the Welsh Guards did that, arriving every morning to
polish anything that needed a very special shine.

All these ceremonial clothes were kept just around
the corner from his own apartment on the same floor.
He would occasionally go there himself if he wanted
to see a particular garment. He took an interest in his
clothes without being too fussy, and he also liked to
know what he actually owned.

His everyday wardrobe, which consists of a dozen
suits, morning coats, and dinner jackets, was much

closer at hand—in the dressing room attached to his bedroom.

I looked after both rooms and planned what he would be wearing. I was given a weekly sheet of all his engagements, and it would immediately be obvious if there was a uniform or robe required to be worn.

This outline, from the Prince's office, is kept on file for advice and guidance. From it I would prepare the clothing we would need. If he had to wear a uniform, I always got it out well in advance to make sure the right decorations, and so on, were there and that all the buttons were in place and nothing was going to fall off.

I also always packed for him when he went away. Sometimes when it was to be a long trip he would say, "Can I help?"

"Please, sir," I would reply, eyes to heaven for deliverance from his efforts.

He did pack for himself once a year, returning after his skiing holiday at Klosters. When I emptied his suitcases I had no fear of him taking over my job!

When we were on a Royal tour I kept a checklist of what clothing we had with us. Each suitcase or hanging bag was numbered and my list told me instantly what was in each piece of luggage. With this system, if he wanted something in a hurry, I could always put my finger on it right away.

He'd say, "I want that pair of beige cord trousers," and I'd look in my list, see which suitcase they were in, and out they came in a trice.

Packing for him was really no different than packing for oneself, except that more outfits, of course, were needed. Putting the right socks with the right suit, working out the type of clothing needed, and then multiplying by the number of days that he was going to be away or have to change. We usually had about six or seven large suitcases, plus two or three hanging bags.

On tour I never actually unpacked. We just used to leave his clothes in opened suitcases and nothing ever came out creased—everything the Prince owns is of very good quality, and I learned to pack extremely well. But if something ever did look rumpled, there was always someone to help. If we were staying at a British Embassy, the Ambassador would always be happy for his butler to come and give a hand to keep everything in proper condition.

Laundry and dry cleaning were kept up to date on route, but I dealt with his handkerchiefs myself. I learned early on not to send them out to be washed as they tended to disappear. Being monogrammed, people stole them as souvenirs, and we could have been spending a fortune in replacing them.

I also did all his shopping. The Prince hasn't set foot in a store for years.

"I think you need new ties, sir," I'd say.

"All right, get some in," he'd tell me. I'd get a large selection from Turnbull and Asser, take them in to him, and he would normally pick out about five or six, having tried them.

"Is this too loud?" was the usual question. If it was, I'd just pull a face. That, along with the other rejects, would be returned—he'd keep the ones with small discreet patterns—and eventually back would

41

come the bill, sent to his office in the Palace and paid by his accountant.

The only colorful ties the Prince ever wore were some of his old regimental or club colors.

For new suits I'd ring the tailor. In the early days it was a chap named Watson from Hawes and Curtis of Dover Street, who first sent in a selection of fabrics. Mr. Watson would ring for appointments for fittings, asking, "When may I attend the Prince?" in tones of deep reverence. Then he would turn up in a large Rolls-Royce.

"What's he in today?" the Prince would ask when I went to announce Mr. Watson.

"The Rolls," I'd tell him.

"No wonder my suits cost so much," he'd grumble.

Today he has his suits made by Mr. Johns of Johns and Pegg in Clifford Street. He still uses the same system. When the fabrics are chosen, Mr. Johns comes to the Palace to discuss style and returns for fittings once the suit is under way.

His shoes come from Lobb's of St. James'. They keep a last of his foot but he rarely bought shoes in those days. Shoes made by Lobb's survive forever. Again samples were sent in to the Palace for him to decide on style and then Mr. Lobb would come to check the last to make sure the Prince's feet had not changed in any way. Then the shoes were made.

The Prince always wears very formal shoes. Having to spend so much time on his feet it is important that his shoes should be comfortable. But since Lady Diana has come on the scene, he has taken to wearing more modern slip-ons and ready-mades, a fact which must cause Mr. Lobb all kinds of distress.

His underwear and socks come from the Bond Street Boutique—a shop nowhere near as trendy as it sounds. Shirts are made to measure by Turnbull and Asser, and again he chooses the fabric and styles in the comfort of the Palace.

This is a very civilized way of shopping and a privileged one. The world comes to him. He doesn't have to go out. The "By Royal Appointment" shops would love to see him cross their threshold, but his arrival would cause chaos. The only time he ever sets foot inside a shop is at Ballater, the little village near Balmoral.

There he calls on a man named George Smith who sells fishing tackle. And even then the Prince waits until after closing time. When George Smith sees a Range Rover pull up at 6:05 in the evening, he knows he has a Royal customer.

I sometimes would pay George out of the "float" or, if the Prince had spent quite a lot of money, the bill went into his office like all the others. The Prince never carries money or a checkbook. And he has no need of credit cards.

Prince Charles has never been in a jewelry shop in his life; he did not even shop for the engagement ring for Princess Diana. A selection was sent to Windsor Castle for her to choose from. He is not particularly interested in jewelry, though he does own five watches and a few pairs of good cuff links, which belonged to George V and George VI, his great-grandfather and grandfather.

Most of his jewelry has been handed down from

other Royals. By far the most beautiful thing in his safe is the diamond Garter Insignia that is worn only on State occasions. The Insignia belonged to George V, a present to him from Queen Victoria.

These days the Royals do not give each other expensive presents of jewelry. In Victorian times they did and so a collection of very valuable pieces was built up.

There is quite a lot of this in the safe, but it is mostly old-fashioned and not often worn.

It was another of my jobs to keep a list of what was in the Prince's safe and to check periodically for insurance purposes that everything was still there.

I have had the fun of dressing up in most of the Prince's regalia at different times. As we are the same height and build I used to wear his robes for the various artists who were painting him; it cut down the time the Prince himself had to spend sitting.

I remember going to dinner at one of the Livery Halls to be confronted by a Leonard Bowden portrait of the Prince of Wales in the Garter Robes staring at me. The head was Prince Charles. The body and the robes were me! I'd worn them for weeks in 1971 when Leonard Bowden was painting the portrait.

When Lord Snowdon came to Highgrove to take the engagement photographs of the Prince and Princess, he, too, used me as a stand-in for the Prince.

The day before the actual session, Lord Snowdon—a very agreeable man—took Polaroids of me in all the different uniforms that the Prince would be in. He wanted to work out his lighting effects in advance. He then lined all the photographs up on the mantelpiece to remind him of the running order.

All that day the Prince of Wales had been out hunting. He came home in the evening, spotted the line of photographs and said, "Ha-ha—who's been wearing my uniforms then?" sounding as if he were one of the three bears.

"Oh, sir," I said. "I do hope you don't mind."

"Not at all," he said. "You look smarter in them than I do."

We had a massive photo session at Windsor some years ago, when the Prince wore practically every uniform and robe that he possesses. It was just like working in the theater. Off with one; on with another. I had to have everything ready for these quick changes, having prepared the running order the day before.

The atmosphere in the studio was totally workmanlike. The Prince hardly spoke. He just did as the photographer told him. It was only near the end as I produced something else for him to wear that he groaned and said, "Not another one!"

At the end of it he pronounced himself exhausted. So was the photographer. And so was I.

∽ 5 ∽

Bed and Breakfast

ONE THING I learned very quickly is never to try to talk to a Royal before eleven o'clock in the morning unless absolutely necessary. Anyone who does is liable to get a regal glare that says without words, "Go away."

The Prince's day always started quietly. He liked to be awakened by the radio, and my morning routine was to tiptoe into the room at 7:50, draw back the curtains very quietly, then turn on the radio which would gradually waken him. I'd then slip into the bathroom and start to run his bath. Back in the bedroom, I'd look for signs of life and then leave.

Fifteen minutes later I'd return to say, "Good morning, Your Royal Highness, it's five past eight." Behind me would be a footman pushing his breakfast into the sitting room.

He always dressed to eat his breakfast; then at 9:30 I would go in and ask about lunch and so on—sorting out what he wanted to eat for the rest of the day.

The Prince likes to sleep in total darkness, a problem in some hotels. I had to make exactly sure where the light switches were for the morning so as not to blunder around into strange furniture, looking for the curtain pull.

On tour, breakfast was also my responsibility. I took everything we needed with me. Our own cereal (he liked bran flakes) and our own honey, our own Chocolate Oliver biscuits, for which he has a passion, and enough lemon refresher to last us for however long we were going to be away.

He had acquired a taste for this drink at Broadlands, where Lord Mountbatten always served it. He much preferred the lemon drink to any alcohol. I would stock up with Malvern Water if we were going somewhere that was really tricky, like India, but this is not as necessary these days. The water is pretty good in most places around the world, and the stories of the Queen taking cases of the stuff wherever she goes are completely out of date.

When we traveled we either stayed at Government House, the British Embassy, or a hotel; very rarely at people's homes. When we were in a hotel, the manager would be most anxious. Having the Prince under his roof, he would be determined to put on a good show and the breakfast trolley would come up groaning.

Suppose the Prince asked for a croissant. At least six would arrive. God knows how big an appetite they thought he had. Piles of food would cover the breakfast trolley, and I'd cut it down to a reasonable size, then put on our own cereal and honey and wait for him to ring.

I learned over the years to ask for breakfast fifteen minutes earlier than it was really required to give me time to sort things out. It was important to have time on my side. If something had been missing, the waiter might have to go downstairs; perhaps as many as twenty-three floors if it were one of the skyscrapers we stayed in. That takes time.

It was much calmer to have everything arrive a little early, check it out and take off half the debris, like the hotel matches and all the other props of hotel living.

The language barrier could create strange problems. In the Gold Coast where they speak a sort of pidgin French, I asked for butter and got a huge lump of ice cream. The Prince likes ice cream very much but not for breakfast.

I'd grab a slice of toast myself while organizing breakfast. The Prince would be dressing and when he rang and I took in the breakfast he always said, "Have you eaten?" He'd then peer at the trolley and mutter about there being enough to feed a family.

For me it was a great rush while he ate; tidying his room—we always seemed to leave places early in the morning—gathering up his blue pajamas, razor, and his Macleans (toothpaste), putting his hair and clothes brushes away. There would be the mad scramble to the airport again, sirens screaming, police all over the place—quite normal for him—and on the way out I'd grab our cereal and our honey off the breakfast trolley.

His first question on the plane was unfailingly, "Did you bring the honey?"

"Yes, Your Highness," I would say trying to keep a note of weariness out of my voice. I always brought the honey. He was paranoid about the honey. If there was half a spoonful left, it still had to be gathered up.

The other thing I learned over the years was never to travel without safety pins, loads of them, as they were useful for all sorts of things, particularly on one occasion in Papua, New Guinea, where they really saved the day. The Prince was there to give the country independence. He also conducted an investiture on behalf of the Queen, and some of those receiving medals were ladies. Almost topless ladies, as is the norm in Papua.

I could see that the Prince was perturbed as he stared through the window at his assembled band of medal recipients.

"Where will I pin them on?" he asked, nonplussed. He could hardly pin a medal right on the narrow covering of the lady's bosom, and around the waistline is not the normal place.

Safety pins solved the problem. I made necklaces of them, strung the medals on, and he solemnly hung the result around the ladies' necks.

We both laughed afterwards. "I doubt if I'll ever carry out an investiture like that again," he said.

The Prince is very healthy so we didn't bother to travel with medicines except for some special pink pills for stomach upsets and he rarely has to use even these. He dislikes taking any kind of drug or patent medicine. The Royal family are great believers in fresh air, exercise, good food, and if necessary, homeopathic medicine.

On the rare occasions when he was feeling poorly and had to go to bed, I would keep an eye on him. No one was allowed near him except me. I would bring in his trays, worrying about whether he was all right. He enjoyed being fussed over. He became much more dependent when he had one of his attacks of flu—his only real health problem. He'd be miserable, fed up, and not wanting to see anyone.

"I feel awful, Stephen," he'd say, sad, but still bathed, shaved, and with neat hair. "Don't let anyone near me, will you?"

Actually the other Royals never go near each other if one is suffering from a cold or anything infectious or contagious. The Queen would chat to the Prince on the phone when he was ill, but she wouldn't go around to his apartment and chance catching it herself. This wasn't lack of motherly love. When the Queen has to cancel an engagement because of ill health, she disappoints a great many people.

In a way my job developed into the role of acting as a barrier between him and the world outside. This could lead to a slight resentment from other people who felt they could not get through to me and, therefore, to him.

But that was what I was paid for.

Household or members of his office would ask to see him, and I'd see the Prince. "Oh, no, not today," he'd say. "Tell them I'll see them tomorrow, Stephen. You fix it."

I'd report back and the person concerned would

say suspiciously, "Are you sure you've asked him? Why can't I see him?"

"Because he has another engagement," I'd say.

Sometimes it was easier to pretend I couldn't find him though I always knew exactly where he was. The only privacy the Prince has is in his own room.

Being the person closest to him at that time, we developed a friendship—only a working friendship, of course. I was the one who was there first thing in the morning when no one else was about; his office not even open. I was there in the evening when he stayed in. Once he had eaten his dinner, I would go in and say, "Good-night, sir," wait for his "Good-night, Stephen," close the door and leave him in peace.

If he wanted me, all he had to do was ring. If he was staying in, it was because he wanted to, and he rarely troubled me. He might ring me and ask where a particular book was. I looked after all his books. I had cataloged them and turned them into a proper library while he had been in the Navy.

"Would you like me to come around and find it for you?" I'd ask.

"No, don't bother," he'd say. "Just tell me where it is."

I had to remember who he was, to the extent that I never sat in his presence, not unless he specifically asked me to do so. It was interesting that after I resigned and the relationship subtly changed, he would ask me to sit down with him more often.

But for the most part he was friendly, he was kind, but he was always Royal.

He always expected to receive what he wanted instantly. He would be impatient, but I never went away feeling as if I could throttle him. It was little things that annoyed him, particularly any inefficiency on the part of his office. It would enrage him if they told him an engagement was going to take one and a half hours and then it stretched to two and a quarter.

"An hour and a half is quite long enough to be with people," he maintained, and if an engagement ran late it meant his own time was cut short. His private time is very precious to him.

"Can you believe what they did!" he'd grumble. "Squashed God knows how many extra people in for me to see, without even telling me. Ah! Sometimes I give up!"

Silly things would annoy him, too. He has, as I've said, a large wardrobe. Suddenly he'd say, "Do you remember that suit I wore when I went to so-and-so? Is it there?"

"No, sir," I'd say. "I do not have it handy. And it is six months since you wore it."

His suits were generally wearable at short notice, but after six months anything would need some attention. That fact didn't stop him pulling a long face.

There were four things that would really make him cross. The noise of plumbing, gurgling away in the night, the hiss and drip of an air conditioner, not being able to open windows because they had been sealed, and perhaps most of all—miserable little hotel towels.

"I need six of those bloody things to dry myself," he'd complain. "Why doesn't somebody *check* the place."

But mostly he'd just sigh deeply and look wounded if something went wrong.

Fortunately he rarely became annoyed with me. On tours before we started off, he would warn me, "Stephen, if I shout at you, don't take any notice. You know I have to let off steam somehow."

I didn't mind. I understood.

He, on the other hand, from his high position doesn't understand other things. Money being one of them.

When he talks about money it is always in thousands, as donations toward charities and trusts, and he is, indeed, generous and quietly so. But when he sees great chunks of money disappearing to pay his office, he can't understand why it should all cost so much.

He is careful with his money. He doesn't like to spend it, and he moans about the price of everything. Hunting and his polo ponies are his only great extravagance, and they do cost him the earth. He is always harboring a sneaking suspicion that someone is ripping him off because he is the Prince of Wales.

It used to amuse me that he grumbled so much about the cost of things, complaining he couldn't afford them. If, for example, he wanted to buy someone a present, he'd have a selection of gifts sent in.

"Gosh, aren't they *expensive*?" he'd say.

"I don't know what they cost," I'd say, deliberately expressionless. "I only know what's on the label."

"Oh, all right," he'd say grudgingly. "I'll have this one . . ." picking a middle-priced item ". . . I suppose I can afford it."

I used to carry his money for him and he was very trusting. All those years that I did his shopping, he would just leave it to me. If he wanted something I would buy it, the account would go to the office, I'd sign the bill and that was the end of that.

He is a generous tipper. Wherever we stayed it was my duty to deal with the gratuities. Generally I'd leave the butler £20 a night, which broke down to £10 for the Prince and £5 each for the policeman and myself. If we stayed three nights, I would leave about £50.

Often we'd be in the car driving away from a weekend and the Prince would say, "How much did you leave?" and when I told him he'd grumble, "That was a bit steep." Other times, when he'd really enjoyed himself, and I was about to leave the usual amount he'd say, "Leave them a little extra. That was an enjoyable weekend."

I used to carry his money in the form of a float which the office gave me, and expenses were written down in a small book. I personally was being paid £434 a month when I left, plus perks, good food, and a good address. And I must say he was never ungenerous with me, even though he doesn't throw money around.

He was careful about what was spent on Highgrove. When the Duchy of Cornwall, his main source of income, bought the house, he was determined not to be extravagant.

He said to me one day in August 1980, "I may . . ." (he always starts off statements "I may") ". . . I may have found somewhere to live. The Duchy are investigating." Then later he asked if John Maclean and I would go and look at the house.

"See what you think," he said. "I've only seen the

place once myself. But it will be very convenient for hunting."

John and I thought the house was lovely. Maurice Macmillan, Harold Macmillan's son, had lived there for a few years and had left it in good order. It's quite a small house, though it looks enormous from the outside, being rather long.

"I think it's a very manageable house," I told him when we got back to the Palace.

"*I* think I'm going to buy it," he said.

"You do realize that there's not even a bed there?" I told him.

"Well, go and buy one," he said.

Highgrove became his in September 1980. The first weekend we went down was in the middle of October after our return from Balmoral. In the meantime loads of things that had been in storage for years at the Palace had been taken there, presents the Prince had been given on overseas tours, bits and pieces of furniture he owned, and a small amount of furniture from the main collection at the Palace.

The kitchen was bare; we had a rather ancient gas stove, a very small fridge, and not much else. I went off to Heals and Harvey Nichols to buy the necessities but with strict instructions from him. "Don't spend too much," he said firmly.

I bought the bed, a big double one, at Heals, and all the lamps and linen at Harvey Nichols. It was moderately good quality, not the best because he decided that when he eventually married what I was buying could go to the staff quarters.

"When I marry I shall get all sorts of things," he

said. So it seems that he was already deciding he must settle down.

So, as instructed, I didn't spend vast sums of money. There was no point. There was so much at the Palace—glass, china, linen. And it would have been silly to move good items to Highgrove until the decorators had finished work.

The Prince, the policeman, and I did all the moving, and the Prince thoroughly enjoyed himself. He's a strong man—he likes doing physical things. Everything that had been brought down to Highgrove was stacked in the rooms, and we just worked from there, sorting out. We had a couple of dailies who had been sent to the house to clean the cupboards and wash everything before it was put away. It was just like anyone moving into a new house, except in this case it was the Prince of Wales rattling around on floorboards. We inherited some curtains the Macmillans had left behind, which gave some privacy, but other than that the house contained just the bare essentials.

"How's your cooking?" he asked me that weekend. "Can you make us something to eat?"

There was spinach in his own garden which the gardener picked for us, and we had eggs and basics in the little fridge. I made Eggs Florentine and we ate them together off trays on our knees. He was enjoying himself, discovering things he hadn't seen for years.

"Look at those," he said, pointing out a pile of rather nice straw mats. "Do you remember when they gave me those on that trip to the Pacific?"

There were many ornaments, presents from trips everywhere imaginable. We found them all a home, and then the three of us collapsed in the one habitable room, formality gone, and sat and watched the telly, exhausted, eating bacon sandwiches.

It was, in fact, a fabulous weekend. We were working hard, but enjoying ourselves.

From then on he went down to Highgrove every weekend from Friday morning to Monday evening. He would hunt every Saturday, and it amused John Maclean and me to think how he had once been so disinterested in hunting. In the early days when he was trying it out he would ride in jeans and a pair of boots. Four years ago that all changed. Now he wears a blue Windsor hunting coat copied from the one George III wore.

Back from hunting, he actually enjoyed the discomfort of the house. The Royal family always enjoy "picnicking" as they call it—as long as it doesn't go on for too long—and they don't have to do the washing up. I'm afraid it wasn't my idea of bliss—so I let my assistant take over my duties every other weekend.

The Prince pottered about there very happily. Highgrove was his first home, and he wanted to hang his own pictures, arrange all his own treasures. He liked those weekends because he was doing something ordinary that everyone who buys a new house enjoys.

The only thing he was lacking was a companion. Though we were always about, I doubt if he really thought of us as companions. In some ways, his life was quite solitary.

But then the Royals are used to this, and when he joined the Navy one of the most difficult things for him those five years was the lack of privacy. At the beginning of each year he would look very pessimistic and say, ''Oh, God, I'm never going to be able to do a thing this year.''

But the Navy was pretty accommodating. In the end he managed to get a fair amount of leave. It was really only in 1976 when he was Captain of the minesweeper *Bronnington*, based at Rosythe, that I hardly saw him. The Queen was, as usual, at Balmoral during that summer, and he would try to get leave on a Friday or Saturday and make a mad dash on Monday morning to get back by eight o'clock.

We'd have a dawn breakfast of bacon sandwiches and an apple en route, he driving as fast as possible through the Highlands. The Prince's face would become glummer and glummer as we neared Rosythe. Even glummer when John Maclean and I set off back to Edinburgh to get the shuttle back to London. His expression said loud and clear, ''Why not me, too?''

I didn't live on board ship with him; nor did his policeman. It must have been the first time in his life that he was without constant police protection. We were always waiting for him when his ship tied up, but the only time I went onto any of the vessels in which he served was to set things up. I would put his clothes and his personal things in his cabin ready for his arrival. But I never stayed.

He always had a steward on board, whom I would advise on dos and don'ts. All I had to do was keep things going smoothly. He was anxious for the Navy not to appear to spoil him, and he didn't want to have it easier than anyone else. In fact, he wasn't treated any differently. The only concession to his being

Royal was the safe installed in his cabin in which to keep State papers.

When he first started in the Navy in 1971, everything was strange to him. He had been so used to having a policeman and me around all the time, he missed having someone to do everything for him. But I believe he came to enjoy being more self-reliant. He had discovered a small independence.

"I must admit the experience did me good," he said when it was all over. But it wouldn't be true to say he loved every moment of it.

As for me, to occupy my time, I became a page while he went to sea for long periods. Things were busy at the Palace, and I was able to help out.

One morning I met the Queen in the lift. Her Page of Presence was escorting her, and I was escorting the Page of Presence. She said to me, "Good morning, Stephen. You're keeping your hand in, are you?"

"Just until the Prince comes back, Your Majesty," I said.

He left the Navy in 1976, and life went back to normal for both of us.

❧ 6 ❧

Family Homes Away from Home

WHEN I WAS a very young footman, I was sitting minding my own business in the vestibule at Balmoral where we footmen waited to be called for duty, when I heard voices that I knew didn't belong in the Queen's Scottish holiday home.

Two young girls, dressed in T-shirts and rolled-up jeans, were coming through the long windows that led into the vestibule. They were dripping water and they looked remarkably disheveled.

"Can I help you?" I asked, wondering where on earth they had sprung from.

"Yes, please," one of them said, her accent Swedish. "We've come to see the Queen."

"I beg your pardon?" I said.

"We've come to see the Queen," the other said patiently, as if she thought I didn't understand English.

For a moment I was nonplussed. Then I said, "Will you just sit there, please, and I'll see if I can get her for you."

"Thank you," one of them said, sitting herself down.

I left two beaming young women dripping all over the tartan carpet and scuttled off to find the Queen's policeman. He was upstairs resting, but he was in the main hall like lightning, gently sweeping the girls out of the house and grounds. They had come by climbing down an embankment and wading across the River Dee. Once into the grounds they had slipped into the house through long windows left open to let in the summer air. They very nearly did see the Queen and certainly caused security to be tightened.

These young girls meant no harm. Very few people who make extraordinary efforts to get near to the Royals do mean any harm. In Britain we have to guard them more from enthusiasts than from mental cases.

It is unusual to have intruders at Balmoral. The house is very remote, and it is used for only ten weeks of the year, from August 14 to about October 20, and then closed again. In recent years, though, holidays seem to have become shorter because of a series of Royal tours.

The Court calendar goes from Balmoral to Balmoral and we always thought of the year as starting there.

After Balmoral, the Queen returns to Buckingham

Palace, ready for engagements like the State opening of Parliament in November and her prescribed order of work and pleasure.

The Royal year is very precise. Christmas is spent at Windsor. Then to Sandringham in Norfolk for six weeks in January. Back to Windsor for Easter. Return to London in June for overseas visitors, like President Reagan's visit in 1982, and then back to Windsor for Ascot week. London again in July for the garden parties, on to the *Britannia* for Cowes week in August, then, using the Royal yacht if she is available, back to Balmoral.

The highlights of those ten weeks in Scotland for the staff are the two Ghillies Balls, which the Queen gives for all the estate workers and some local workers. These are annual summer dances that take place in the lofty ballroom at Balmoral Castle. They start at 10:00 P.M. after everyone has dined. Jack Sinclair's musicians, a well-known Scottish band, play from the gallery, and long dead stags stare down from the walls at the goings on.

When the Court is at Balmoral, a detachment from one of the Scottish regiments is stationed at Ballater to guard the Queen. A representative group of these men are asked on both occasions.

Back at the barracks, heaven knows how many hours have been spent preparing for what they probably consider an ordeal while the Sergeant Major puts them through their Scottish dancing steps.

This does pay off. The Queen makes a great point of dancing with as many of the soldiers as she can.

All the Royal ladies dress and wear their Royal Stuart sashes and tiaras and the men wear their kilts. The mixture of guests creates a marvelous melting pot. Everyone from the forester to the Duke of Argyle (if he's asked) join together. It's a lovely gathering and great fun with dancing being fairly civilized until after the midnight refreshments. Then the noise grows and the dancing becomes wilder while the music is punctuated by Highland whoops. But at least at Balmoral there is no fear of disturbing the neighbors.

A couple of years ago the King and Queen of Belgium were staying for a Balmoral house party and they came to the ball. The band always played a Paul Jones to get everyone well mixed and when the music stopped, Queen Fabiola landed up opposite the estate carpenter. Off they went in a stately waltz, and to make polite conversation she said, "Tell me—what do you do?"

"I'm the estate carpenter, Your Majesty," he told her.

"How interesting," she said, obviously trying to think exactly what a carpenter was. Then her face brightened. "Ah yes—my husband would have liked to be a carpenter—had he not been the King."

A bemused carpenter spent the next day going around saying, "Can you imagine! He wants to be a carpenter. He doesn't like being a king at all."

Most of the Balmoral holiday is spent shooting for grouse on the moors, and in Scotland they go out earlier and finish later in the day because that far north there is so much more light. The Royal family, fresh-air fiends to a man, have barbecues at night, taking the food out to primitive cottages (invariably ones without electricity) on the estate in a special trailer that has been adapted to be pulled by a Land Rover.

Prince Philip designed this trailer and had it specially made. The food and drinks are kept in sections, some of which are refrigerated. It is a very efficient way of producing a meal for a great many people without needing any cooking facilities. And it gives the Royals the opportunity to look after themselves without any staff at all.

Of course, in the daytime when they are shooting, there are beaters, loaders, and ghillies about, and the ladies come from the house to join the men for a picnic lunch. This is a very brief affair. There is no alcohol for those shooting or loading, although all kinds of drinks are provided, a few sandwiches, then on with the shoot. At lunch the Royals sit on their section of the moorland, while the staff sit a respectable distance away on their bit of territory. The family do stick together; they are very close, and they are happiest when they are rid of all staff. But only for a while. They don't mind serving themselves. They don't even mind cooking. But clearing up is out.

It always struck me how we could be shooting all day with everyone being so friendly; then at six o'clock, when we were all back at the house the family unit would take over. The Royals became totally Royal. The staff became one hundred percent staff. We were all back in our rightful places again.

Not surprising, really. At the Palace the Royals are always just passing each other on the corridors or dashing out here, there, and everywhere. Meeting each other is a hit and miss thing. It is not unusual for them to eat alone, simply because there is no other member of the family about at the time. The Queen, who frequently lunches alone, does the *Telegraph* crossword puzzle as a little relaxation while she eats.

She needs relaxation. Her work never stops wherever she is. Boxes and dispatches are sent up to Balmoral, Sandringham, or wherever she happens to be. She deals with what are called "boxes" every day.

The blue telegram boxes from the Foreign Office keep her up to date with Government affairs. The others are red and inform her of what she personally is doing in the future—arrangements and suggestions for forthcoming tours and engagements. Balmoral, because Parliament is in recession, is the easiest time for her. She has no parliamentary reports to read.

Although there are masses of staff to do everything, when the Queen has guests she acts just like any hostess. In the afternoon before her guests arrive, she checks every room, making sure that there are flowers, clean linen, and water, etc., in place. Her house parties are, nevertheless, very protocol oriented. Guests are asked to come for drinks at six. On arrival they will be met by an equerry or a lady-in-waiting who takes them into the drawing room where the Queen is waiting to greet them. Their luggage is taken upstairs, unpacked, and laid out by one of the maids. Then after drinks the Queen herself shows people to their rooms. We always knew when she was coming with her guests because her dogs go everywhere with her. They run ahead like an early warning system. Hearing them pattering along the corridor signals that the Queen can't be far away.

Between six and seven is the "quiet hour" when everyone does what he likes: rest, change for dinner, read, or watch television. Then the entire party meets downstairs at 8:00 and dinner is served at 8:30.

I never saw anyone, however friendly they might have been, kiss the Queen. She is never greeted intimately in public. Even her closest friends will say, "Good evening, Ma'am. How are you?"

Her guests don't vary a great deal. In fact, it is the same friends who come year after year. Very few new faces appear on the scene. The Duke and Duchess of Wellington, Colonel and Lady Zena Phillips from Luton Hoo. Lord and Lady Porchester, the late Lord and Lady Rupert Neville, and Lord and Lady Westmoreland are probably her closest friends. Her circle is a small one.

Country house visits with the Queen are not exactly restful. What with the shooting, the walking, and the general activity that goes on, one guest was heard to say, "I'm exhausted. At least it's Sunday tomorrow and we can have a lie in."

One of the greater traps is missing the Queen's departure for bed. She usually goes up about midnight or earlier, and this gives other guests the chance to retire as well. If they miss the cue, they're up until two in the morning listening to Princess Margaret playing and singing at the piano. While she is holding court, there is no escape.

Any guests who think they are going for a weekend's rest are quickly disillusioned.

All these activities take place in the country because, at heart, the Royal family are country people. The Queen's great interest is in breeding horses and dogs. She trains her own gun dogs and works very hard with them. All the dogs she breeds are named by her, and she gets enormous pleasure out of seeing them work. A properly trained gun dog can save his master a great deal of effort tramping to find and retrieve shot birds.

Approaching Balmoral one sees a notice board for car drivers. It reads: "SLOW. Beware horses, dogs, and children."

The Queen trained and bred the Prince's golden retriever, Harvey—a large friendly animal the Prince says has soiled some of the best carpets in Britain! He's by no means house-trained, and when we went away for weekends, I'd have to follow him around with soda water and blotting paper.

Another of my duties was to walk Harvey at Buckingham Palace when needed. This was a treat for me as the gardens at the Palace are very private. The only time we would see them was at a garden party or photographed in a book. Today staff are allowed to use the gardens at certain hours. They can also use tennis courts after 6:00 P.M. but this is a fairly recent privilege. The Royals do try to ensure some privacy, and the garden is one of the few places in London where they can find it.

Before taking out Harvey, if the Queen was in residence, I would always ring her Page to make sure she was not going to be in the garden herself. Pages are the link—the mouthpiece—between the various Royals, communicating their messages and their wishes. The Prince didn't have a page so I acted as one for him.

One afternoon when Harvey needed to go out, I made the usual telephone call.

"Is the garden free?" I asked the Queen's Page.

"Yes," he said. "She's in the sitting room. It's all right."

So off I set with Harvey bounding before me.

After a while I saw this figure in the distance. There were corgis running at heel, a headscarf, and a very characteristic walk. "Oh, dear," I thought, "she isn't in the sitting room. She's here."

I had forty acres to maneuver in, so I shot off in another direction, dragging Harvey. All went well until I spotted the pack of corgis again and did an abrupt about turn. About twenty minutes later the corgis unfortunately spotted Harvey and rushed over to join him. With them came the Queen. We were face to face, and I just wanted to jump into a bush.

"I'm sorry, Your Majesty," I said. "But I did ring the page."

"No, no, no," she said. "It's perfectly all right. I've been trying to catch you up for the last half hour. I want to see how Harvey's getting on. I hadn't realized he was in London."

She had bred Harvey, and the dog was so rarely at the Palace that when she suddenly spotted him in the garden from her sitting room window, she had set off in pursuit. While I had been trying to avoid her, she was trying to catch me.

Harvey is a most handsome dog, so handsome that people keep writing to the kennels in Sandringham for him to service their bitches. Harvey always obliges. He has progeny all over the place. There's money in dogs—and Harvey helps pay for the Sandringham kennels, but his great moment of glory was when he was shown at Crufts—as a Royal representative of the dog world.

"Will you show him?" the Prince's office asked me. "The Prince can't do it himself."

I declined. I'd have been embarrassed walking around Crufts in plus fours, hoping Harvey would behave.

He may have wreaked havoc on the finest carpets in the land, but the Queen's dogs, on the other hand, are beautifully house-trained. When she is away they are looked after by a very pleasant woman at Windsor named Mrs. Fenwick. Mrs. Fenwick has more dogs than the Queen, and at my last count, the Queen had eleven.

They give her a great deal of happiness, and they breed so quickly that she gives them to people who she knows will provide them with good homes. Then she still keeps an eye on them. She often will recognize the dog before she recognizes the person she gave it to. But her own eleven, which include a few varieties from mistakes with other Royal dogs, live in her apartments and go wherever she goes, pattering at her feet, or sleeping around her when she sits. They don't bite as many people as is rumored.

It is at Sandringham that the dogs are bred, and where they are buried. If a dog hops on the train at Liverpool Street, not looking too healthy, you can take a bet it may not come back. When dogs get very old and the Vet recommends they be put away, the Queen always has them buried at Sandringham. When we see one of the gardeners start to dig a hole, and the page orders a posy and the carpenter provides a little wooden box, we know we are set for a dog funeral.

One morning toward the end of a Sandringham

holiday I was in the Prince's room and he said to me, "I can't bear it. They're going to bury Heather."

Sure enough the telltale signs were there. Heather, a three-legged, one-and-a-half-eared, long-time favorite with a habit of getting into fights that she always lost, had fought her last battle.

She was placed in the lawn where her resting place can be seen from all the garden windows.

There is no proper little graveyard. The dogs are just buried under trees and in particularly pretty spots. Walking the Sandringham grounds one often comes across a small stone with a name carved on it. Originally these were just along a garden wall, but now the Queen is spreading them further afield.

What with the dogs, the pheasant shooting, and the fact that it is run as an agricultural estate, Sandringham is the most viable of all the Royal properties. The family go there every January, into the freezing Norfolk flats where the wind whistles off the North Sea, and the Royals find it so bracing!

In some ways they are quite extraordinarily predictable. The life in Norfolk in winter is very much the same as that in Scotland in summer. The only difference is that they shoot pheasants in Norfolk and grouse in Scotland. The guns go out at 9:30; the ladies join them for lunch at 12:30.

Also because of the bitter weather the lunchtime picnics at Sandringham are held in various village halls on the estate, meeting places that are more used to accommodating the Women's Institute than a Royal gathering.

When I first went to Sandringham, I couldn't believe it. There we were in a bare-boarded hall with an enormous table covered with linen cloths, napkins, and silver. It looked like the dining room of a West End hotel, with footmen waiting at table in full livery. The food was brought out in hot boxes hours beforehand, and after eating a very good lunch, the ladies went on to accompany the gentlemen shooting for the rest of the day.

Nowadays, shooting lunches are less formal. The Royals now help themselves to food; the footmen are no longer required. The coffee, for example, comes in thermos flasks. In my early days a footman served it in a silver coffee pot, kept warm over a small burner. I will always remember the embarrassment of one young footman who picked up the coffee pot and advanced on Princess Margaret to refill her cup. What he hadn't noticed was that the burner had stuck to the bottom of the pot, and just as he reached the Princess, down it fell, landing on her napkin and setting it alight.

The Royals love anything that alters the even tenor of their lives. They fell about laughing, delighted, and the Queen called out, "Oh, look—they're trying to burn Margo!"

It was just as well it didn't happen in the house. At that time Sandringham was like a tinder box—it hadn't been fireproofed for years. It is a very large house—about 150 rooms—and just to be on the safe side fire practices were held every January. These caused chaos for days afterwards and gave the Royals a lot of fun.

The bell would generally go about 4:30 or 5:00 when all the guns were back in the house again. The drill was that everyone marshaled on the lawn to be counted. Royals as well as us. They went to one corner of the lawn by the front door, while we went to the corner by the ballroom. In the house some senior staff had to "rescue" blankets that were planted to represent valuable fur coats, tapestries, paintings, etc. My job was to grab the Prince's valuables and run. People would be rushing about everywhere, snatching blankets, and the Royals would troop from their rooms on to the lawn where the Equerry counted them and their houseguests. The Sergeant Footman counted all of us, and in the house, the estate staff who formed the house fire brigade were all running around in tin hats, looking like Dad's Army, putting out an imaginary fire.

Eventually, the fire engine would come clanging in from King's Lynn. With a great show of efficiency they would run their hoses about the outside of the house. There would be dozens of firemen on the front drive—probably everyone at the local fire station had wanted to get in on the act. And when everyone had proved they could be in the right place at the right time, and that the fire brigade could cope, it was all over.

One evening after the routine the Queen, as usual, told her Page to tell the Yeoman of the Cellar to give the firemen some beer in the ballroom.

Later in the evening she saw the Yeoman of the Cellar and said, "Whiting, how much did they drink?"

"Six dozen bottles, Ma'am," he told her.

"Good heavens!" she said. "Six dozen bottles! I dread to think what they'd have drunk had it been a real fire!"

Dinner is always late after fire practice, and the

73

whole routine of the house gets upset. Like children, the Royals love it. They think it's fun, that all are suffering together. Any hiccup in the routine is a divertissement in their lives.

I remember another fire practice which took place in the morning when the Queen was out riding and missed it. The bells went off and the usual routine went into action.

The Queen Mother was being escorted downstairs when she met Princess Margaret's Scottish maid on the staircase looking very distressed.

"What's the matter?" the Queen Mother said.

"Oh, Your Majesty, it's fire practice and Princess Margaret won't get out of bed," she said.

The Queen Mother smiled her sweet smile.

"Ah, well," she said, fingering her long strand of pearls, "she'll just have to burn, won't she?"

Eventually major restoration had to be done at Sandringham, and the house was uninhabitable for two years. The Queen decided they would all "picnic" as she called it, at Wood Farm, a much smaller house on the estate. The house is normally used as a shooting lodge and it only has four bedrooms and a staff extension. Extra staff were put into the couple of cottages at the end of the drive, and the houseguests were put up at local hotels.

No one was going to miss their family gathering, though, and Princess Anne arrived with Mark Phillips in a caravan. They wired it up for electricity to the kitchen, and there they lived, coming into the house every evening for dinner and then going back to the caravan to bed. People imagine the Royals live very grandly. A lot of the time they don't, but it does take a bit of imagination to think of Princess Anne roughing it in a caravan in freezing January.

It was at this time that we spent New Year's Eve at Wood Farm. Maybe the Queen Mother was tired—I don't know—but she *was* living at another house, Hillington, three miles away.

Her Page came into the kitchen looking somewhat perplexed.

"They want to have New Year's Eve now," he said. It was not quite ten o'clock. "We've got to put the clocks forward."

Every clock in the house was duly put forward, and at ten o'clock they had New Year's Eve. "Auld Lang Syne" was played on the record player, and the darkest-haired footman had to be first foot, coming through the front door and handing out lumps of coal.

The Page who always made a rather good hot punch for the occasion was decidedly put out.

"They can't have it. It's not ready," he said crossly.

So they toasted each other with God knows what— and went to bed.

We then put the clocks right again and had a double ration of punch.

Even staying at Wood Farm it was still business as usual for the Queen, and she rather enjoyed the diffi- culties that the small house created.

The telephone rang incessantly, but there was no efficient switchboard to deal with the calls and Chef usually landed up answering.

One evening he called up the stairs to Mr. Bennett, the Queen's Page at that time, "Mr. Bennett, it's Prin- cess Margaret for the Queen."

"Thank you, Johnny," the Queen's voice floated down. "I heard that."

Then the Governor General of Australia, Sir John Kerr, arrived in Britain, and the Queen decided that she should receive him in Norfolk at Wood Farm. We thought we'd make him feel at home so we scratched around to find something Australian. The footman unearthed a small rug embroidered with a map of Australia which had been relegated to a staff room, and I found a cigarette box we had never used that also had Australia on the lid. We put these out as rather pitiful props.

The entrance to Wood Farm is through the kitchen. The Governor General, who lives in considerable style in Canberra, stood, waiting to be announced, somewhat bewildered, in the kitchen, while the chef got on with his cooking. Then, at the appropriate moment, we led him out into the hall where the Queen was waiting to greet him. It all went rather well, really. The Queen can carry off any situation with dignity.

The Australians always seem to land up in Norfolk and they must find it exceedingly cold. Dame Zara Holt, the widow of Harold Holt, the Australian Prime Minister, came to visit the Queen for lunch at Sandringham. It was 1969, just shortly after her husband died.

Unfortunately she arrived very early and the Royal family, with the exception of Princess Margaret, were all still at church. Dame Zara went off for a car ride to kill time, and someone informed Princess Margaret, who was still in her bedroom, of this premature arrival.

Eventually she wandered down—the Princess does not like to be hurried—and was sitting in the drawing room waiting for Dame Zara to return.

Prince Andrew, aged six, was also in the house, exuberant as ever. He could see his aunt was waiting for someone, and he could see two footmen hovering at the door. He bounced in to see Princess Margaret—literally bounced. He had been given a kangaroo ball—one of those bouncing toys with ears to hang on to that were so popular at the time.

"Who are you waiting for?" he wanted to know.

"Dame Zara," the Princess told him. "She's come a long way. From Australia."

Prince Andrew considered this and then he said, "If she's from Australia, perhaps she'd like to play with my kangaroo."

"I don't think so, darling," Princess Margaret said gravely. "She's just lost her husband, so I don't suppose she wants to play with anyone today."

When the Royals set off for their holidays it is somewhat more complex than the rest of us getting ourselves off to the Costa Brava. At the Palace there is a staff of about 160 people. On holiday, about eighty of these travel with the Queen.

Everyone travels, including the switchboard, post office, secretaries, chefs, footmen, pages, butlers, housemaids, and, of course, policemen, valets, and dressers.

Going off to Balmoral or Sandringham were expeditions. Balmoral was the more complicated. The Royals used the Royal train if not using the yacht, but a completely separate train was reserved for the staff. Chauffeurs went ahead with cars for the Royal family and their household, and everyone's luggage was put on freight lines. In the south, for Windsor or Sandringham, the staff went in coaches, Royals in cars, the Army moved our luggage, and all we had to worry about was hand baggage.

On holiday there are generally four servants to every Royal and guest. The Queen's cinema also traveled with us. This was, and still is, operated by the Pipe Major. The Pipe Major travels, because each morning at 9:00 he pipes the Queen; a tradition which began with Queen Victoria who liked the sound of bagpipes. Now every morning the Pipe Major can be seen marching up and down outside the Queen's window, puffing like mad. And he has to get it right. The Queen has a very good ear for music.

She is no longer entertained by him at Sandringham. There he was cut out as an expendable extra by the Master of the Household in an economy campaign—along with the staff ushers who were employed to look after the senior staff.

The only person unaffected by that particular economy was "Bobo" MacDonald—the Queen's dresser for fifty years.

Bobo had always had her meals brought on trays by the staff ushers and on being informed that from now on when at Sandringham she would have to go downstairs and eat with all the other staff, she said whatever is the Scottish equivalent of "Not on your life."

Her poor assistant dresser had the job of smuggling food to her for the first few days. Neither of them could seem to be going against the Queen's wishes.

Then Bobo struck on the idea of having a cold. Such

a bad cold that her meals had to be delivered on trays. As before.

The cold has proved permanent. She is still the only member of the staff who is served her food when the Royals are at Sandringham.

∽ 7 ∾

Season's Greetings

AT CHRISTMAS, the entire Royal family, from the Queen down to the youngest arrival, get together at Windsor Castle, which makes a lot of people. Christmas used to be spent at Sandringham, but during the twelve years I worked at the Palace there was a boom in Royal babies. The children who had been babies inevitably grew up. Sandringham became too small to house everyone, so now Christmas is spent at Windsor.

The Castle is big enough to accommodate everybody. Each branch of the family has its own tower. In the Queen's Tower all her immediate family have rooms, and this part of the Castle is very much the Queen's real home. The Queen Mother lives in Lancaster Tower, where President Reagan and his wife stayed in June 1982. The Gloucesters are in York Tower, the Kents in Edward III Tower, and the staff mostly in Brunswick Tower. Personal members of the staff were housed near their own Royals. I was in a most splendid room near the Prince.

Most of the staff see little of the Royal family as they like to make Christmas very much a family affair. Still, behind the scenes, everything is very organized for them. The three main drawing rooms in the Castle are all in use. The White Drawing Room—a most beautiful room decorated in white and gilt—is used as a sitting room. The Green Drawing Room, with its green silk walls, is used for gatherings before dinner. And the Red Drawing Room goes through a complete transformation.

Every piece of furniture is removed and a long, wide trestle table is put down one side. By early afternoon on Christmas Eve this table is an amazing sight, piled with presents, all colorfully wrapped. The table is divided into sections. The first section is piled with gifts for the Queen, next come the Duke of Edinburgh's, then the Queen Mother's, and so on down to the youngest Royal arrival.

The room has red silk wall coverings, the carpets are taken up to reveal polished wood floors. An enormous brightly lit Christmas tree dominates and the chandeliers blaze down on the bright wrapping papers. The Royal family have filled the table—all of eighty feet long—with their presents to each other.

I would spend hours wrapping the Prince's gifts, knowing that in the excitement of opening them, all my work would be destroyed in seconds. Royals, particularly the children, are just like anyone else. They can't wait to see what is under the wrapping paper!

For weeks prior to Christmas I would have been busy, rushing around London or going through Christmas catalogs with the Prince, searching for present ideas for the family who have everything.

It is all much simpler for the Queen. About four weeks before Christmas one of the drawing rooms is turned into a miniature Harrod's. A Mr. Knight, who has taken care of the Queen's Christmas shopping for years, brings in a vast selection of expensive and not-so-expensive gifts, all of which are laid out for her inspection. She goes shopping, in one of her drawing rooms, every evening after dinner.

Everyone else in the family is also planning, without such ease, but with a lot of connivance between their respective staffs.

"If anyone asks you what I want for a present," the Prince would say, "tell them something to do with fishing."

The message would be duly passed on when one of the pages rang me for suggestions. In turn, I would ring the pages and strange requests would come back. The last year I was there I got hold of Princess Anne's Page.

"The Prince is trying to think what she wants," I said.

"Easy," he said. "She wants a doormat."

On this totally reliable information we bought one, and it is, as far as I know, still at Gatecombe Park.

At the end of all this, with about thirty members of the family, there are enough gifts to open a bazaar. And interestingly, the present-opening ceremony takes place on Christmas Eve, at teatime. The entire family congregates in the Red Drawing Room, the door is shut firmly—no staff are allowed in. And then we would hear shrieks of delight. Cries of "Look what I've got" ring out, and eventually the children pound around the Castle to try out new toys or show them off.

Actually they don't buy each other very exotic gifts. One would imagine that they give each other gold or Fabèrge or something precious. Not at all. The presents tend to the practical side—a doormat, lamps, a car rug, books or ties or some new piece of picnic equipment. In other words, the type of useful things that they would not be presented with in their official capacities.

The reason why the ceremony of the gifts takes place on Christmas Eve dates back to Queen Alexandra's day. She was Danish, and Danish people always open their presents the night before.

After the opening ceremony, the presents are left on display in the Red Drawing Room overnight. The staff go in and clean up the mountain of wrapping paper, leaving the room looking spotless, ready for Christmas morning.

They do keep some presents back for Christmas morning. These are just little things, which are put into old shooting socks and slipped into the bedrooms.

"I'll do the Queen's stocking," the Prince would always say, and another of my jobs was to run around buying small things like soap, smelly candles, oranges, and all sorts of odds and ends with which we would fill the socks.

The Prince also made one for his father, and I don't doubt that there will be one for the Princess of Wales every Christmas.

The Queen lands up with a lot of stockings. Not that all the Royals do this—it's not something that Princess Anne bothers with too much.

On Christmas morning each branch of the family stays together in its own tower and has its own private little gathering before meeting for church and lunch in the State Drawing Room.

This lunch is totally private, except that the chef comes up from the kitchen to carve the turkey. The Royals all pull snappers, wear paper hats, eat plum pudding, and make a great deal of noise. Meanwhile the staff are having their own marvelous time with a table groaning with food in their quarters. Because I lived so near to Windsor, I missed this and went home, but I was always back by four.

Traditionally at this time the Queen receives the personal staff to wish them a Happy Christmas and give each one a present. This is considered, and indeed is, a great honor. In her private sitting room there is a table laden with presents, a fire blazing in the corner, and portraits of ancestors looking down from the walls, as she stands waiting for them to come in.

She knew I liked good glass—I suppose the Prince had told her—and every year I received a piece of crystal, shook her hand, wished her a Happy Christmas, too, and said, "Thank you, Ma'am."

The Royal family love Christmas. Naturally they receive hundreds of cards from all over the world. The Prince spends hours pinning those he receives on a screen in his Windsor sitting room. The Queen hangs hers on old-fashioned wooden clothes horses. They think Christmas cards are "cozy," a word that rattles through their vocabulary, and there is no Twelfth Night superstitious nonsense. The whole lot—clothes horses, screen, and cards—are packed up and taken on to Sandringham where they are on display until the end of January.

So anyone who sends the Royals a card can bank on it being truly appreciated.

The buildup to Christmas is fun, too. The Chief Housekeeper goes out weeks before to buy the presents actually requested by each member of the staff. They are all given a price guide—usually between £12 and £16 depending on length of service.

On December 19, the Staff Christmas lunch is held at the Palace, and everyone from top to bottom is invited. Afterwards, everyone lines up outside the Bow Room and files in one at a time to receive a present from the Queen. There are a lot of staff at the Palace. The ceremony takes a long time, and the Queen shakes every hand and has a word for everyone. She must be exhausted at the end.

But neither her day—nor the staff's—is over. That night she gives the Staff Dance where she is very much in evidence.

And the next morning the Court moves to Windsor.

The Queen considers Windsor her main home. She uses it at weekends unless she is away or invited to friends. And therefore, before Highgrove, it was the Prince's home as well. This meant that once I became his valet, I had my own permanent room there and was not moved around like the rest of the staff.

They are all very fond of Windsor. It is grand—very large—but it is comfortable as well. Windsor Castle itself may be grand, but the Royals simply do not live in grandeur. The Queen keeps an F-registration car there in which she potters around quite happily. She also has a K-registration Rover. (Cars are given an alphabetical rating according to year of manufacture.) If a car still gets from A to B and causes no trouble, she is quite unconcerned about its age. She enjoys driving herself, but only in private. It would be too complicated if she had an accident on a public road. Not that this is likely because she is a very safe driver.

Princess Anne is much more interested in cars and speed. The Prince loves his old blue Aston Martin. It has a J registration, making it thirteen years old, but he treasures it and treats it like gold dust. Everyone else connected with the Royals uses Fords and gets a new model yearly. And in the country, Range Rovers are the favorite form of transport.

But there is little real extravagance. The bill for the staff is, of course, enormous, and there are always moans when the Civil List comes up for review and the family ask for more money.

This is no problem to the Prince as his income is mainly derived from revenues from the Duchy of Cornwall.

It's a Royal joke that Willie Hamilton stood up in Parliament and he had the green book in his hands. The green book is the Royal handbook listing all members of the various households. He solemnly read out the ladies-in-waiting and their names, women-of-the-bedchamber and their names, plus extra women-of-the-bedchamber—he didn't seem to realize all these are honorary positions—and then he said, "How big is this bloody bedchamber?" He gave the impression that the Queen has dozens of ladies-in-waiting. In fact, she has four. Those known as the Women-of-the-Bedchamber, all titled ladies, are her personal friends. And they do a lot of work. They write her thank-you letters to women's organizations, schools, children—and deal with all sorts of small tasks.

They do not get paid for any of this, but they are given expenses which probably just about pay for their clothes for the special occasions when they accompany the Queen to engagements. But then most of them are not short of cash for themselves.

If Willie Hamilton had wanted a stronger point, he should have gone for the kitchens. There is a kitchen staff of about twenty, including professional chefs and their helpers. And the waste of food used to be appalling. The Queen gets the blame for the waste and cost, but in fact it has little to do with her. Staff used to say casually they would be in for lunch and then just not turn up. The chefs were constantly cooking too much. Today things have improved with a booking system. If you don't book your lunch, it isn't cooked and you go without.

The Royals themselves are very frugal. If someone extra turns up for lunch on a Sunday it is difficult to find another portion. If the Queen is eating alone, just one small piece of chicken will be cooked, or a chop. There is no question of an entire roast being prepared and the remains put in the fridge.

The Queen, of course, has a professional personal maid, a dresser, and two assistant dressers. Bobo MacDonald, who beat the Sandringham serve-your-self-system, is still with her, but doesn't do much because she is beginning to age. The others do most of the work. They seem to be forever in and out of suitcases, and there is always tissue paper floating on the corridors outside the Queen's chamber as one passes.

"She's off again," we would say.

Another expense of the Palace is the heating bill. The Queen only has to sniff, and someone rushes to the phone and up goes the heating until the whole place boils. The running of the Palace is a series of contradictions when it comes to money. On the one hand there are stringent economies, like no more waiting on table, but there is no cutback on actual staff. It is true to say that the Royals do absolutely nothing for themselves. Everyone who works in the Palace has a function and the end result is cosseting the Royals. The chefs are there to cook, the footmen and pages to take in guests, visiting dignitaries, and run around, the housemaids to clean. On a higher level, the Household deal with all money matters and paying of bills. I doubt if the Queen has ever signed a check in her life.

But, of course, they do work themselves. Another Royal chore is being painted. The Yellow Drawing Room at the front left-hand corner of the Palace is used as a studio for the portrait painters because it has windows on two sides and the light is good. Sometimes there will be four or five half-completed canvases in there, all by different artists, painting different members of the family.

I often remember coming down the corridor at some odd hour of the day to see the Queen in full evening dress, regalia, tiara, diamonds, sailing down toward the Yellow Drawing Room, the dogs pattering around her, off for a sitting with an artist.

There is a certain charm in these encounters. One might meet the Prince in his Welsh Guards dress uniform or Princess Anne in a ball gown. The end result is that the Royals, when being painted, look exactly like a child's view of royalty. To grown-ups tiaras and diamonds look faintly quaint when worn just after breakfast. But once dressed up, my goodness, the Royals look royal! They put on royalty with the trimmings.

Yet what looks like enormous personal wealth is not at all. If the Royal family were truly broke, many of the treasures would not be theirs to sell. Some of the jewelry and most of the pictures in the various homes are owned by the State with the Queen as guardian of this national treasure.

The Prince and Princess of Wales' actual wedding presents do belong to them, but all the jewelry that the Princess has been given will stay in the Royal family forever.

They never sell jewelry. It is all kept securely in safes in the Palace and will be handed on to future generations. Although there is a considerable amount of this, avid followers of royalty must have noticed that they usually wear the same favorite pieces.

The big question at the time of writing is what will happen to all the jewelry that the Duchess of Windsor acquired on her marriage to Edward VIII. It is all British Royal family jewelry: much of it belonged to

Queen Alexandra. What causes anxiety in Royal circles is that the Duchess, now completely senile, might leave it and other valuables to France as a thank-you for her home, which is on loan from the French Government.

Since Lord Mountbatten was assassinated, no one really knows what is happening to the Duchess. At one time he would go to see her at her Paris home in the Bois de Boulogne and bring back information. Then he had a row with Maitresse Blumm, the Duchess' lawyer and guardian. She was convinced that Lord Mountbatten was pressuring the Duchess into returning the jewelry and other family treasures to Britain, and he was refused admittance. So even that source of information dried up.

The younger Royals don't mind the Duchess so much. I suppose for them, the scandal was too long ago.

I remember once when we were in Paris, the Prince called on her for tea. We had been to Rheims for a champagne charity gala for the United World Colleges—a pet project of Lord Mountbatten. On the way to the airport he stopped off to see the Duchess and to my chagrin did not take me with him. I would have loved to see this living legend. He said very little about the meeting when he came back. "She is very frail and seems ill," he remarked, but no more.

When he became engaged one of the three thousand telegrams that arrived was from her. It just said, "Best wishes, Great-aunt Wallis." He did wonder whether she had sent it herself, or if Maitresse Blumm had sent it for her.

I was working at the Palace when the Duchess came

to the funeral of her husband, the Duke of Windsor, in June 1972. There was an enormous amount of curiosity regarding her in the Palace. Everyone—even the Royals—wanted to get a good look. After all, she had changed the course of our history. The Queen had met her a couple of times before. She went to have tea with her on visits to France. (The Royals always see people they don't much want to see for tea. They can get away quickly, but they have been polite and called.) But when the Duchess arrived at the Palace, here was the woman everyone had speculated about for years. Some of the older long-serving staff remembered her well, and those with long memories remember how resented she was and how autocratic.

One of them told me, "She used to say to the King, in her heavy American accent, 'David, I don't want to see that man around, if you don't mind.'"

Now here she was in the house where she might have been Queen, but never achieved it. Admittance only came with her husband's death.

No wonder we all wanted to get a look at her.

The staff were told to prepare one of the guest suites on the first floor at the front of the Palace, and when the Duchess arrived she was so tiny and so frail that she aroused a lot of sympathy among the younger Royals. The Prince was particularly kind to her. He, in fact, is quite fond of her.

"Well, she is family," he said one day with a little sigh.

Lord Mountbatten also liked her. He had been the best man at her wedding, and he did try for years to get her back to England to live, but the older Royals were implacable. Her only guarantee is that she can be buried at Frogmore alongside the Duke. Today nobody really talks about her.

There is a story, of course, that the Queen Mother will never forgive the Duchess for marrying King Edward VIII and precipitating her husband, George VI, into a job for which, as second son, he had not been trained. She is said to believe that the strain of being King throughout the war caused his early death in February 1952.

I suppose all rumors have some truth, but with the Royal family it is very difficult to know. They *never* speak in public of anything that might be an embarrassment to them. If Princess Anne is stopped and fined for speeding, it is never spoken of. Princess Margaret's friendship with Roddy Llewellyn was a taboo subject. No one would have dreamed of discussing Angus Ogilvy's, Princess Alexandra's husband's, difficulties in the city, which caused something of a small scandal. And most certainly not in front of the servants. Equally certainly not in front of their friends. It would only be to other members of the immediate family that they might mention any royal misdemeanor, but they work on the principle that these things are best ignored.

They lean on each other. They have no need to leave their own safe, enclosed, privileged circle. There is no one in the family that the rest of the family doesn't like, though they are a little cautious about Princess Michael of Kent, but mainly because she is "new."

The Queen Mother still has a lot of influence over all of them, particularly on Prince Charles, who is probably her favorite grandchild. He spent a great deal of his childhood with her when the Queen was away on world tours, and up until his marriage he would still go to Birkhall, the Queen Mother's Scottish home, if the Queen were away. On the weekends when the Queen was not at Windsor, he would stay with his Grannie, as he calls her, at her home, Royal Lodge, at Windsor. He hated staying in the Castle alone and the Royal Lodge is more homey, anyway. He visits her regularly at Clarence House and even though it is only a few hundred yards from the Palace he has to take a car. He tried to walk to see her once and was nearly mobbed.

I used to go to Birkhall and Royal Lodge with the Prince, and whenever I met the Queen Mother she knew my name, greeted me kindly, and enquired if everything was all right. She is the embodiment of the Royals' favorite word—cozy—and a wonderful homemaker. The Prince describes pieces of china or glass he particularly likes as "very Royal Lodge" or very "Birkhall."

These two houses are his ideal homes, and the Queen Mother's presence in them adds to that impression. The houses have smaller rooms and less staff. She herself loves watching TV, and when the Prince dined with her it was usually TV dinners on their laps in front of the box. She also loves entertaining and can wear out people who are a great deal younger than she is.

Much later in the holidays at Balmoral she gives her own version of the Queen's Ghillies Ball. This is very much a family affair for the staff and estate workers. As there is no ballroom at Birkhall, a little tent goes up outside the staff hall for the band. She greets everyone personally, dances with everyone. Food is served, the bar is thrown open at 11:30, and everyone finishes up in a merry state.

It's just as well that Birkhall is deep in the Highlands. Driving back from the Queen Mother's Ball I have often seen cars parked—or abandoned—in the most extraordinary places.

It's what you might call a memorable evening.

There is one custom the Royal family share that few people know about. Every year when we were on the Royal yacht, we would anchor for the day off the coast near the Queen Mother's tiny Castle of May. This is a very comfortable home in spite of its rather grim medieval look. The gardens were all made ready by the Queen Mother's gardeners for her August visit, and we arrived in time for a very good lunch. Everyone was encouraged to wander through the grounds before tea was served and then back to the yacht by launch before sailing on to Aberdeen.

As we steamed away the Queen Mother always sent up big rockets from the turrets of her castle for a dramatic farewell, and her staff would wave big sheets from the battlements. In return, the *Britannia* would send up flares, scorching streaks of light into the sky. Unfortunately, being Scotland, some summers were rainy and foggy so we couldn't see the Queen Mother's fireworks nor she ours. But we could all hear the bangs and crashes as they exploded into the damp sky.

Set as it is in the far north of Scotland, the Castle was too far from anywhere for anyone else to enjoy our firework display. This, therefore, became a very private little ceremony, and one which signaled the end of the working year and the start of the much anticipated summer holiday.

From July on the Prince would be saying, "I'm exhausted. I can't wait to get to Balmoral."

After the Castle of May, that was our next stop.

8

Mother and Son

DURING THE TIME I worked for Prince Charles, I cannot remember a day when, if they were in the same place, he and the Queen did not spend some time together. Each morning between 9:00 and 9:30 the Queen's Page would ring and ask me if the Prince would be down for dinner that evening. If they were both in the Palace, they always dined together.

Every day I received a circular in a folder which listed each member of the family's movements for the day. The Prince rarely bothered to look at this. He would ask me, "What is the Queen doing for lunch?" Or I would inform him that the Queen was going to the premiere that evening. All the Royals relied on their personal staff for this sort of information.

The Prince is very fond of his mother. He still calls

her "mummy" when they are together, but becomes very Royal should anyone refer to her as "your mother." She is the Queen and he always speaks of her to others as "the Queen." If he is going out in the evening, he'll nearly always say, "Tell the car to wait for me at the King's door. I'm going to say good-night to the Queen."

The male apartments at the Palace are traditionally to the right of the building, so the King's door is on the right of the inner quadrangle. The only time the Queen uses this door is when she rides off for the Trooping the Colour.

He always visits the Queen in her apartments—she never comes to his. I have not seen the Queen in his second-floor corridor since Princess Anne's wedding day in 1973. Princess Anne's rooms were alongside her brother's, on the left-hand side of the corridor, and the Queen visited her then as mother of the bride.

The Prince still depends on the Queen for guidance. "The Queen is very wise," he would often say. He sees her as being in charge of a huge family business. She receives the State papers, boxes, and telegrams—top secret things—most of which she shares with him. They have the same information fed to them, and this pooling of knowledge is helping to train him for the job of King that will one day be his.

He believes that the longer the Queen does the job, the better she becomes at it. He says she is brilliant, and he values her guidance enormously.

She has been a good teacher, training him for kingship since the day he was born. But the speculation that she might abdicate and let the Prince take over the throne is nonsense.

When this was suggested in the newspapers, he read the reports, snorted, and said, "What rubbish!"

He thinks about it, of course. Three years ago he used to say occasionally, "We will see what happens when I'm in charge!" But this remark was never made about important policy. More likely he was complaining that the chef had turned out a bad meal or an arrangement had been mishandled. It was always to do with the running of the Palace, and not the running of the monarchy, that caused him to make this remark.

Abdication, the Royals say, is not part of the British tradition. It is simple enough for the Dutch monarchy to hand over the throne because they are not crowned in a religious service. Their ceremony is merely a civil one. But Kings and Queens of England are anointed and consecrated by the Church. It is like marrying a nation.

It is possible that in years to come as the Queen becomes older and wants to slow down, the Prince of Wales might change his title to Prince Regent, but he himself does not believe this will happen. He is quite prepared to be a King-in-waiting for a very long time. He said to me one day, "What's the rush?"

He is *not* interested in rushing into the job because he understands the restrictions. When I was with him, we could go shooting, fishing, flying—just the Prince, the policeman, and I. Once he is King all those freedoms will go. The throne will clip his wings, and he knows it.

For the meantime the Queen is doing a marvelous

job. She is totally dedicated to her own, her family's, and Britain's heritage. She would not want to see everything she and her father built up after the Duke of Windsor's abdication in 1936 crumble. And the task of assuring the continuation of the monarchy in a form that pleases the people of Britain is hers.

This is the reason for her preoccupation with the Princess of Wales' baby. And why she insisted a doctor come immediately when the Princess slipped down some stairs at Sandringham in January 1982 before the birth. She was concerned as a grandmother would be, but she was perhaps equally concerned because the baby is second in line to the throne.

When his time comes the Prince will be a subtly different monarch from his mother. Brought up in the sixties when everything was changing, he knows the monarchy must change, too.

"We have to adapt all the time," he says, but there is no question that the Royal family will ever become like the Dutch, riding bicycles in the street.

"It's a fine balance," says the Prince. "To be modern—but to keep the mystique."

So far the British Royals have succeeded where the Dutch have failed.

The Prince and I went to Amsterdam for the 1980 coronation when Queen Juliana handed over the monarchy to her daughter, Princess Beatrix. To our astonishment the crowds had to be controlled by the National Guard—armed with tear gas.

The Prince said, "You can't imagine that happening in Britain, can you?"

The thought of tear gas in the Mall is unthinkable.

But the Prince has faced the possibility that the monarchy could become unpopular.

"If they wanted me to go—I'd go," he says.

And for the time being the training goes on. When the Queen goes abroad all the information she acquires is handed on to the Prince. The Duke of Edinburgh, although a very good consort, does not have the same interest. He will never get the job. The throne is a two-person show—the Queen and the future King.

Yet the Duke, too, is wise.

"The Duke is the most knowledgeable person I know," the Prince used to say to me.

He can be fatherly and is very much the man in charge in his own home. People rarely realize this as he always appears to be the man two paces behind the Queen with his hands behind his back.

But it is the Duke who will storm down to the kitchen to tell the chef he thinks that dinner was bloody awful. And it is he who makes family decisions when the Royals are on holiday.

He brought the children up strictly, and he is still inclined to get irritable with the Prince. He used to tell him off for being slow. When we were out shooting the Prince would potter around or start chatting to one of the Keepers. He is easily distracted if something he thinks might be interesting is happening elsewhere.

Then you could hear his father calling, "Charles—come *along.*" He is always trying to speed him up.

"Coming, Poppa," the Prince would say.

But they rarely row and at the end of the day are close.

Even though he is slowing a bit, the Duke still has tremendous energy. He is quick and does a great deal of work. We all thought he was becoming very irritable with the Prince because he wasn't settling down; however, with the engagement and wedding, all this seems to have passed.

But the Duke has blotted his copybook over the years with both the press and the public with his habit of making unfortunate remarks. He once told the British workingman to get his finger out. This certainly caused the Palace Post Office to get *their* fingers out. We were deluged with angry letters.

Today his public irascibility doesn't seem to matter so much. The people are more interested in the Prince and Princess of Wales than any of the other Royals. And he and the Queen are getting closer as they get older. There is terrific unity there; and even though they have been married for thirty-three years, it is certainly not a marriage of tolerance. They call each other "darling," and mean it. They live together as man and wife in their own apartments, just like millions of other couples. She would miss him most dreadfully if anything ever happened to him. And it's really rather lovely.

But though the Duke has a knack of putting his foot in it, making statements that would have been better left unsaid, I've never heard any of the Royals express an opinion regarding politics—except that Lord Mountbatten did say that he did much better with a Labour Government than he ever did with the Tories. In the years when Labour was in power, we all knew that a great respect had grown up between the Queen and Sir Harold Wilson. The old guard who make up some of the Household were very suspicious.

It is tradition that Prime Ministers always see the Queen on a Tuesday at 6:30 P.M. and when Parliament was in session, Harold Wilson spent a good deal of Tuesday evening keeping her up to date with all that was going on.

The Palace staff used to say that he had weighed up his monarch's character very cleverly. The Royals love a diversion. They enjoy some little drama that breaks the monotony. Sir Harold had developed diversionary tactics to a fine art. The Queen always leaves for her Windsor Castle weekend on a Friday, but it seemed to us that the Prime Minister would often have something to impart on a Friday, something of which she simply must be informed.

In the normal way we could set our clocks by the Queen's routine. By three o'clock every Friday she would be gone. And when the Queen goes away, the Palace just folds. Like a theater, it goes into darkness. But one Friday instead of darkness all the lights were blazing and the atmosphere expectant.

"What's happening?" we were all asking each other. The Queen was waiting to receive Harold Wilson. Something was undoubtedly up.

In fact, the pound was down.

He came later in the evening to tell her that the Treasury had decided to devalue.

Prince Charles particularly liked James Callaghan when he was in power, but he felt that Edward Heath was difficult to communicate with.

Margaret Thatcher? No one ever seems to mention her.

Even in the Palace, not everyone gets intimate and unexpected glimpses of the Queen. Staff like the chefs, the housemaids, the livery porters—the people who really work below stairs, or in the cellars—never see her and could work forever in the Palace without doing so.

However, on Jubilee Day, the staff were allowed the rare treat of lining the corridor to the Grand Entrance when the Queen left for St. Paul's and the Service of Thanksgiving. As she came into the Grand Entrance, which is like a well, and gave everyone a good view of her, the entire staff just broke into cheers.

She stood stock still for a second, looking totally stunned, almost as if she might cry. Then she recovered, smiled and waved at the people who work for her, and in her marvelous pink outfit, the baubles on the hat jauntily swinging, walked to her carriage. The Prince was waiting on horseback beside her car and rode at her side to the cathedral as her A.D.C.

The cheering that started at her own front door just grew and grew in volume all the way down the Mall, the Strand, Fleet Street—until she reached St. Paul's. It was the most wonderful day. We drank champagne at the Palace; we toasted the Queen—many of the girls in tears. We were stunned by the public emotion. And so was the Queen.

The Jubilee was very much the Queen's year though the Prince was involved. The limelight was hers. We did a lot of looking out of the Palace windows, watching the crowds and marveling at the enthusiasm. It was very exciting, with the Palace all ticking together. The bands seemed to be playing all the time. The Prince has always loved bands since he was a little boy. Even then he would look out of the window and listen to the music, and we had plenty of that to do while the Jubilee was going on.

"One thing about this job," he used to say, "is that you have your own orchestra most mornings."

In London, at 11:30 A.M., when the Guard is changed, one of the regimental bands plays down in the courtyard, and the music drifts into his rooms.

In Jubilee Year he did one or two things the Queen simply hadn't time for—like a helicopter trip to the Western Isles—it was just a three-day mad hop of late nights and early mornings, with the Prince wearing a kilt most of the time, representing the Queen in the outer reaches of the British Isles.

But the best day was Jubilee Day itself, June 23, 1977. Watching the crowds gather outside from the Palace windows and hearing the incessant cheering that went on from early morning to late at night, the Prince turned to me and said, "I can hardly believe it."

But he did not know that an even greater tidal wave of affection would sweep over the family four years later in July 1981 when he married Lady Diana Spencer.

∽ 9 ∾

Royal Tragedy
and Royal Security

On JUNE 11, 1981, Trooping the Colour took place on a glorious hot and sunny day. It was also to prove a historic day, but I did not know that until the Prince came back to his Buckingham Palace apartment at 12:30 P.M., after the ceremony. He was wearing his Welsh Guards scarlet tunic, and for him he looked hot and bothered.

He handed me his sword and began wrenching at the gold buttons of the tunic.

"Do you know what happened?" he asked.

I had no idea what had happened. After he had left that morning, I'd peered from the window of his room, parting the curtains to see down the Mall and watch the Royal procession leave for Horseguard Parade. Then I'd started rushing about, packing and preparing for the Prince to leave for Windsor for polo when the Trooping was over.

Assuming some Guardsman had fainted—a fairly usual occurrence—I just said, "No, what happened?"

"Some idiot fired shots at the Queen."

"Oh, my God!" I said, shocked, and hesitated before asking tentatively, "Is everything all right?"

"Fine. They were blanks as it happened." He was wrestling his way out of the tight tunic while I tried to help. "The noise startled the horses, but the Queen managed to stay in control." He shook his head. "It makes one realize how vulnerable one can be."

Indeed, the Royal family are vulnerable. As I have said, most of the time they need more protection from enthusiasts rather than from mental cases or terrorists. Nevertheless, as the Prince himself frequently says, the possibility of assassination is just one of the risks of the job.

In this instance, the shots were harmless. The seventeen-year-old gunman was immediately grabbed by Alec Galloway, a Scots Guard NCO, and all ended well.

But there was one occasion—on August 27, 1979— when the Royal family's vulnerability became a horrible fact.

It was the most unhappy morning of the entire time I worked for Prince Charles. His great-uncle, Lord Mountbatten, had been assassinated by the IRA and I was sitting at Heathrow Airport waiting for the Prince to return from his fishing holiday in Iceland. He was flying back to see if he could be of some assistance in any way.

Lord Mountbatten was seventy-nine years old. He and most of his family had been aboard their boat, the *Shadow V*, which was moored at Mullaghmore Harbour near his Irish home at Classiebawn Castle.

They were going fishing and had hardly left harbor when there was a murderous blast from fifty pounds of explosives planted on board. Lord Mountbatten was killed instantly, along with the Prince's godson, fourteen-year-old Nicholas, and a seventeen-year-old boatman.

The Dowager Lady Brabourne, who was eighty, died later in Sligo Hospital, and Lord Mountbatten's daughter, Lady Brabourne, and her son, Timothy, were in critical condition. Lady Brabourne's husband, John, was also injured.

Immediately after the news broke, the Prince's office had begun the process of getting the Prince back from Iceland. They sent an Andover of the Queen's Flight—the same one that had flown him there only three days previously.

When the plane landed on the south side of the airport where all V.I.P. landings are made, I went on board. He was walking toward me from the rear of the plane, looking very pale and drawn, and already wearing a black tie. I always packed one wherever he went, never thinking it would actually be used.

As he came toward me I stammered, ''Your Royal Highness—I don't know what to say.''

He just looked at me and said very quietly, ''What was the point?''

There was no answer. Neither of us said any more.

He already had packed his briefcase with the work he takes everywhere. I took it from him and left the plane ahead of him. He followed when his car was in position at the foot of the aircraft steps.

It was a silent drive to Windsor while the chauffeur threaded through the traffic. When we arrived at the Castle I unpacked the picnic lunch I'd brought from Buckingham Palace, and as it was such a glorious sunny day he said, "We might as well eat outside."

He has a favorite spot in the gardens, and I settled him down there. Slowly he began to unwind as he sat quietly watching swallows dart about the Castle walls.

"I hope this hasn't ruined your holiday," he said as I unpacked lunch.

"No, sir. I was going later in the week."

He was silent for a moment and then said, "It was good of you to come."

His meal was set out and I was standing at the side of the table, waiting to help myself after he was served.

"How did you learn the news, sir?" I asked.

"When the Ambassador telephoned. At first he just said it was bad news." He stopped for a second. "My immediate reaction was that something had happened to the Queen Mother. But he said that wasn't so. He said they had just heard and were waiting for confirmation that there had been an attempt on Lord Mountbatten's life. That he had been injured."

I just listened as he toyed with his food.

"I felt so helpless," he said. "So far away."

It had been later in the day before the harsh facts were told to him.

"I felt immense gloom," he said. The death of his godson, Nicky, had hit him almost as much as that of Lord Mountbatten. "Such a waste of a young life," he said.

When lunch was finished and cleared away, I brought a telephone out to him in the garden and left him to talk to the Queen who was at Balmoral with the rest of the family.

He also rang Norton Knatchbull (now Lord Romsey), Lord Mountbatten's heir. He had gone to Ireland, and the Prince asked him for the latest reports on the condition of Lord and Lady Brabourne. They were both very seriously injured, and Lady Brabourne was on a life-support machine.

In between phone calls I went out to see if he wanted anything.

"I must go to Ireland and help," he said.

But as his office firmly pointed out, this was quite impossible. Politically his appearance in Ireland would have caused tremendous problems.

It was a dreadfully sad time. He was quiet and said little. He was obviously deeply shocked and very unhappy. During the three days I was with him before leaving for my holiday, I went to London twice a day to collect lunch and dinner from the Palace. Not that he was eating a great deal. He was so upset that it was best to leave him alone. He wasn't in the mood to see anyone. All he wanted to do was keep in touch with the situation in Ireland and he spent hours on the telephone.

He said one day, "I can't understand it. Why

should someone like Lord Mountbatten, who has done only good, be attacked? And Lady Brabourne. She's *eighty*." His voice was despairing.

The weather continued superb. It seemed to make it all worse somehow.

He had always looked upon Lord Mountbatten as a grandfather, never having known one, and indeed, his funeral wreath carried a card that said: "From H.G.S. to H.G.F." From honorary grandson to honorary grandfather.

As a compliment to his honorary grandfather he said to me when the funeral arrangements were being discussed, "I'm going to wear every decoration I'm permitted. Lord Mountbatten would have liked it."

Mountbatten would have. He loved to dress up, and I remembered with a pang how when we were all in Nepal for the Nepalese King's coronation, Lord Mountbatten had said gleefully as I weighed him down with all his own decorations, "I'm going to look like a Christmas tree."

Before the funeral, on September 5, the Duke of Edinburgh, who had regarded Lord Mountbatten as his honorary father, flew down from Scotland, and he and the Prince went to Eastleigh Airport, near Broadlands, to wait for the return of the bodies.

Then later the Queen and the other members of the family came south for the funeral. Afterwards the Prince went back to Scotland with them all.

Lord Mountbatten had been truly fond of the Prince. They spent a great deal of time together at Broadlands, Mountbatten's home, when the Prince was on shore base at Portsmouth in the Navy in 1973. They talked together for hours. Lord Mountbatten enjoyed the conversations. He liked going over his own naval career again and encouraging the Prince to talk about his.

He always wanted to know what Prince Charles had done that day, and he was a great one for saying, just faintly disapprovingly, "In my day we did it differently."

I never went to the funeral. I wish I had. But my own holiday had been arranged, the tickets bought and the Prince insisted I go.

Reluctantly I left him, and he said, "Thank you for all your kindness."

I have never felt right about going, but there was nothing more I could do. His uniform was ready with the decorations that would have so pleased his great-uncle. My assistant was there if anything had been needed.

But I wish I had been at the funeral. I had liked Lord Mountbatten very much.

The Prince has pondered the possibility of being kidnapped. A few years ago, before Lord Mountbatten was murdered, the IRA had the Prince on their hit list and he knew it. It wasn't something that was discussed; the security services had warned him to be careful and security itself was stepped up. But he did say one day, "If I'm kidnapped, I'm kidnapped. If I'm gone, I'm gone. I'd be delighted if anyone got me back. But no one should ever pay ransom."

And eventually we were told that the IRA had abandoned (permanently one hopes) their plans for the Prince. They couldn't get near him.

I don't know for sure, but I strongly believe that the

Royal family have an unwritten law that ransom should not be paid for any of them. Obviously kidnapping is always a possibility and one that they have faced.

They know the dangers and so do the security services. People see the police who guard the Royals in their morning coats, walking around Ascot, trying to blend into the surroundings and still looking what they are. But they are not alone. There is a very good backup system, apart from the man on the spot.

There was one Royal Ascot meeting during the Prince's naval days when he was nearly barred from the course. He was stationed at Portsmouth and, having managed to get away early, decided he would go up to Ascot and see the family and their guests. Not having time to get to Windsor Castle, he headed straight for the course and went by the Golden Gates to wave at the Queen as she passed in her carriage on the way down. As he was waiting, an official saw the distant figure and shouted, "Hey, you can't stand there!" The Prince shouted back, "But it's *me!*" "I don't care who you are," said the official coming closer, "you can't stand there." Suddenly it dawned on the poor man to whom he had just refused entry— and he retreated with a lot of bowing. "I needn't have waited anyway," the Prince told me. "They all went by in the carriage and looked the other way."

While I worked for the Prince, he had a team of three policemen, but the two most senior of them at the time were John Maclean and Paul Officer. Paul, who did not always agree with the Princess, left on the day of the wedding, and John Maclean is due for retirement in 1983. John has always been with the Prince. He's fortyish, a good honest man, and one of the few people who can keep up with his boss. They share the same interests; they both enjoy sports, wind surfing, diving, fishing—all the energetic things. Paul is more reserved—comfortable at garden parties and at Ascot. But John, even in white tie and tails, still looks what he is. Play "spot the policeman" and he'll be picked out every time. But that in itself is probably an added protection.

"A handy man to have in a fight," the Prince used to say, though I don't believe either of them were ever in one.

The good old days when policemen attending Royalty just had to carry a coat or help with the shopping are over. Today security is all.

The Prince himself has terrific instinct, is very cautious, and unlikely to put himself in a position where he could be at risk. When he is driving himself, which he loves to do, he notices if anyone seems to be following. His first reaction is that it must be the press, but just to be certain, the policeman in his car makes a radio computer check on the number of the following vehicle.

Only on two occasions were we really worried by a car that wouldn't go away, but in both cases we were driving down a long A road. In the end the Prince decided that our tail was just someone who couldn't be bothered to overtake and who was going exactly the same way.

Balmoral is one of the few places where he can really go walking—the chances of someone springing at him from a bush are remote. But if anyone tried the

Prince would probably have already sensed they were there. He has an animal instinct in the country—no doubt brought about from all those years of stalking stags. He knows how to move silently, and is aware if anything human or animal is about.

He has this habit of wanting those around him to share what he enjoys. So, he took me stalking with him once at Balmoral.

"No need to take a car," he said. So we walked. And walked. And walked. By the end of the day I could see him striding further ahead in the growing dusk. At one point he must have been a mile in front of me, and I was beginning to get rather nervous. We were stuck in the middle of nowhere, and I was thinking I'd never make it home as he plunged deeper and deeper into the moorland. In the end he waited for me to catch up. But I assure you, even a fit terrorist would have had trouble stalking *him* in the country-side he knows so well.

A lot of Royal security is unseen. In their homes there are panic buttons around the place which set off silent alarms, bringing assistance in an emergency. It is necessary to know where they are and how to use them.

Indeed, bells are a great feature of Royal life. Most Palace staff are summoned by them. We used to say that the first thing that Nanny teaches a Royal is how to ring for services.

In the Prince's study there is a special bell under his desk. This is not meant to be used as a defense against attack. It was there to summon me.

Anyone who gets a chance to talk to the Prince about a project—like the head of a charity or the purveyor of some new scheme—is liable to become carried away with enthusiasm. If an appointment overran, the Prince would just gently touch the bell under his desk drawer and after a few moments in I'd glide. He'd look up, all surprised: "Oh, Stephen—is it really that late?" and turning apologetically to his guest, "I'm so sorry—I'm running out of time."

It was a marvelous way of tactfully ending an interview.

But his kind heart could cause the Prince trouble. One year—it must have been about 1978—he was driving through the moorland in Scotland on his way back to Balmoral when he saw a very disconsolate girl, deep in the countryside, thumbing a lift. He stopped, and she told him she was lost.

"She turned out to be some sort of student," he told me as he was preparing for dinner, "so I just took her back to the main road and dropped her."

A year went by, and he came back to Balmoral Castle having been out on the same road. "Can you believe it!" he said to me. "I saw a girl thumbing a lift, stopped—and it was the same one as last year."

"You were set up, sir," I told him. "The lady obviously had her timing down to a fine art."

Security is different now with a much tighter guard on the Royal family, even more so since the awful security breach when, last year, a man managed to enter the Queen's bedroom. Not so long ago the Royal family seemed to move around with fewer restrictions and in a more relaxed way with the police being a formality rather than a protector. There is a charming story involving the Queen Mother and her policeman.

The Queen Mother spends her weekends at Royal Lodge, her country home near Windsor Castle. One Friday, as usual, she set off, her policeman in the front seat beside the chauffeur. It was a warm afternoon and he nodded off. On the way out of London the car suddenly halted in traffic. The policeman woke with a jolt and immediately jumped out of the car and opened the rear door. "Where are we?" inquired the Queen Mother. The policeman looked around and to his horror realized that they hadn't arrived at Royal Lodge. "Hammersmith Broadway, Your Majesty," he stammered. "Oh, well," she said, smiling, "perhaps we'll go a little further today"— and on they drove.

Yet Buckingham Palace itself is very secure. There are all sorts of beams in the garden which if broken by intruders bring the police screaming in from miles around. The sentries aren't entirely there for the pageantry and since three German hitchhikers managed to get in and sleep the night in the Buckingham Palace grounds, believing they were in Hyde Park—only six days after the incident at the Trooping the Colour— the walls around the Palace have been made even higher.

The job of guarding the Prince is very much sought after in the police force. The reason is simple—he is the pleasantest of the Royals to work for. He's easygoing. He cares about his staff and he likes people. And so his staff stay. Princess Anne's turnover of staff is quite enormous. She loses her temper and shouts, and they simply will not stay with her. Prince Andrew tends to be the same.

The Royals, I'm afraid, are birds in gilded cages.

10

A Prince of Wit and Warmth

THE STRONGEST WORD I ever heard the Prince of Wales use was "bloody." I never heard him utter a four-letter word in the twelve years I worked for him. Nor does he go around kicking the furniture or throwing things. That sort of behavior is simply not his style.

When annoyed, he generally groans, his head gently bent, and pulls a clown's face, all more in sorrow than anger. He has been known to shout— usually at the telephone answering machine—when things go wrong. It's an original way of letting off steam as the recipient of his wrath can't hear him.

One thing that makes him very tight lipped is smoking. He cannot abide it. His car has no ashtray, so if people ask if they may smoke, he says, "Of course, but I'm so sorry there are no ashtrays."

No one is likely to scatter ash over the Prince of Wales' car rugs so that usually ends that.

He has no ashtrays in any of his private apartments, though they will be produced for a dinner or cocktail party. We had one equerry who used to smoke what the Prince called "those dreadful French cigarettes."

The poor man always had to go and stand at the other end of the plane, the room, from wherever we were so that the smell didn't float in the Prince's direction.

I remember one evening when we were in Yellowknife, in northwest Canada, attending a big political dniner. Four hundred people were in an overheated banqueting room while outside the temperature was subzero. The Prince had particularly asked our host, the Commissioner for the Northwest Territories, to request that no one smoke until after the Royal toast. There were rumblings of discontent when this was announced.

When eventually the toastmaster said his "to Her Majesty the Queen" line there was an audible sigh of relief. All that could be heard were handbags opening, cigarette packet paper rustling, matches striking, and lighters clicking. The room looked like a torchlight parade, and the Prince looked horrified. But he was quite unrepentant at having made them wait. He genuinely believes that smoking is bad for the health.

If smoking annoys him, tardiness truly angers him. He loathes being kept waiting. If he's ready to go, he wants to leave. He wastes no time. He can change his clothes in minutes. Many's the time I have heard him come in from an appointment, go straight through from bath to dress and out the door in the space of ten minutes. I never liked to go in when he was dressing and thought to myself, "I'll give him a few more minutes"—and I would miss him.

If I wanted to catch him to ask him about his plans for the next day, give him telephone messages, ask what time he wanted to get up in the morning, or remind him of an appointment, I had to be quick. I had to catch him in those vital minutes before getting out of the bath and going out of the door.

Miss him and he was halfway down the corridor shouting out, "Good-night, Stephen," as he tore down the stairs to the car, running as always. He and his father Prince Philip are just the same. Both of them are always dashing.

It was a great joke once when he was running back from the swimming pool during a State visit from the President of Zaire. The Prince had dressed in a suit and tie after his swim and was tearing along as usual. Out of a room popped a black gentleman, one of the President's entourage, who stopped him.

"You press," he demanded imperiously, thrusting a bundle of clothing into the Prince's hand.

"Certainly, sir," said the Prince of Wales, and without missing a beat, took them off down the corridor until he found a footman to pass them to. A rather bewildered footman, I might say, who could not imagining why Prince Charles should be handing him a bundle of someone else's dry cleaning.

"Guess what happened," he said back in his sitting room. "I nearly got your job."

But all this rushing about makes him impatient with people who are slow—just as his father was impatient with him. He has quite a collection of stock phrases. When people keep him waiting he says, "I don't know why I *bother*."

Another is "The things I do for England!" when called upon to eat something quite disgusting which protocol demands he swallow. He has eaten and drunk some very strange things in different parts of the world. Raw liver and blubber in the Arctic regions, snake in Hong Kong, and some questionable cocktails in Africa.

He's even tolerant about some of the poorer food which is served at the Palace. He lifts up the cover, looks at whatever is on the plate, sighs and says, "They haven't done very well, have they?" Considering there are about twenty people in the Palace kitchens he has every right to be angry, but another of his stock phrases as he picks at his meal is "Anything for a quiet life."

About the only thing that really caused near rebellion, while I worked for him, was when he had to wear a stiff-fronted shirt on State occasions.

"Have I absolutely got to?" he'd grumble when I produced one.

"I'm afraid so, sir."

"I loathe these things—" looking at it as if it was designed for strangulation.

Soothingly, "I know, sir."

"Oh, all right"—and he'd begin to struggle into the thing.

Basically he is a contented person, happy with his lot and his position. Considering the restrictions on

From my little house on Lillie Road in London to a rather larger house. You can see my rooms in the Palace circled.

Carriage duty as a young footman in Park Lane.

The Royal family when I entered Royal Service. (*UPI*)

The investiture of Charles as Prince of Wales marked his entry into adulthood — and signaled his need for a valet. (*UPI*)

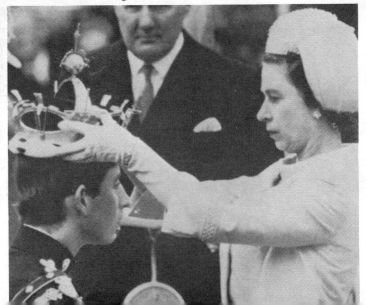

Fun at Balmoral. One of my favorite photos of the Prince is the one of him dancing the Highland Jig with his young cousin, Lady Sarah Armstrong-Jones. (*UPI*)

A typical day at Buckingham Palace — with my assistance, the Prince was able to do two things at once. (*Allan Warren*)

Two of the three ladies who have influenced the Prince's life: his grandmother, the Queen Mother, and Lady Susan Hussey, one of Queen Elizabeth's ladies-in-waiting. (*UPI*)

The Queen in a rare moment of informality — wearing slacks.

The sporting Prince: in the saddle during a race and out — a dreaded nightmare at polo. (*UPI*)

Windsurfing at Cowes — a calmer sport. (*UPI*)

My outdoor job: loading the Prince's shotgun at a game fair. (*Anwar Hussien*)

Travels with My Prince

Looking out the window of
the Royal Andover aircraft
until it's my turn to
disembark.

Left, snake for lunch in Hong Kong with the
Ghurka regiment. (*UPI*)

Below, watching the mudmen dance in Papua,
New Guinea.

A red Indian tribe in Canada made the Prince an honorary chief.

Another crown of feathers to grace his Christmas card Jubilee year.

The Prince and his staff in the Arctic — from one extreme to the other.

Stephen

WITH ALL GOOD WISHES FOR
CHRISTMAS AND THE NEW YEAR
1977

and my thanks for all your hard work throughout this hectic year —

Charles.

CANADA 1977.

Candidates Over the Years for "The Job":

Lady Jane Wellesley (*UPI*)

Davina Sheffield (*UPI*)

Lady Sarah Spencer
(*Anwar Hussien*)

The Lord Mountbatten with
his candidate, Amanda
Knatchbull, his niece. (*Anwar
Hussien*)

And the winner! (*UPI*)

The Royal Calendar

Summers at Balmoral in Scotland. (*Anwar Hussien*)

Winters at Sandringham in Norfolk. (*Anwar Hussien*)

Weekends at Highgrove — the Prince's first house of his own.
(*Anwar Hussien*)

Christmas at Windsor Castle — I took this view from my room.

Mother and Father

A proud mother shows her affection and pride after a successful polo match. (*UPI*)

A saddened father and son after the tragic murder of Lord Mountbatten. (*UPI*)

Inside and Outside Buckingham Palace

Left, I took this view from a window looking out at the crowds. *Below*, the family on the balcony after the Trooping the Colour. (*UPI*) *Bottom*, away from it all: the Queen, Princess Margaret, and other Royals at Badminton Horse Trials. (*UPI*)

I went to a wedding . . .

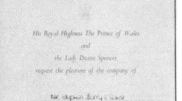

His Royal Highness The Prince of Wales
and
the Lady Diana Spencer
request the pleasure of the company of

Mr. Stephen Barry Evans

at Mark's Club on Thursday, 16th July, 1981

Black Tie   *7.30 for 8.00 p.m.*

My own invitations.

ER
The Lord Chamberlain is Commanded by
The Queen and The Duke of Edinburgh to invite

Mr. Stephen Barry

to the Marriage of
His Royal Highness The Prince of Wales
with
The Lady Diana Spencer
in St. Paul's Cathedral
on Wednesday, 29th July, 1981 at 11.00 a.m.

One of the best seats in the cathedral. (*Serge Lemoine*)

And on the honeymoon, too

H.M.S. *Britannia*, the Royal yacht.

The unpublished route of the sixteen-day honeymoon cruise.

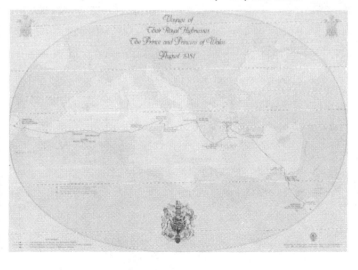

A ship's concert: the staff join the crew in entertaining the honeymooners. That's me dancing out of step on the right.

The only outside visitors on the honeymoon, the late President Sadat and his wife arrive for dinner when the ship anchored at Port Said *(UPI)*

The honeymoon party near the end of the voyage. As you can see, we all had a marvelous time.

The Prince and Princess' farewell photo to me — and my favorite one of them.

Charles 1982 Diana.

Out of Royal Service and back to private life. (*Jarry Lang*)

his life, and the fact that he is the future King, he really is very nice. He enjoys being who he is. He loves his family and his job and performs his duty cheerfully most of the time. He only pulls a long face when he is tired.

Of course, there are plenty of compensations for the restrictions of being Royal. Often in conversation he'd ask me if I had seen a certain film.

"Yes, sir," I'd tell him.

"Would I like it?"

"Yes, sir, I think you would."

That film would then be brought up to Balmoral to watch during the summer.

I love the theater and go quite often. He'd use me as his own personal theater critic and ask for advice on what to see on one of his rare free evenings.

A theater visit requires special arrangements, but believe me, even a full house miraculously isn't if the Prince of Wales wants to take a party.

"Do you ever go to night clubs?" he asked me once.

"No, sir, I do not," I told him. "I can't afford to."

He looked thoughtful. "Yes, I suppose the cost of going out must be very high," he said.

We—the policeman and I—used to go along to the big formal parties with him, and we enjoyed ourselves enormously. The Prince, on the other hand, was always being annexed by the hostess, perhaps having to meet her plain daughter, her maiden aunt, or some long-lost relative from America.

John Maclean and I would be laughing in the corner or talking to the pretty girls, and we'd receive the odd wish-I-were-there look as the Prince answered the same boring questions and asked the same boring ones back. Eventually he'd manage to break away for a moment and get over into the corner with us for a bit of light relief.

"Who have you been talking to?" he always wanted to know.

He's good at hiding boredom, but he does fall asleep quite a lot. Usually at private dinners. People who know him well know that he likes to nod off and the lady sitting next to him—usually the hostess—will carry on talking as if he's fascinated by her conversation. There have been occasions when they didn't even realize that forty winks were being grabbed. But he wakes up, refreshed, bright and cheerful, and carries on talking as if nothing has happened.

He sleeps on airplanes and in cars. He has a great gift of being able to catnap and wake up the better for it.

With all the traveling that he does, it is fortunate that he does not suffer from jet lag. Because he drinks so little—one dry martini a day and he'll often skip that—he adjusts very well after a long-distance flight.

When we would return to England after hours on a plane, he would just come into his apartment, head for his bedroom saying, "Phew, I'm exhausted." But after a very brief rest he'd be fine again.

At the Palace he used to sleep in a huge four-poster bed with curtains around in the same pattern as the curtains and walls. Now that he has moved to Kensington Palace the bed has gone there.

There were a pair of rather fine eighteenth-century tables on each side of the bed and two large chests of drawers on two walls of the big, comfortable room.

Heavy curtains, white with green climbing plants and birds on them, covered the long windows.

He had a fireplace, but he never lit the fire. He can't abide heat. A really freezing wind would have to blow down the Mall and into his bedroom to force him to turn on even one bar of the electric fire which stands in the grate.

"If you're cold, put on a pullover," is another of his little sayings. A pullover is the Prince's idea of central heating.

Power cuts never disturb the Royals in the slightest. The Prince puts on an extra pullover, and the Queen sits tranquilly at her desk, wearing her mink coat.

Power cuts are just another temporary crisis, a little discomfort to enjoy.

It was ironic that people were always very grateful when the Prince and his retinue were guests at a country house party in the winter. The host would put the central heating on full blast for his arrival.

"We haven't had the heating on for weeks," the staff would tell me. And the only person who didn't appreciate all the warmth was the Prince himself.

When I worked for him he had four rooms. Two of these, the bedroom and the sitting room, had been designed by the interior designer David Hicks, who married Lord Mountbatten's daughter, Pamela. His study he decorated himself with dark brown hessian wallcoverings and lots of picture lights.

It is a big room—big enough for fourteen people to dine and in the early days he used to give dinner parties there. He hadn't done so for years after he left the Navy. The last big lunch he gave in his own room was for the officers and their wives from H.M.S. *Bronnington*, on his twenty-eighth birthday, when the ship was in the Pool of London. It was a marvelous treat for all of them.

"It's a bonus having a Captain who is also a Prince," one of the officers said to me as we showed them round the Palace afterwards.

In his study he keeps his desk that he had at Cambridge, and it is here that he spends most of his time, working at what he calls "doing bags."

The "bags" are blue plastic pouches, zip fastened, and sealed with a plastic seal so that he can check to be sure no one has tampered with them. A huge variety of papers come in these pouches. Lists of his engagements, requests for audiences, details of future tours. These pouches are filled and sent to him by his office every day, regardless of where he is. He sees most things that arrive from the Government, but a lot of the mail he receives is dealt with by staff. He only gets the personal letters.

Children and schools write and send in drawings. Years ago a child sent him a marvelous drawing of the Prince as the Prince of Wales and drew him as a whale wearing a crown. He was enchanted by this and had it framed. It now hangs in his bathroom.

The children's letters are handled by the office, but it is amazing how efficiently things get dealt with if someone writes to him. The letter will be marked for action and forwarded to an M.P. who then usually jumps to it. The Prince expects an early reply. Three private secretaries and an assistant look after the bulk of his correspondence and all letters are answered— unless they come from lunatics. We had one who wrote three times a day. An abusive letter came with every post. But it's fascinating how people still turn to the Royals as a last resort. And sometimes it works.

Most of his day is spent seeing people and he is also involved in Duchy of Cornwall matters and interested in his tenants. He listens to Radio Four when he can—taking the radio into the bathroom and carrying it around with him. His one paper is *The Times*. The Princess of Wales on the other hand reads everything she can lay her hands on.

Even on Windsor weekends the work does not cease. There he tries to work out of doors. He loves sitting in the fresh air snd sunshine and his favorite place is along by the garden wall, near the Queen's Tower. We take out a card table which we set up for him, with a comfortable chair and a telephone. And there he is, if anyone wants him. This south-facing spot is tucked under the wall by the East Terrace, where a big cage full of budgies live. They make a perfect alarm system, twittering excitedly if anyone walks down the path, so he is always aware if someone is coming.

He would often go and spend the night at Windsor, particularly if he were riding the next morning. This wouldn't cause any complications, as there are always a few staff in residence. I would just ring up and say, "We're coming down tonight," and the rooms were basically ready and waiting. The Palace kitchens would provide a picnic and off we'd go.

His rooms in Windsor Castle aren't grand. They are cluttered with the kind of bits and pieces that we all collect over the years. Someone gives him a bowl for Christmas or a piece of glass, and it finds a home in

Windsor. His rooms are a housemaid's nightmare to dust! He keeps all his polo trophies there—and there are a lot of them—and the general effect is one of comfort. The furniture is plain and modern with good fabrics. There are watercolors on the walls. But none of his own are hung, even though he paints a lot and even managed to complete a couple of pictures when he was on his honeymoon. His paintings are framed, but just lying around. He's not vain enough to hang them.

"Do you recognize this place?" he was always saying, rather shyly handing me his latest masterpiece. If I could say, "Of course, it's a Craigowan view," he was delighted.

On weekends he usually answers letters from friends who have invited him to shooting or fishing weekends months in advance. Anyone wanting the Prince of Wales as a houseguest has to ask him early.

He now sees less of his friends than he did. In the old days before the Princess came along, he would often say, "Stephen, we have six coming for drinks, and afterwards we are going on to dinner."

Or, he would ask me to arrange a 10:30 P.M. after-theater supper party. During the mid-seventies he did have a busy social life, but as his friends married, settled, and had children, he became more isolated.

There was the added problem that sometimes people were afraid to ask him out, convinced he would be too busy. It used to amuse me how even his close friends would approach the subject. The dialogue usually went, "I'm sure you're far too busy to come to dinner, but we'd love to see you if you can."

"When?" the Prince would say.

He loved being asked out, but people held back for obvious reasons. As he could hardly ring up and invite himself, quite often he'd find himself eating alone or with the Queen.

He himself can be disorganized about arrangements. He loves opera and would book the Royal Box at the Opera House and then forget to ask anyone to join him. I'd remind him he was going to the opera.

"My God!" he'd say. "So I am. Who with?"

This was always something of a problem. He tried to avoid asking people he knew would be bored stiff but might feel they should accept. So we'd scratch around at the last minute, trying to find opera enthusiasts who were free. I always went as he knew I loved it. The author and explorer Lawrence Van der Post and his wife were frequent guests, so was Sir Isaac Berlin, an Oxford philosopher, Hugh and Emily Van Cutsem, very old friends who have managed to become close to the Princess. But more often than not Lady Susan Hussey, the Queen's Lady-in-Waiting would be dragged along to fill up the box. Not that she minded. She too loves opera but most of the Prince's friends aren't that keen.

The Prince is the Patron of the Royal Opera House and a night at the opera as his guest is a performance, both on stage and in the Royal Box. We always took dinner with us. Behind the box there is a small dining room, and little do the audience realize what is going on. For two hours footmen have been in the theater, laying out silver, beautiful glassware, and linen. When they have finished the table looks like one from the Palace—not surprising as everything has been brought from there.

When the first intermission comes, the Prince takes his party through the door at the back of the box and into the dining room. They then sit down for the first and the main course.

My principal job of the evening was to wait for the five minute bell and then nod to him.

"Five minutes, sir," I'd say.

I'd then remind him when the two minute bell went, which meant down with knives and forks and lights out, so that when the door to the box was opened he and his guests could slip through quietly without causing a hiccup. He was anxious not to inconvenience people who had paid a lot of money for their seats.

In the second interval, pudding and coffee were served. At this point the principal singers from the opera would come up and take a cup of coffee with him. He rarely missed a Joan Sutherland performance; she always popped up to see him—in full stage regalia. Another favorite is Placido Domingo.

The Prince, of course, does not pay for his tickets. The Royal Box is owned by the Royal family, and they share it among them. The Duke and Duchess of Kent often go and try to make sure they don't clash with the Prince. But he usually hears when they want to see a performance and often asks them to join him.

It's rather a pity that the Princess Diana dislikes opera as it is one of his great pleasures. Those were wonderful nights out, and the old-world touch of having dinner in the theater made them perfect. He looks forward to his opera nights and they are arranged well in advance—like all his engagements.

Very well in advance, in fact. Twice a year, in June

and December, he holds a meeting with his office to plan the next six-month's engagements. Requests for his presence will have come in from all over the country. Working from this meeting, he tries to keep himself free in the mornings until 9:30 and leave himself a small gap in the afternoon. And he tries to keep a long weekend free from engagements whenever it is possible. This leaves him a very crowded four-day work week, but he prefers to work longer hours followed by a longer break. If he is going away for a weekend, he tries to fit engagements into the journey, saving both time and money.

Wherever he stays, local vicars always ring to ask if he will be coming to church. The answer is usually no.

"I can pray while I'm fishing, but I can't fish in church," he says.

I would occasionally go fishing with him, and personally I found it hard work, just watching, standing all day long, casting, and sometimes catching nothing. Not that this bothers the Prince. He's a good fisherman and doesn't get upset if he comes home empty handed. I've known him to go two days without a catch and still stay cheerful. I think a lot of the appeal of fishing for him is because with a rod in his hand and his feet in the water, he doesn't have to talk to anyone.

One of his favorite places to fish is at Anne, Duchess of Westminster's home on Loch Moore, in the Western Highlands. He usually managed to land a salmon in either the loch or the stream that runs into it. This he would give to the Duchess who promptly would give him one back. She is a particularly pleasant Duchess. She even gave me a salmon once.

We fished in all the best places. In the summer on the Wye where the Duke of Beaufort has a stretch of river. At Broadlands, Lord Mountbatten's home. He was a dedicated angler.

Prince Edward is following in the Prince's waders. He likes to fish. Prince Andrew shows no interest whatsoever. Edward and Andrew are chalk and cheese, but Edward is more like Prince Charles. They have a lot in common—the same basically easygoing temperament. They are both gentle people.

Like Edward, the Prince at heart cares more about family and home than anything. He used to tell me how happy he was on school holidays when he was at Balmoral and how he dreaded the return to Gordonstoun.

"I had this schoolboy dream. I was going to run away and hide in the forest. Somewhere I couldn't be found so I didn't have to go back to school. I hated school and hated leaving home," he said.

It wasn't that he was soft. He just loved his family and his home life.

"When you're having a perfectly good time," he said once, "you don't want to go back to cold showers at seven in the morning and cross-country runs before breakfast."

But I think he'd send his own children to the same sort of school. In retrospect he knows it was the right thing for him.

Even when I first knew him, when we were both twenty-one, he was still very shy and people would try to take advantage of him and manipulate him.

Now it is the other way round. He is totally in command of the situation. If he picks up the phone to say he wants something done and done immediately, no one leaves it until the next day, as used to happen. His wishes are carried out.

When he was younger, his office used to sneak off early on Fridays and I'd find him on the telephone with no one there, making strangled noises of fury.

Now he is confident, and it was the Navy that changed him. In those five years of service, he matured. He even looked more mature when he grew and sported a splendid full beard for a while.

The beard made its first public appearance at Badminton Horse Trials and was very popular in the family—except with Princess Margaret who hated it.

"I cannot bear the look of that thing," she told him that day. "For heaven's sake, shave it off."

The Queen thought it suited him. "You look just like your great-grandfather," she said, and indeed it did make him look like George V and very impressive at that.

But it had to come off. He was about to be installed as the Great Master of the Order of the Bath and had decided to wear his Welsh Guards uniform for the ceremony. The Navy is the only service allowed to grow a "full set," so it was reduced to the smart mustache which Guards officers are permitted. Then, came the summer, he shaved the whole lot.

"I'm going to grow it again, though," he said. But never did. A beard would have been a problem with any other uniform than naval. That's the trouble belonging to three services—the Army, the Navy and the Air Force, all at once.

133

But growing up took a while for him, just like anyone else. He used to love to play practical jokes. He no longer does this anymore—and thank heavens, say his nearest and dearest.

When he was a cadet in the RAF and stationed at Cranwell, he issued an order to the College that the boot issue was wrong, and would everyone please hand in his boots at the porter's lodge. Every cadet duly did as he was told, and at the end of the day there was a huge pile of unmatched, muddled boots slung outside the poor unfortunate porter's lodge.

I don't think he was enormously popular when it was discovered he was the joker responsible.

Another of his less grown-up habits was throwing bread rolls around at barbecues. I remember he once neatly wrapped a bap—a sort of soft, Scottish bread roll—around Lady Tryon's face. She didn't seem to mind, being one of the ladies in his circle who wasn't remotely stuffy. But then few people voice a criticism of what the Prince of Wales chooses to do.

He used to tease his younger brothers. Before Prince Andrew had a car, he was always begging to borrow big brother's Range Rover.

"Certainly not!" the Prince would say, but he always gave in at the end.

But he was pretty impressive even as a twenty-one-year-old. I remember accompanying him to the Albert Hall where he was to address the National Institute of Directors.

He'd been in a sweat for days over the speech, and the end result was truly brilliant. I sat at the back of the hall listening to him talking so convincingly and sensibly to all those captains of industry, reminding myself how young he was and feeling very proud of him.

Back at the Palace, in his sitting room at teatime, I said, "What a brilliant speech, sir."

"Did I come over all right?" he wanted to know.

"I thought so, sir," I told him.

"Good. It's a weight off my mind, I don't mind telling you."

Even as a young man he never let the Royal image slip. He was fortunate in that he never had teenage spots. The Royals all have good complexions—fresh air and rain water helps no doubt, but more than that, he simply never looks scruffy. His hair always stays in shape. He washes it himself, brushes it, all with the minimum of fuss. Hair to him is not something on which to waste time.

When he needed a haircut, I rang up Mr. Willison from Trufit and Hill in Jermyn Street and asked him to come over. It would be either when the Prince was getting up in the morning or in the evening before he dressed for dinner. He worked on the principle that if he was going to get his shirt messed up with bits of hair, he might as well get the job done when he was going to have to change anyway.

Mr. Willison gave me basic lessons in haircutting so that I could cope with a trim when we were on long tours or in Scotland. In the end I nearly always played barber as it saved time. I suppose I can be held to be directly responsible for the moans from the hairdressing world that his style was awful. Now the Princess' hairdresser cuts the Prince's hair making two for the price of one and a whole new look has developed.

Mr. Willison was only one of many who attended

135

him. If he bruises himself playing polo, his physiotherapist comes along to the Palace. In fact there are only two people he visits—his dentist in Wigmore Street, and if he takes a spill riding, he goes to the King Edward Hospital near Windsor for X-rays. Chiropody he doesn't bother with. He is quite capable of cutting his own toenails.

As I have said, he is very healthy. A fervent believer in exercise, if he's stuck in London, he'll go for a run around Buckingham Palace gardens. And he eats very little as well.

His insistence on neither eating nor drinking too much can cause problems.

We—the policeman and I—were always having to tell white lies on his behalf. People are terribly generous when we stay with them, and they sometimes put a bottle of champagne and a drink tray in his room.

"Oh, dear," he'd say, seeing it sitting in its ice bucket. "Champagne" —in tones that suggested it might be arsenic.

He hates to hurt people's feelings, so we always had to have a glass (my personal preference is red wine) so that when the butler took the bottle back he could report to the lady of the house that the Prince had something to drink and everyone was pleased.

His favorite foods are cold, fishy dishes. Salmon mayonnaise or prawns are always welcome. He likes cheese and puddings. He is not really a meat and two veg man. What he does loathe is chocolate puddings. Chocolate on a biscuit, yes—but never in puddings.

I remember years ago when we were in Tasmania staying in a private home and the hostess had hired a cook to prepare dinner.

The Prince went upstairs to his room, and as I generally tried to warn people of his likes and dislikes, John Maclean and I went down to the kitchen. We were too late. There was this Julia Child of Australia cooking away, very pleased with herself.

John looked at me and I looked at him. She was making a wonderful-looking chocolate mousse. I hadn't the heart to say anything. Then suddenly, she took a great handful of nuts and smothered the pudding with them. Another thing the Prince can't abide is nuts. Poor woman, her heart would have been quite broken if we had told her, so we just quietly crept from the kitchen.

We came upstairs to find the Prince tying his bow tie, just about ready to come down to dinner.

"Everything all right downstairs?" he asked.

"Yes," I said. "You'll love the pudding."

He looked at me suspiciously, "What is it?"

"Well—"

"Not chocolate?"

"It's chocolate. With nuts."

"Oh, God!"

I always had to warn him so that his face wouldn't drop. When the chocolate mousse was produced, he managed a bright smile.

"Oh, lovely," he said, "chocolate mousse! But just the tiniest amount, please. The first course was so good I haven't a lot of room left."

The Princess of Wales' taste in food is rather more sophisticated than her husband's. She likes hot soufflés and Cordon Bleu cooking, so things have slightly changed in the kitchens. At least it gives the chefs more to do.

But the Prince genuinely enjoyed cooking for himself—well, to be frank, playing around with food and generally making a mess. Some years ago he took over Wood Farm at Sandringham as a weekend retreat for himself. He used it when he was at Cambridge and could get away for the odd afternoon. We had a Mrs. Hazel who used to cook for him, but then in 1970, when his policeman and I started going there with him, he used to enjoy coming into the kitchen to help.

His idea of cooking is grilling steaks and making bread and butter puddings, which he really does like. We used to have to eat vast quantities of it otherwise it would be served over and over again.

We also used to spend similar weekends at Craigowan, where he liked to fish. But wherever we were everything had to be eaten. There was no waste at all.

"It's my Scottish meanness coming out," he'd say.

By the end of these trips we were reduced to what he called "scrap meals." Bits of this, that, and the other. I can remember Lady Diana's very first visit to Highgrove, and her face dropping when she was served with one of his leftover lunches.

If it was good enough for him, it was good enough for everyone else.

His Scottish meanness also came out in that he'd check in the kitchen every morning to see how much milk had been ordered on his behalf and how many chickens there were in the deep freeze.

He said in suspicious tones to a chef one day, "Why are there sixteen chickens in the freezer when I'm only here for three days?"

"Well, Your Highness, you do like your vol-au-vents," the chef said.

The Prince was not convinced.

But food is not high on his list of priorities. Up until the time he married he would often pop into the nursery for breakfast, particularly in the days when his little brothers were still there. The nursery was a family unit within the Palace and he needs family. He doesn't drink coffee at all and tea only at five o'clock, so his breakfast drink was cold milk. He ate cereal and toast—no sausages, no eggs, no kedgeree at all.

This sense of family closeness probably explains the Royal fascination with barbecues and picnics. It's impossible to be formal and Royal when eating out of doors, frequently in some discomfort. But they do let others join in occasionally.

But for most of his life when he eats out, he is eating with complete strangers, at some formal dinner or another. He has no favorite restaurant as he rarely goes to them unless it is in a private room or for a friend's birthday. He is more likely to be in a public place like the Savoy or the Dorchester, dining with 100 to 150 people. The routine on these occasions is precise. Over the first two courses he talks to whoever is on his right. Come the pudding and the coffee, he turns to the left. He is constantly squashed between frequently boring Mayors and their wives or faintly belligerent trade union leaders and their awed wives, with the notable exception of Joe Gormley who he thought was fascinating. He certainly gets to talk to a great cross-section of people and enjoys this. He likes asking questions and is intrigued by what makes people successful.

He really does like people and enjoys going out and meeting them—as long as it's not too many at once. He particularly likes the elderly and always makes a great effort to see them. In a crowd he looks ahead for someone whom he thinks he can talk to. Anyone with a broken arm or in a wheelchair or with some obvious problem is the one who will always get his attention. "People want to talk about their broken leg," he says.

He'll trot over, ask a few questions, make a little joke or say something sympathetic, and move on again. I could always guess which face in the crowd he would pick on. Choosing someone a little different made meeting so many people simpler and made those who didn't catch his eye less disappointed. This, combined with his quick humor and ability to make people laugh, gives him an advantage in most situations. What used to impress me is that his French is so good. He can even make jokes in the language.

When the threesome—Prince, policeman, and I—were out, he was always spotting some ridiculous situation that used to make us all laugh.

We were in Barbados once and he spotted an enormous black lady jumping up and down. She was shouting, "Hallelujah! Now I've seen my earthly Prince, I'm ready for my heavenly one!" He dined out on that story for weeks and his imitation improved every time.

He collected little gems like that. Another favorite story that improves with the telling happened just before Princess Anne married the then-Lieutenant Phillips.

The Prince had gone for a ride along what is called The Long Walk—a three-mile ride on the Windsor estate. He had stopped and was sitting looking out over the view when a small boy appeared.

Parking himself by the horse's head he said, " 'Ere. You Lieutenant Phillips?''

The Prince looked down at him.

"So sorry. No."

The child gave a disappointed shrug.

"Well, all right then," he said and trotted off back down the hill.

He does have a considerable sense of humor which sometimes took the form of winding us up. We all wanted to hang on to our jobs because we liked what we were doing.

Riding along in the car he'd say, absolutely straight faced, "I'm going to make some changes soon. I'm sure you're all ready to do something different, aren't you?"

Not quite sure whether or not he was joking, response was difficult.

One day when the police had all been given a raise by the Government, he said to John Maclean, "Well, how much do you earn now?"

(The Prince does not, incidentally, pay his policemen. They are paid by the Home Office.)

"I'm not going to tell you, sir," John said.

"Oh, come on. Tell me. Is it as much as a captain or a major in the Army?"

John, whose rank was Chief Inspector, nearly choked. He had a strong suspicion, without knowing, that majors earned a good deal more.

"I'm not sure, sir," he said. "I don't know what the Army are paid."

Joining the conversation, I said thoughtfully, "Perhaps I should ask for a payrise,'' working on the principle that timing is all.

John, anxious to change the subject, said, ''You'd better see your shop steward about that.''

''I *am* his shop steward,'' the Prince said, ''and he can't have one.''

But afterwards he looked into what I was earning, and I did get a small raise. His Scottish meanness (as he himself called it) is always in conflict with his natural generosity.

11

Courting Danger

THE PRINCE does take risks, far too many for both the Queen and now the Princess of Wales' comfort. For years he has fought to do exactly what he wants, and most times he wins. It's known at the Palace that the Queen cringes every time he goes hunting. People in his own office are always trying to persuade him to be "sensible," as they call it. But he is very much in charge of his own decisions.

Yet it is unlikely that he'll ever get away with his greatest ambition. He yearns to ride in the Grand National, but the weight of opposition is too great. I doubt if it will ever happen. When he came off his own horse, Good Prospect, in 1981 at a steeplechase meeting at Sandown, that probably finished all his chances of a crack at the National. Particularly as he fell from the same horse four days later at Chelten-ham.

These falls were dangerous enough, though all he did was bruise his back and his ego. Nevertheless, he was not amused. The horse, he insisted, had no shoulders. He said grumpily, "It's going." And it went. Irritatingly, since then it has been placed several times.

But it is a long way to the ground from a horse and the Royal family have before them the example of the Duke of Buccleuch. In 1971 when he was the Earl of Dalkeith he fell in a hunting accident and has been in a wheelchair ever since. But his passion for hunting is so strong still that the Duke follows the hunt—sadly from a specially designed mobile cart.

Probably the most dangerous thing the Prince ever did was in the Northwest Territories of Canada. We went there to visit the Eskimo population and the marvelous Commissioner for the area, Stuart Hodgeson, arranged the whole visit.

The Prince wanted to get as near to the Arctic as he could and we finished up at a place called Resolute Bay. This is a small settlement of huts, inhabited mainly by Eskimos and scientists. There was nothing else except a great deal of snow. Once there, the Prince embarked with great enthusiasm on activities that are not normally found in kinder climates. He went dog-sleighing, husky-trekking, and even ate blubber.

The Prince was having a whale of a time, if you'll excuse the pun. So was I. It was a fascinating adventure for all of us on the trip—John Maclean, Sir David Checketts, the Prince's Private Secretary, and me.

At Resolute Bay the scientists had dug a great hole in the ice and one of them, Joseph MacIniss, was taking photographs of marine life under the Arctic.

Before we left England the Prince had heard about this. "I'd love to go down with him," he had said, and his office with some reluctance had arranged with Stuart Hodgeson that this should happen.

The Prince is, of course, a very good skin diver, so it was reasonably safe for him to go. They had to put him in a strange-looking, double-insulated diving suit, bright red with blue stripes, and once inside, the scientists inflated him like a Michelin man to keep out the cold of the water. Had that suit popped, we would have had an instant deep-frozen Prince on our hands.

A tent had been placed over the hole in the ice and there we all gathered for the descent. The hole itself was the size of about four manhole covers, the depth of the ice twenty inches, getting thinner all the time. The water below was jet black; no light could get through.

Once he got into the suit, someone brought him a red helmet and mask and just before it went over his head, silencing him, he said, "What have I let myself in for!"

Indeed, I thought, what have you let yourself in for.

He disappeared down the hole like a big red and blue balloon while about nine of us stood around the edge. Lamps had been lowered into the water to guide him, and he and Joseph MacIniss, who was accompanying him, had underwater torches.

145

John Maclean and I were wondering if we would ever see him again.

"God!" I said. "We might be looking for another job."

"Heaven forbid!" said John.

It seemed awfully quiet, the water was so black and we couldn't see or hear anything. The others seemed confident nothing could go wrong, but until these things are over one never knows. He was gone for about ten minutes. It seemed like ten hours.

When he finally bobbed up again, was pulled out, and the mask came off, he was looking frightfully pleased with himself.

"That was fascinating," he said. "I enjoyed it."

What it was all about I never did find out. There didn't seem to be a great deal to look at except for ice caves and icicles, and I wouldn't have gone down that hole for all the ice in Greenland.

Another thing that he would really liked to have a go at is ballooning, but this has never been allowed. In 1980 there was an invitation from Britain's top balloonist, Don Cameron, to go ballooning over Wiltshire. Everyone, from the Queen's Flight, who advise on flying activities (he can't even go on a private plane without their approval), to his office, disapproved so heartily that he finally agreed to forget it.

It ruined his day. He could see all these beautiful balloons floating about the sky on one of those crisp October days when the sun shines so sharply. He had come from a house party at the Tryons and with them he watched from the ground.

"I don't see why I couldn't have done it," he grumbled. "It doesn't look that dangerous."

As it is, he is qualified to fly helicopters and turbo-prop planes, but not jets. He hasn't had sufficient time to learn about jet piloting which is apparently a totally different flying skill.

He can fly Andovers of the Queen's Flight and frequently does. When we went to Ghana and the Gold Coast in 1975, he did practically all the flying. But now he just likes to take off and land. He leaves the boring bits when the plane is on automatic to the co-pilot.

John Maclean and I used to give him points for his landings—rather like Come Dancing or the Ice Skating championships. We had some cards with numbers on them which we'd hold up when the plane was down. A bumpy one rated under five. A smooth finish gave him up to ten.

"You try and do it better next time," he'd say, laughing, when we were both pretending to be ill. When we gave other staff a lift, they'd look on in amazement, wondering what the hell was going on. John and I could get away with a lot more than anyone else.

Polo, of course, while a gentleman's sport (though I did sometimes wonder hearing the language coming from the field) is hardly a gentle one. It's a very fast game, but the Prince is fearless. He has had some nasty crashes. He cut his chin rather badly once and has the scar to prove it, and no doubt there's another from the bloodied mouth he got at Windsor in June 1982.

He says scars do not matter. "I'm not a pop singer," he announced.

Extraordinarily, even on the polo field he never

147

seems to get untidy or rumpled looking. I don't know how he does it.

But polo is his great relaxation and he personally is reponsible for the current popularity of the game. When the Duke of Edinburgh gave up in the early seventies, interest in it declined. When the Prince became interested, it revived immediately.

It does cost dearly to play. It's necessary to have sufficient cash to keep four or five polo ponies, all of which eat their heads off. Grooms and stabling have to be paid, plus vet's bills. The Prince's ponies are kept at Windsor, where the Queen breeds them. He normally plays at Smith's Lawn, Windsor, but has to borrow other people's ponies if he plays abroad or far from home. The expense of transporting the four ponies needed for a game is too great.

Polo is probably his greatest extravagance. Then comes hunting which, thank God, is only a short season. He always thought he was doing me a favor by saying, "Do you want to follow the hunt today?"

"I'd love to," I'd say bravely and get in the car and sit there for hours, watching a herd of overdressed people occasionally charge past on horses before they disappeared into the distance.

It was boring. I much preferred watching polo. When I had first joined the Prince he had said, "Do you know anything about polo?"

The answer was no.

"The only way you'll understand it is to watch it being played," he said. "You'd better come along."

I liked being on the field and talking to people. Also I was useful. When we were abroad we took a huge golf-type bag with us—full of polo sticks. Each stick is a different height to go with the height of the pony. They vary between 49 inches and 55 inches from the player's hand to the ground, based on the height of the horse.

It was my job to "do the sticks" and remember the playing order of the ponies—in other words measure them against the animal to be sure which stick went with each horse. If the Prince played with the wrong one, the stick would not have made contact when he swung at the ball.

The biggest scare he gave us was once when he was playing polo and I thought we'd lost him. We'd flown in a luxurious private jet with all modern conveniences from an engagement in Vancouver, right across the American continent to the Wellington Polo Club, a new complex in Florida, some way from Palm Beach.

He was going on to Eleuthra, a Bahamian island where his cousins, the Brabournes, have a home. And it was an ideal opportunity to stop en route for a little polo.

It was blazing hot in Florida. He had practiced in the morning and then played a very fast game in the afternoon. When he came off the field he sat down on the golf cart, looking very pale and rather peculiar. He was scheduled to present a prize in a few minutes' time but he didn't look at all well.

"Are you all right, sir?" I asked.

He was breathing very erratically. "I'll be all right in a minute," he said. He wasn't. Paul Officer and I hovered anxiously, and when he suddenly said, "I do feel unwell. I don't think I'll be able to present that prize," Paul went into action.

He summoned a car from the U.S. Secret Service (who were there in droves), and we immediately took the Prince back to the cottage where we were staying. Once there he said he thought he might lie down for a minute or two.

Paul and I were worried. This was all very out of character, and Paul, having a vague knowledge of medicine, said to me, "I think he's dehydrated. We'd better get the doctor from the polo field."

Paul made the telephone call while I pulled the Prince's polo boots off as he lay on top of the bed. The doctor was there in minutes. He took one look at the Prince and said, "Hospital."

The transit van we had been using was brought to the door by a security man. I folded the white bedspread over the Prince where he lay, and Paul bodily picked him up and carried him to the van. We made him lie down in the back—there was plenty of space.

By this time the Americans were doing everything possible. Two police cars arrived to escort us to the hospital, both with sirens, one driving in front, the other behind. It was all very dramatic, but rather worrying to think that the next King was stretched out behind us, wrapped in a bedspread, and looking very ill.

The journey took an interminable ten or fifteen minutes. When we got to the hospital, the Prince was paler than ever. He was rushed in as they had been warned that a V.I.P. was arriving. The hospital staff seemed to think it was the Governor of Florida or some film star because of all the fuss and curiosity was rife. When they discovered it was the Prince, people seemed to emerge from the woodwork, all trying to get a look at him.

Not many of them managed it. With all speed the Prince was taken to an emergency room. I stayed with him all the time while a team of medics performed all sorts of tests on him. He was given a glucose drip, and he lay there very quietly while it was all going on.

"Are you all right?" I asked him.

"Yes," he said, but his voice was very weak.

Oliver Everett, the Prince's Assistant Private Secretary, who was with us, rang London to forewarn the Palace what was going on. He was anxious that the Queen did not hear the news from the media.

The hospital found Paul a room next door to the Prince, and I went back to the cottage to get pajamas, dressing gown, and a toothbrush. We hadn't bothered to take a thing as we'd rushed out of the door. He was sound asleep when I returned.

His collapse—and it was dehydration—cast a shadow over the weekend. There was a party that night, but the guest of honor was in hospital, and none of his team wanted to go without him. Oliver Everett and I stayed at the cottage. The party went on, but it was just not the same.

I rang Paul at the hospital the next morning, and he told me that the Prince would be coming out after lunch. Could I send a suit as the only clothes he had were his polo gear. I packed for both him and Paul, sent the clothing off, then waited for them to return.

"Are you sure you're all right, sir?" I asked as a shaky Prince appeared out of a huge Mercedes. I always seemed to be asking him if he was all right. But then it was my job to be sure that he *was* all right.

"I think so," he said. "But I did feel most peculiar yesterday. I didn't feel as if I was dying, but I felt very strange." He shook his head. "I've never passed out in my life so I don't know how it feels, but I felt as if I might be about to faint."

He was well enough to eat lunch the next day, and he spent the rest of the time there watching the polo, like a child with measles, watching others have fun. The trip was spoiled for him.

The following week he went off to Eleuthra, and I went down to Fort Lauderdale for a holiday of my own.

"When are you coming back?" he asked as I saw him off at the airport.

"The day before you," I told him.

"Why don't you fly back with me?" he suggested. "It's a scheduled flight."

I was pleased to be asked and delighted to accept. He did rather like me to be with him. I was a face he knew. It was much easier to ask me to do things for him than someone else. He was comfortable with me.

So I changed my booking and was there in case he needed me on his flight home.

~ 12 ~

Travels with My Prince

IT WAS President Sadat's funeral that finally confirmed my decision to leave the Prince. Once so excited at the thought of traveling round the world, I had had enough. I felt when we returned from that short and alarming trip to Egypt that if I never went five miles further than the King's Road I wouldn't care.

I no longer feel antitravel, but that particular funeral was not a pleasant experience.

The news of the President's assassination came through while we were at Craigowan on the Scottish end of the Prince and Princess' honeymoon in 1981. I had heard from the four o'clock radio news program.

The Prince was out stalking; the Princess resting.

One of the policemen said, "Shall we tell the Princess?"

I thought about it and said no. I felt the news should come from the Prince. I knew the President and his wife had made a considerable impression on the Royal couple when they dined on *Britannia* on their honeymoon and I guessed she would be upset. A minute or two later, the Prince's Private Secretary rang and asked if he would ring him immediately he came back.

"Ah," I thought, putting down the phone. "Another funeral."

I met the Prince in the hallway just as he came through the front door.

"Mr. Adeane called, Your Highness," I said. "Can you ring him. I'm afraid it's not very good news."

He was pulling off his rubber boots. "Who is it this time?" he asked, his voice resigned.

"It's President Sadat, sir," I said. "He's been assassinated."

"Oh, dear," he said. "How awful. How did you hear?"

"First the radio, and then Mr. Adeane, sir," I said.

He nodded and then asked, "Where's the Princess?"

"She was resting. We haven't told her," I told him.

"Fine." And shaking his head he went off to tell her himself.

It was immediately decided that he would represent the U.K. at the funeral as the Queen and Prince Philip were in Australia. He wanted to go. He had genuinely liked the President. The Princess wanted to accompany him, but he wouldn't hear of it. There was such uncertainty about what was happening in Egypt that he wouldn't put her in any danger. The Prince, who has a great deal of personal courage, thought it was better he went alone. He explained to the Princess that women rarely went to Muslim funerals, and her appearance could cause diplomatic problems.

The newly wed Princess did not wish to part with her husband and went around muttering, "I wish I could go, too." She was anxious for his safety and would have been happier if he had stayed at home.

We had two days to prepare before the Prince left for Cairo.

"What are the weather conditions there?" he asked me, a familiar question before every trip.

"Very hot, sir," I said.

"Then ask if naval tropical kit will be all right," he said.

He wanted to wear his full-dress naval uniform. It is the one he is most entitled to after five years in the service. The Navy is, of course, the Senior Service. Our only anxiety was if white tropical kit was correct for a State funeral.

His office checked with the Foreign Office, who checked with the Egyptian Embassy, and tropical kit was pronounced O.K. I told his orderly in London where to find the uniform, and when we flew in an Andover down to Heathrow and transferred to a VC 10, his clothing was already on board.

We were quite a small party—the Prince, the Foreign Secretary Lord Carrington with two of his staff, Mr. Adeane, two police officers, and I.

We stayed at the British Ambassador's residence in Cairo for one night after we arrived. The plane was to fly us back next day directly after the funeral.

The atmosphere in Cairo was uncomfortable. People crowded the streets in excited groups; trouble seemed to be bubbling under the surface as if something must erupt.

By the morning of the funeral the tension intensified. The Egyptians had tremendous security problems with the Prince, three former U.S. Presidents and Henry Kissinger, as well as assorted royalty and heads of state all in their town. There was anxiety among our Embassy staff. They were well aware that most of the assassins had not been caught and could still be roaming the streets.

Eventually the Ambassador said to Mr. Adeane, "We've decided it will be more sensible if Lord Carrington's staff and Mr. Barry wait at the airport while the funeral is taking place. Then if anything goes wrong, we only have to get the Prince, Lord Carrington, and you back to the airport and the VC 10 can be underway."

Lord Carrington's secretaries and I spent five hours on the tarmac in the blazing heat, hanging around the plane, wasting time, and worrying that all was well. The tension was almost unbearable. We felt we would rather have been at the funeral than with this dreadful waiting, not knowing if anything was going wrong.

I was also beginning to doubt the wisdom of the Prince wearing white. He would be standing out in the crowd, totally conspicuous; a sitting duck. Ex-Presidents Carter, Ford, and Nixon, and Henry Kissinger, were all in bulletproof vests, and they were safely back in the air by two o'clock, long before the Prince. He had stayed behind to speak to Madame Sadat and to deliver a personal letter from the Princess. He did not reappear at the airport until after five that evening, still wearing the gleaming uniform.

Nevertheless he and Lord Carrington were shaken when they boarded the aircraft, almost the last of the visiting dignitaries to leave.

"We had one bad moment," the Prince said. "It was a very strange feeling. There was a group of guards who seemed to be on crowd control standing in front of us. Quite suddenly they turned around and were facing us with their guns pointing straight at us. John and Jim [his two policemen] nearly had apoplexy. I suppose it was just a question of bad organization, but it gave us quite a fright. We weren't sure exactly what they were going to do. Then they just moved on."

"You should have worn a bulletproof vest, sir," I said, knowing that he had never worn such a thing in his life.

"I couldn't be bothered," he said. "If it's going to happen, it's going to happen."

Funerals were always very tiring. I attended four with him: President Sadat; Kirk, the Prime Minister of New Zealand; Robert Menzies of Australia; and Jomo Kenyatta of Kenya.

Idi Amin was at that funeral, sitting in the same row as the Prince, who told me he thought he was the most evil person he had ever seen. He refused to speak to him or to meet him.

People always seemed to die when we were at Balmoral. This complicated things for me, getting the

Prince's wardrobe together, particularly as funerals were always very quick trips. Board the aircraft, get there, attend the ceremony, turn around, and come back. New Zealand was the worst. One minute we were enjoying Balmoral, then precipitated into an interminable, thirty-hour flight. Then straight back to Balmoral via London before we had time to gather our breath.

The most difficult thing about long-distance funerals was trying to stay awake. There are only two beds on the VC 10 that we used on these occasions. Naturally the Prince had one. The Prime Minister, or whoever was representing the Government in power, had the second. The Leader of the Opposition would either get a chair or do what the rest of us did—stretch out on the floor.

Flying to Prime Minister Kirk's funeral, James Callaghan was Prime Minister. He had the bed. Ex-Prime Minister Edward Heath got the floor.

If we had to stay anywhere that had once been a colony it was always Government House. Their existence creates a network of Royal homes around the world that seems to have survived the death of the Empire. Because we always stayed in these generally quite splendid mansions, and their staffs rarely changed, they knew the Prince's likes and dislikes. Mine, too, come to that. In other countries we would stay at the British Embassy if possible. Hotels were always a last resort.

It was on the plane where I worked hard. I never slept before the Prince had settled down. And I literally slept at the foot of my master's bed. I had to be on call in case he wanted anything.

No matter who else was flying with him, the Prince was in charge. When he wanted the lights down, the rest of the passengers slept, too.

I had to be up well before him, checking the time of landing, and giving him an hour and a half to wake up, breakfast, and dress before we left the aircraft. It was a mad dash sometimes.

The VC 10s we flew are RAF planes, normally used for troop movements and not equipped with any luxuries. There are no full bathrooms. The interiors are very basic; the toilet facilities are much the same as on any commercial flight. The Prince always used an electric razor to shave so there was no question of him cutting his throat at 20,000 feet. But it was amazing how often we'd come in to land and I'd still be belting on a sword or fixing an order in its right place before he made a majestic appearance on the plane steps. At Sadat's funeral he was wearing an Egyptian order which belonged to the Princess of Wales. President Sadat had conferred an order on both of them on the honeymoon. The boxes were identical, but neither of them had been opened. They'd been lying around the office, and the wrong one had been taken in the rush. Nobody noticed.

We had a very set routine on the VC 10s. Once we were on board, off would come his good suit and he'd change into cords and a sweater. We had to be careful doing this. Windows on planes have a habit of being at knee level, and he might have been treating the outside world to a glimpse of the Royal knees. His suit would go on a hanger, ready to be put on again on arrival, unless of course he was leaving the plane in uniform for a State occasion or visit.

The first time I really flew with him was three months after I started the job. We went to Fiji to confer independence on the Islands and from there we went on more or less around the world. When the last Prince of Wales did his world tour by battleship it took him many months. When we went, using an RAF VC 10 part of the time and traveling commercial for more lengthy trips, it took four weeks.

We preferred to use the RAF planes because we could adapt our timings. A commercial plane has to be caught. With the RAF we would come and go at our own pace and the planes were incredibly reliable. There were rarely any problems or hair-raising flights—except for the very first time.

On the way to Fiji one of the engines broke down and we had to land in Bahrain. It wasn't an arranged stop—but a forced one.

"I'm sorry," the Prince said to me. "This really doesn't always happen."

I was relieved to hear it. I'd been thinking to myself, "If it's starting like this, what next?"

We stopped three or four times at RAF bases for refueling and to stretch our legs. The whole lot of us—nine people in all—were always taken off to the C.O.'s house where, if there was a pool, the Prince would swim. But generally he just wanted a little peace and quiet.

He did not always get it. For the C.O.'s wife, this was a moment to savor—entertaining the next King. He did not want to be entertained. He wanted to rest.

We always slept on board the aircraft, and I wasn't sorry to see Fiji and a proper bed again.

The Prince and his Equerry, Nicholas Soames,

went to a number of solemn functions. They would both come back and mimic the whole thing. We laughed a lot.

I was fascinated by the Fijians. They all seemed so enormously tall; I felt like Gulliver and it seemed a long way from home.

Just how far away we were was rather brought home when the Prince asked the Governor's wife what time it was.

"Where?" she asked, and rolled up her sleeves to show four watches on each wrist. She could tell the time anywhere in the world.

From Fiji just four of us went on to the Gilbert and Ellice Islands to deliver a message from the Queen. We flew in a tiny aircraft; first stop Funafuti. There we stayed at what John Maclean christened the Funafuti Hilton—a large hut, just off the beach, divided by screens. This made it somewhat like sleeping in a hospital ward. The Prince had the most private area. He had two screens.

It was pretty primitive. At one end of the hut there were a few bamboo chairs and not much else. All the food was flown in specially from Singapore and served by a rather bewildered local lady. And this narrow strip of desert island with a superb beach was strictly not for swimming. The island was lacking in the usual conveniences, so the sea was to be avoided.

Those we had left behind in Fiji were staying in a luxury sports club.

"Who gets the best time?" the Prince asked.

"They do!" we chorused.

However, we managed, ignoring each other's snores throughout the night and keeping out of each other's way in the morning. I had the Prince's clothes hanging all round the walls. He hadn't much with him anyway, and all I really had to do was make sure his things didn't disappear to souvenir hunters.

Over the years I was to encounter a lot more of these novelty Away Days.

These journeys may sound like jaunts, but they are really hard work, undertaken in strange places and usually in very hot temperatures. They had their comic moments, of course. I remember one island where we commandeered the only car in the place. Overnight this beat-up old Morris Minor became the Royal car, and everyone else in the procession had to pedal behind on bicycles. It was one of those situations that only the British can carry off with dignity.

That first trip was a marvelous experience for all of us. The Prince himself had not done all that much traveling before. It was his first major tour. He had been to Japan, representing Britain, the year previously, and it was there that the Sony people mentioned they were thinking of putting a factory into Europe. Immediately the Prince said, ''Why don't you build it in Wales? There's a nice place near Bridgend.''

They took up the suggestion, and he was, and is, naturally very pleased with himself. Early in 1982 the second phase was opened by the Princess. The papers complained that she had given a Japanese firm incredible publicity by wearing a hat with Sony printed on it. They seemed to have missed the point. That factory is the Prince's pet, and it has brought much-needed employment to a depressed area of his Wales.

But I digress. When we left the islands on our way back we stopped off in Mexico and stayed in the late Merle Oberon's house in Acapulco. Prince Philip and she were old friends, and he suggested that staying with her would be pleasanter than a hotel.

Of course, she was quite old when we went to her home, but still beautiful. A tiny little lady of immense charm. She was married to a Mexican tinman—very rich, of course.

Time meant nothing at her house. It was 10:30 at night before dinner was served and 2:00 in the morning before it finished. The Prince had his is-it-ever-going-to-end face on.

I could always read what he was thinking. Fortunately other people would rarely have guessed.

Most of the time everything went smoothly on our travels. Before a major trip is undertaken, someone from the Prince's office goes and covers the ground —a kind of advance man. Usually the Private Secretary, the policeman, and the Press Secretary will go ahead and plot the whole trip in advance, checking that every room is going to be suitable. They know exactly where he is staying and who he will meet before he even sets off. When they come back, they make final adjustments and recommendations to the programs. They bring him up to date with the background of everyone he will meet. It's very much a professional job, planned to the last detail before we climb into the plane.

The Fiji trip was a major one, and it gave me a great deal of experience quickly as to just what sort of preparation these operations take.

On the plane I would be in constant liaison with the

cabin staff, checking how long the next leg of the journey would be and what time we would be arriving. We'd be juggling time and meals constantly. If we were arriving, say, at 11:00 at night, instead of having lunch and dinner we'd just make it one meal—probably dinner—and do everything possible to minimize jet lag.

In the plane the back-up crew were behind the cockpit, then came the galley, then, behind a curtain, the Prince's section with his bed, his table, and four chairs. Down the aisle and behind another screen there were about six seats where we would sit. Then the rest of the plane would be used, if possible, to move military personnel from place to place. We'd drop servicemen off at places like Cyprus or Singapore all the time. The flight was rarely entirely for the Prince's benefit—mainly because using the plane for another purpose made for economy.

There were times when it seemed we spent our lives in the air, trying to keep some pattern to time so that we were not completely disoriented when we got to the other end. It bothered the Prince very little. He likes moving on. Three days anywhere is enough for him—unless it's Balmoral or Highgrove. After that he becomes restless.

The Prince would sleep, wake up, eat breakfast at what seemed like a suitable hour. When lunch was possible, we'd take turns to eat with him. If he wanted a rowdy lunch, he'd invite John Maclean and me. It would depend on his mood whom he chose to eat with him.

I would inform the cabin crew of his likes and dislikes and just act as a general liaison between everyone. As we traveled with the V.I.P. RAF crews we all got to know each other.

When we flew commercial it was quite different, of course. These flights were rather boring. The Prince never drinks so none of the rest of us would take advantage of all that lovely free first-class champagne. Also, people don't realize until they get to the airport who is going to be traveling with them. It only dawns when airport authorities make a very positive search of everyone's baggage. The full-fare-paying passengers get irritated when the plane is late leaving. They will have checked in at the correct time—only to discover it will take at least another two hours before the aircraft gets off the ground.

Just to calm everyone down, when we did take off, the Captain always apologized for the delay and then said, "As a consolation and with the compliments of the airline, may we offer you an open bar."

I'll never forget one flight from San Francisco to Sydney when this offer was made. Loud Australian cheers came from the back. The Prince said, "Oh, God!" and offered his condolences to the crew. Those who had scraped in on stand-by fares had hit the jackpot. It's a long way from San Francisco to Sydney. By the time we arrived, most of the passengers were legless, the stewards walking around in a daze, and the plane was bone dry.

For these reasons we did try to use RAF planes. Traveling commercial throws a lot of people into confusion and ruins the bar profits.

A lot of surprised first-class passengers have found themselves sitting near the Prince, and it creates a very silent flight with everyone on his best behavior.

Rather like the parties which he attends. The noise level always increases by several decibels after he has left. His presence unfortunately can be a dampener—and he realizes it. "What happened after I went?" he always asks.

Of course, people are still pleased to have seen him in the flesh. And when he leaves a commercial aircraft, he always pops his head through the curtains to where the second-class passengers sit so they can get a look at him, too.

I must say working for him gave me some spectacular treats. Once we flew the Concorde to New York just to go to the ballet and then came right back again. Another time we flew from Vancouver to Florida to play polo at the new Wellington Club complex.

That trip, of course, had a sad ending because the Prince was so ill. But our journey was marvelous. I played steward, handing out trays of food with the Prince saying, "Let's see if you've learned anything from Qantas."

(Qantas was a favorite airline as they were always so agreeable about sending an aircraft if the Prince needed one.)

On our private jet, the crew shut the door and left us to our own devices. The plane was full of gadgets so the Prince was a happy man. We played the Bee Gees nonstop on the stereo and as there was a telephone, the Prince decided to use it.

"Would you believe," he said, "I'm ringing from forty thousand feet, and the number is engaged."

When the Prince of Wales travels he becomes a Howard Hughes character. He can never go out.

When he's not at an official engagement, he is virtually locked up at the top of some hotel, surrounded by security men. In fact, when we were in Vancouver once we stayed in the same hotel and the same suite of rooms that Howard Hughes had used.

The Prince said, "I know exactly how he must have felt."

If he wants to go for a walk, he has to take about ten policemen with him. When he wanted to swim or go surfing in Australia, a whole mob had to go along, too. The security is intense. But at least Howard Hughes achieved privacy with his security. The Prince has absolutely none. He is a prisoner of his own circumstances.

He can never escape. In the twelve years I worked with him, I never knew him to creep off to a nightclub or take a girl out while he was abroad. All his relationships with ladies were in Britain, and he most certainly wasn't set up with a girl when traveling, like so many visiting dignitaries are.

When he was away, all he really wanted was to get back home. He loves Britain; he loves being here. In years to come I believe they will have to lever him out of this country for State visits and overseas tours.

There is not much pleasure in traveling when you are the Prince of Wales.

"I'm just a roving Ambassador for Britain," he says.

Some trips are more fun than others. He had this great ambition to see the United States and one day at Balmoral, when we were out with the guns, he said to me, "I may be going on a tour of America. Would you like to come?"

"Try to keep me away," I said.

The soundings for the trip had been done from Washington. The British Ambassador had contacted the Foreign Office to say there was great interest in the Prince making a visit.

The Foreign Office then contacted the Palace. Would Prince Charles like to tour America?

For once he agreed with alacrity. He had been there before with Princess Anne in 1970 when Nixon was President. And Nixon had made a fairly determined attempt at matchmaking his very pretty daughter, Patricia, with the Prince. Nixon saw it as a great double. The Prince had other ideas.

"At least I won't have a daughter to face this time," he said before we left.

Normally he has to have a specific reason for a tour—he obviously can't just go and sit at Palm Beach for four days. But on this occasion the brief was simply to tour the States.

There were so many American friends who wanted to see him; all kinds of links with Britain—the English-Speaking Union, Friends of Covent Garden, all asking for him to visit. He really wanted to go and the Embassy in Washington thought a visit from him would be marvelous for Britain. They put a program together and arranged for him to go to seventeen cities and places in thirteen days. The object—to meet as many Americans as possible.

It was an easy trip for me. There were no uniforms to take. It was just what I call a suit job.

We flew on British Airways to Chicago, stayed at the magnificent Drake Hotel, on to Detroit, and then to the South—Atlanta, Georgia.

The Prince is quite a show business fan and does enjoy meeting the artists whose work he admires. He very much likes Gladys Knight and the Pips and they were in Atlanta, their hometown, playing the Fox Theater. So we went. A reception was given for him on the stage after the performance, and the Prince was fascinated to meet Gladys Knight.

From Georgia we went on to Texas where we stayed with Anne Armstrong at her ranch, which, as well as being amazingly luxurious, is also a business where cattle are bred.

The Prince knew Mrs. Armstrong as she had been Ambassador to Britain. He played polo at the ranch on the Sunday and that evening she gave an enormous party for him.

About a hundred people came in by private jet, and when the Prince asked his Private Secretary how his accommodation was, Squadron Leader Checketts said ruefully, "Rather like sleeping at the end of Runway One, London Airport."

The Prince was intrigued by Texans and their lifestyle. The American millionaires at that party may have been fascinated by him, but he was equally fascinated by them. He is rich, of course, but they are rich in a different way. And success and self-made money interest him.

After the dinner he said to me, "Do you realize that the amassed wealth in the room tonight is supposed to represent our National Debt?"

After Texas it was day-hops until we arrived at Los Angeles for a three-night stopover. We lodged at the Beverly Wilshire Hotel in the most beautiful rooms in the private Tower—the same luxury dwelling where

Warren Beatty has a permanent suite. Our rooms were all two-floor maisonettes with a spiral staircase to link them and the Prince went roaming around all our accommodations, joking that ours was better than his. Not true. Our rooms were never better than his.

One of the engagements was a huge charity dinner for a thousand people which had been arranged by the Variety Club. Ronald Reagan, as a former Governor of California, came, and the Prince, as usual, ended up sitting next to an older American lady, whose husband had arranged the whole thing. Squadron Leader Checketts was delighted to find himself next to Sophia Loren.

Every now and then he caught his boss' eye glinting at him down the table. Afterwards the Prince said, "It's all very well. I pay you *and* you land up with the beautiful ones!"

He did better the next day when we were invited to lunch at 20th Century-Fox film studios. There were about thirty people there, including the late Henry Fonda and the entire cast of *M*A*S*H*. The lunch had already been arranged back in London, and the decision was made that on this occasion the Prince would sit next to Lauren Bacall—one of his favorite actresses.

Possibly slightly overcome by her proximity, he blurted out, "I so enjoyed all your black and white films, Miss Bacall."

"I really put my foot in it," he said to me afterwards. "She was annoyed. She said, 'I'm not that old, Prince!' "

That day he really enjoyed. Charlie's Angels were on the next set and we were taken there to watch the filming. He managed a brief chat with Farrah Fawcett

Majors, but it was cut short because they were rushed off to be photographed together.

"They're all very glamorous," he said afterwards, "but aren't they small? Particularly Farrah Fawcett Majors. She looks much taller on the screen."

A faint note of disappointment? Maybe. The Prince likes his women tall.

The 20th Century lot itself is interesting. As we drove in off Pico Boulevard, a complete reconstruction of a New York street that had been made for *Hello Dolly* was pointed out. The studio had even built a mock-up of the old Third Avenue elevated railway. The Prince was fascinated to see this.

A fan of Barbra Streisand, he has seen every film she has made. When he was in the Navy in 1975 he had met her. Someone had asked him then, "Which Hollywood star would you most like to meet?"

"I'm sure they thought I'd say Raquel Welch," he told me, "but I said Barbra Streisand. I wanted to meet the woman behind the voice."

I'm a fan, too, and when he got back to U.K., I said to him, "I hear you met Barbra Streisand, sir."

"Yes," he said, "but I think I caught her on a bad day, though. She was terribly busy."

The meeting wasn't entirely a success. At the time she was "voicing over" for *Funny Lady*, and she really gave him very little time and she seemed to be nervous of him.

He wasn't at all disappointed. Just pleased to have seen her. He likes her music and said that it had been an enjoyable experience watching her work.

Though he met a lot of glamorous women on that trip in 1977, as usual there was no romance or even dallying. It was sheer hard work, but for once, enjoyable.

An awful lot of girls kissed him which he quite liked, but the kissing began to get out of hand. We were going to a college football match and when our plane landed, he showed signs of alarm. Peering out of the window (as he always did to see what was awaiting him) he had spotted about sixty cheerleaders. The thought of them all trying for a kiss quite unnerved him.

"My God! They'll smother me if they charge," he said, staring at all the baton-twirling, short-skirted, All-American girls waiting on the tarmac.

We got him through in one piece. Happily they parted like the Red Sea.

It was a nonstop thirteen days. He'd get back to the hotel, stagger into the bedroom and say, "That was fascinating. When are we off again?"

Looking at the schedule, I'd say, "Seven-fifteen, sir."

If there was enough time, he would sit down in a chair and nod off. My job then was to keep people out of the room and wake him half an hour before we were due out—just like at the Palace. He did a great many things every day: walking in the heat, meeting people, seeing what sights he could. He was ready for a nap before the evening's activity.

His favorite evening on the trip was, I think, when we went to the San Francisco Opera. We saw *Turandot* with one of his favorite singers, Montserrat Caballé. And he did something he would rarely do in Britain. He went backstage to meet the cast.

The atmosphere was terrific. The curtain was

down, and everyone was on stage, still in full costume and makeup. He and Montserrat Caballé, a large Spanish lady, talked enthusiastically about opera. He had met her before when she sang *Traviata* at Covent Garden.

He enjoyed himself, but sometimes I had a better time, I'm afraid. When he came back for the night, I would say, "Are you popping out, sir?"

He'd just shake his head.

"Then if there isn't anything else, sir. . . ."

"Are you going out?"

"Well, if there isn't anything else, sir."

"No—off you go."

I'd tell one of the policemen where I'd be and go out on the town.

During breakfast the next morning he'd say, "Did you enjoy yourself?"

"Yes, sir," I'd say, and give him a brief rundown on the evening.

"Umm. More than I did," he'd say ruefully. "I was up until two o'clock this morning writing today's speech."

It wouldn't be true to say he resented our freedom, but sometimes there was a slight touch of envy that we had so much more than he did. We were the ones who could join him when we wanted to or go off on our own, while he stayed locked in a hotel's luxurious ivory tower.

We returned to the States in 1981, Wedding Year, and on both occasions he met Nancy Reagan and was very taken with her. He likes bright, intelligent, older women, and Mrs. Reagan qualified on all counts.

He met her at the ballet in New York and in Washington at the White House. And it was then she told him she would be coming to the wedding alone.

"I'm pleased she's going to make the effort," he said afterwards, not showing any signs of indignation about her much publicized refusal to curtsey to the Queen.

Washington was a particularly difficult city for him to enjoy, though. The security was so intense, with Secret Service men coming out of the woodwork, that he felt very hemmed in.

It was just as bad in 1978 when we went to South America, and the Prince was virtually a prisoner in the Copacabana Hotel in Rio. Outside the hotel was the magnificent beach, and below his window a superb swimming pool. The Prince's suite overlooked all this. And what he was looking down at was us and all the reporters following him by the pool and having a marvelous time. There was he, the principal reason for the whole thing, stuck about ten floors up and feeling thoroughly trapped.

We'd even missed the carnival in Rio. We were just too late for it, but the samba school that had won the prize for dancing entertained the Prince one evening at the Governor's mansion. He let his hair down and joined in the dancing. The resulting pictures must have been printed in every newspaper in the world.

We traveled around Brazil quite a bit, ending up in a resort town on the Amazon. The visit was no more than a stopover en route to Venezuela. Astonishingly, the hotel manager came up to us and said, "Do you know that Lord Snowdon is staying in the hotel?"

We did not.

"Why can't they communicate, back in London," the Prince said, cross. "I should have liked to have been told he was here."

Lord Snowdon was photographing the Amazon, but he found time to pop in for a drink before we left for Caracas—a busy, noisy town where everyone seemed to drive with guns on their laps. We were staying at the Embassy—much more comfortable than a hotel as at least there was a garden for the Prince to walk in. He complains most bitterly at the difficulties of getting exercise when on an overseas tour.

It was in Venezuela that we got lost. There was the Prince of Wales, sitting on a dusty road somewhere outside Caracas while his chauffeur tried to find a cafe, or someone who knew the way.

A security man's nightmare.

Frequently we would find ourselves sitting in a layby because the Prince was early, something that made him quietly fume because it meant that whoever had worked out the trip had allowed for normal traffic conditions—forgetting that the authorities would clear the roads for him.

Once in the middle of New Guinea we were so early that the Prince and I went for a walk to the nearest village and back. We were both enchanted by the sight of a stunning black lady, dressed in a black wrap and with a superb, heavy necklace—made of Coca-Cola bottle tops.

We did manage a few days' break in Venezuela. Four of us, the Prince, Squadron Leader Checketts, John Maclean, and I, all flew in an Andover to a dusty airstrip right up in the mountains to a place called Lake Caribou. It was the spot that had given Jules

175

Verne the inspiration for *The Lost World*. We saw his point. All there was when we landed were three or four huts with nobody in them except a few staff to look after us.

Their first duty was to paddle the four of us in a canoe, with all our luggage, further down the river to a camp site. Right bang in the middle of nowhere, it consisted of two sheds, two huts, and a barbecue hut.

The Venezuelan Government flew in very good food, and we were just left to our own devices for two days. It was primitive but comfortable and a complete contrast to Caracas.

The silence was the most extraordinary thing. We were so high in the mountains that the only sound was made by the river as it rushed past—far too broad and rapid for swimming.

The heat made everything shimmer, and we just lay about, eating and sleeping and getting very tanned. The place was so remote that in the cool of the night one felt a little uneasy, wondering how anyone could survive there. But we were surviving with delicious food, plenty to drink, and enjoying much the same kind of barbecue that the Prince likes in the Highlands of Scotland.

"Supposing someone came round that bend in the river and saw us all sitting here, eating," the Prince said. "Wouldn't they get a surprise."

"They would if they realized who you are, sir," I said.

The Prince slept in a hut by himself, in a single bunk. In the shed next door the policemen bedded down, while Squadron Leader Checketts and I shared the other hut with two bunks.

It was a strange experience.

That was a period of freedom. Another was when he visited Paris for the Queen's State visit when Lord Soames was our Ambassador there. The Prince was in the Navy and his ship was docked at Marseilles. He flew up to stay at the British Embassy with the Queen, working on the principle of the more Royals the merrier.

I flew from Britain to join him, and one of the policemen brought his Aston Martin over on the ferry.

At the end of the visit, I went back to the U.K. in the *Britannia* with the Queen, sailing magnificently down the Seine to Le Havre. The Prince drove himself back to the South, through the night, the hood down, cassettes playing his favorite classical music.

He enjoys overnight drives, sharing the wheel with the policeman. On long journeys he likes to start fairly early and keep going, even if it means arriving at around two or three in the morning. Then he will just collapse.

Life was all contrasts, from regal trips in the Royal yacht to roughing it on Venezuelan rivers to the time I shared a bathroom with Cary Grant at Prince Rainier's Palace at Monte Carlo. My mother was thrilled when I told her about that.

I'll treasure forever the memory of arriving at the Ivory Coast in 1977. As we drove from the airport, the streets were lined with enthusiastic large black ladies, all waving flags. Each and every one was dressed from head to toe in fabric with the Prince's face printed on it.

Two sets of smiles greeted him, theirs and his own.

''I'm seeing far too much of myself,'' he observed.

The Ivory Coast had its chilling moments, though. We were staying at the President's guest house which in contrast to the general surroundings was possibly the most splendid accommodation we were ever given. Silk walls, chandeliers, fine food. Nothing was spared in the way of luxury.

One of the sights we were taken to see was a large and murky lake, full of the President's crocodiles. We were shown them being given a dinner of live chickens, but a nasty sense of something more sinister persisted.

"I wonder what else they use that lake for," the Prince said afterwards, rather thoughtfully.

Before the visit to the Ivory Coast, we'd been to Ghana and the Prince was dressing at the back of the plane as it came in to land. Suddenly there was a terrible roar of acceleration, the plane tilted alarmingly and shot back into the sky.

"What the . . ." the Prince said, recovering his balance.

After a minute the chief steward appeared. "So sorry, Your Highness," he said. "But the Ghanese Guard of Honor chose that moment to cross the runway."

And there they were down below, in total disarray all over the landing strip.

In 1980, Rhodesia became Zimbabwe and the Prince went there to confer their independence. It was a twitchy trip; there were still a lot of guerrillas about and an uneasy feeling that they might just appear to cause a little aggravation, but all went well.

The Prince has given several countries and islands, once colored red on the map, their independence.

The ceremony always occurs at midnight, signaling the start of a new day. The proceedings take place in a stadium, or outdoors. Every country sends a representative, and it's a bit like belonging to a club.

The Prince, dressed up to the nines, goes along at about 11:45. In the field, or wherever, blazing with lights, he stands on a makeshift platform and reads a message from the Queen while everyone cheers and claps.

Then slowly the British flag comes down and up goes the one of the new country.

It's then the ruler of the country's turn to get up and make his speech. After, to the playing of the new national anthem and scenes of mass hysteria, it's all over.

Nassau had the best independence ceremonies that I can remember. It was 1973, and the Prince was quite young. There were three large independence balls—two one night and the third the following night. We went to them all. Paul Officer and I had a splendid time. As usual, the Prince had to dance with the general's wife, the first secretary's wife, the Ambassador's wife, and the Prime Minister's wife.

"I never get to the pretty girl in the corner," he grumbled. "Just as I'm looking around for a little light relief, I get dragged back because the hostess thinks I look bored."

He rarely had the opportunity to walk up to someone and say, "May I have this dance?" Even the private dances in Britain where he did have a little more freedom seemed to have dried up before his marriage. And he loves dancing and is very good at it.

He clipped our wings a little at the balls in Nassau.

Not being a late person, he left just when the parties were getting to their height, and when he went we went. And quickly—to get back before him.

After all, we were there to look after him and not to go dancing.

The King of Nepal's coronation in 1975 was one of the most curious episodes of my travels with the Prince. Both the Prince and Lord Mountbatten went and I was looking after the pair of them. There was double the luggage to check and pack—no mean task as Lord Mountbatten who loved dressing up had taken every order, decoration, medal, and shiny bit that he could find. It was from Lord Mountbatten that the Prince learned, "If you've got it—wear it," though he has never been quite as unrestrained about dressing up as his great-uncle was.

We arrived in Nepal from Delhi where we had rested for a couple of days and where Lord Mountbatten took great pleasure in showing the Prince around the Presidential Palace. Lord Mountbatten had lived there when he was Governor General and acted as if he still was. He completely took over—his presence dominated the Palace. The poor incumbent President, a very shy man, was scuttling from room to room trying to escape us as Lord Mountbatten directed his own guided tour.

Most of the servants had been at the Palace in Lord Mountbatten's day and they treated him as if he were a god. The Prince was vastly amused by the whole thing.

In Nepal, the King and his family ran the country and had all the power. The King's brother owned the only decent hotel—a sort of motel—and there we had to stay along with the other old familiar faces from State occasions around the world.

Madame Marcos, of the Philippines, who bobbed up everywhere, flew in with sixty guests, including Mrs. Ford of Ford car fame. The Crown Prince of Japan—another regular—was there, so was the Swedish King and the Governor General of Australia.

The hotel was not exactly grand. It had basic furniture and the rooms were small. It was like a motel anywhere in the world. One afternoon I discovered all these rich and famous people jammed into the Prince's small sitting room drinking tea halfway up a mountain, squashed together on divan beds and acting as though they were in some sort of Palace. He, as host, was carrying off the situation with his usual dignity.

Madame Marcos always caused slight concern to the Prince. She would arrive with expensive, rather useless presents for him which caused slight embarrassment. She always put him in a situation where he had to give something back, and I can remember him staring at a huge volume of some beautifully bound but obscure books and saying, ''What can I give her this time?''

We always had a stock of small gifts ready for people like the Ambassador's wife, etc. They included the ubiquitous box, photographs in frames, cuff links, small pieces of silver. Nothing was overdone, just tasteful.

These gifts were all prepared in London as part of the routine for a tour. Madame Marcos was our little problem, though. We were running out of ideas for her. And she kept pressing the Prince to visit the Philippines.

"We'll get there one day," he'd murmur.

The main difficulty with the actual Nepalese coronation was that no one knew exactly what time the King was to be crowned. We all had to get up very early indeed to get to the temple where the coronation was to take place in the middle of Katmandu.

There everyone had to wait for the sun to come up and for the astrologer to decide exactly the right moment for the crowning. The auspices had to be good.

This was all very well, but I had both the Prince and Lord Mountbatten to dress. The Prince was not so much of a problem but his great-uncle had so much to put on that it took me nearly half an hour to achieve the required effect. Thank God, the Prince only had one or two decorations. Lord Mountbatten had dozens and every intention of wearing the lot.

The Prince and Lord Mountbatten were in the temple waiting for the coronation to begin just after seven, and there they waited and waited, sitting on long hard benches.

Suddenly, sometime after nine o'clock, the astrologer threw up his hands and announced, "It is now."

The King, who had been sitting on a simple throne along with the rest of the guests, sat bolt upright, and someone literally plumped the crown down on his head. He was King in no time at all. There he sat, wearing this turbanlike arrangement with a plume of what looked like peacock feathers in the front. It was all over, except for the elephant rides to the local arena where the new King received everybody.

"No sense of ceremony at all," grumbled Lord Mountbatten.

On the way back to the U.K. we stopped in Teheran to stay at the Shah's palace. Actually it wasn't *the* palace, but a guest palace, so opulent that it almost made Windsor Castle look like a semidetached. The Shah was away and there were only the Empress and the Crown Prince to greet us. A Mercedes took the Prince and Lord Mountbatten from the airport, through the squalor of freezing cold streets to the incredible luxury of the palace. The Shah's chamberlain, in morning coat, was waiting in the vast hallway for us to arrive, and there were guards everywhere—sinister-looking men in expensive suits.

The Prince had quite a lot to do in Teheran—seeing the Ambassador and performing his usual role of drumming up business for Britain. The rest of us rather enjoyed, with a slight sense of guilt, the extraordinary life-style of the Peacock Throne. We had caviar for breakfast every morning but conversation at the table was limited. The Shah's court spoke mainly French, so meal times were rather divided into those who were English speakers and those who were not.

I came home clutching a biscuit-sized tin of caviar which had been a parting gift and shared it with a friend who is a chef at the Savoy Grill. I knew he and his wife would appreciate it.

Every other year the Royals try to show their faces in Australia. No hardship for Prince Charles as he really enjoys both Australia and the Australians.

Perhaps it is because they do not get over-excited by the appearance of the monarchy there. They don't fill the streets to wave as they do in black countries, where he is known as "Him—Number One Son." If an Australian happens to be on a street corner when the Prince or the Queen goes by—good luck. But the Australians don't queue for hours to see them.

The Prince would have loved to have lived there for a while. He loves the space and he finds the people outgoing and generous. He likes their outwardness, in the same way as he likes the Americans. There's no British reserve—in Australia they couldn't give a "monkey's really." They like him and they respect him but that's the end of it. Therefore he enjoys being treated with a certain respect but appreciates that they are at ease with him.

I had the feeling when we went to Australia in 1974 that all the stories of the Australians not wanting the Prince to be their Governor General were untrue.

At that time no one quite knew what the Prince was going to do with his life. And it seemed to me that the Australians were fed up with the Governors General like Sir John Kerr and would have liked someone from the monarchy who would be seen to be non-political.

Another Australian bonus for the Prince is that he always manages to play polo there (that large bag of sticks goes everywhere!) and he has good friends with whom he can be very relaxed.

We spent part of the spring before the wedding touring Australia, and the Prince rested at the home of his friends, the Sinclair Hills.

He spent two weekends there, playing polo and, as usual, eating barbecue food. There was one elaborate barbecue, which took place a four-mile ride from the Hills' home, where I was in charge of making the

Pimms. Sinclair Hill said everyone rode—so everyone rode, including me. I had not been on a horse for about ten years and the Prince spent half the time waiting for me to catch up.

"Are you sore?" he inquired sympathetically at the end of the day.

"Yes, Your Highness, I am," I said with feeling.

He telephoned Lady Diana quite often that trip and she him. A story broke that there had been a telephone leak with someone listening in to their conversations. It wasn't true. His phone calls were made mainly from Government House and they were very brief. If anyone had been listening they wouldn't have heard a great deal.

Of course, he was no stranger to this continent having spent part of his education at Geelong in 1966. He had also accompanied the Queen in 1970 for the Bi-Centenary celebrations. But in 1974 he undertook his first major trip and I also went. Like all tours that have followed it was a goodwill visit and he took time off from the Navy to make it.

We had one extremely funny evening on that tour. We were in Brisbane and invited to a variety concert. The Prince is quite used to these overrunning, and never expects to get away on time, but our Brisbane evening was exceptional.

Winifred Atwell, the honky-tonk piano player, had made a whole new career in Australia, but the Prince remembered her from his boyhood when she had been a top star in Britain.

Winnie was topping the bill, and as the concert stretched and stretched, she had been waiting in the bar and passing the time with the odd drink or two. It was 11:15 when she made her appearance—just when we should have been leaving the theater.

She started to play, watching the box where the Prince was sitting, and every time he applauded she went on playing. And playing. And playing.

Eventually at gone midnight the desperate theater manager brought down the back curtain. Winnie played on. He brought down the front curtain and she could still be heard, honky-tonking behind it.

The Prince still had to say thank you to the stars, to the manager, to the stagehands and the lady who sold the ice cream. It was 12:45 A.M. before we got back to the hotel. And if the manager hadn't brought down the curtain, I'm sure Miss Atwell would be playing yet.

✑ 13 ✑

Prince Charles Was Their Darling

O~N THE MORNING~ of June 17, 1977, the Prince was listening to "What the Papers Say" on BBC Radio Four, as is his habit. He heard to his astonishment that across the front page of the *Daily Express* there was a banner heading which proclaimed: "Charles to Marry Astrid—Official. Engagement Next Week. Sons Will Be Protestants, Daughters Catholic."

The supposed lady of his choice, Princess Marie Astrid of Luxembourg, was probably a pleasant young lady, but one he hardly knew.

He immediately rang for me and asked me to get him a copy of the paper. *The Times*, his normal reading, had no mention of the story.

He didn't know whether to laugh or be angry when he read the piece which revealed that "Although their association has been kept secret by the Palace—even to the extent of denying they had even met—a close friend said last night, 'They fell for each other at that first meeting.' "

The Prince's comment to me was, "It's absurd!" Then tongue-in-cheek he added, "I'm sorry I didn't tell you about my engagement. I promise I will next time."

"Please do, sir," I said, "just so that I can tear down to Ladbrokes and put some money on it."

Princess Astrid's parents are friends of the Queen, which is how the story began. The Princess had been in Britain, studying languages, which added fuel to the fire. Not one of his staff had ever met her. We weren't even sure if he had. The whole episode must have been as embarrassing for her as it was for him. Happily she has since married an Austrian. The Prince received an invitation to the wedding, but he did not go. I seem to remember he sent her a pair of sheets as a wedding present and that was that.

The story that he might be courting Princess Astrid as his bride was just one of the many that appeared in 1977—Jubilee Year. We called this "speculation year," because both press and public were certain that the Prince must announce his engagement at this time. The result was that every girl he so much as said good-morning to took on the mantle of a possible Princess of Wales. This was tiresome for them and for him, too.

All through the seventies the newspapers were researching every girl in his circle who was white,

Church of England, and under thirty. He said pub-
licly, "I have fallen in love with all sorts of girls and
fully intend to go on doing so. But I have made sure I
haven't married the first person I have fallen in love
with."

There *were* a lot of girl friends, but not as many as
the newspapers thought. Many of the girls they
linked with him were either no more than the daughters of old friends of the family, just trumped up
stories, or sheer speculation.

He is, of course, enormously attractive to women
and is good at conversation. So when he heard that
the Welsh Guards in Germany (of whom he is
Colonel-in-Chief) were having trouble talking to the
local girls, he did something about it.

He wrote a little booklet—a guide to "chatting up"
girls in German—and sent it out to the regiment. Considering his German isn't that good, it was quite a
feat.

Another of the Jubilee rumors was that he would
wed Princess Caroline of Monaco. As in the case of
Princess Astrid, the speculators gaily ignored the fact
that the late Princess Grace's and Prince Rainier's
daughter is a Catholic and by our British Royal standards, Royals have to marry Church of England.

He only met Princess Caroline once when we went to
Monte Carlo for a huge charity ball given by Prince Rainier. He sat next to her at the Sporting Club dinner
which caused all sorts of excitement. Unfortunately for
the speculators he was not remotely attracted by her.

Princess Grace was sitting opposite him at dinner,
and he found her much more interesting. Her daughter was not his type—he likes blondes. Caroline is

dark. He likes good English complexions. To be truth-ful, Caroline's skin wasn't that perfect at close-up range.

If it had been a courtship or the beginning of some-thing big, their meeting had little time to develop. We flew to Nice, drove from there to Monte Carlo in cars sent by Prince Rainier. I helped the Prince into his black tie and diamond neck order for dinner, and af-terwards there was the most marvelous firework display and dance.

We stayed the night at the Monaco Palace—that was the occasion where I shared a bathroom with Cary Grant—and the next morning we flew back in the Andover.

That was the beginning, middle, and end of the so-called romance with Princess Caroline.

What people never seemed to realize was just how cautious the Prince was with girl friends. He was really quite happy being a bachelor. After his engage-ments were completed, he was free to do exactly what he wanted to do—with no woman to interfere with his sporting activities. Whichever girl was the current fa-vorite, he was very much in charge. He would always ring her—usually quite late in the day. It was very un-usual indeed for a girl to ring him, and he preferred it that way. He did all the running, and if he wanted to change his plans, he wasn't stuck with an evening out when something more interesting had turned up.

He rarely collected his girl friends before a date. They always arrived under their own steam and they generally departed back from whence they had come the same way.

I don't think it ever crossed his mind to wonder

about their transport. It was only the special girls who received preferential treatment, which usually meant sending someone—usually the policeman on duty—to pick them up.

This never seemed to bother his girl friends. I think they quite enjoyed the perk of arriving at the Palace or at Windsor. But there were snags in the end. At the start of a new friendship, a girl friend enjoyed all the attention and speculation from the media. For a while it was all very flattering. Then it would begin to dawn exactly what they had taken on. Being watched by the press all the time can get out of hand. They began to think, "This could spoil my chances with someone else. Will anyone want one of Prince Charles' castoffs?" And gradually many of his romances just fizzled out.

The relationships he did have were arranged with the most enormous discretion. In all those twelve years that I worked for him if he was meant to be in his bed in the morning when I went in to wake him up—he was in bed. Alone. And his girl friends would never have talked. He stuck to his own kind—wealthy, socially acceptable young women. Had they so much as whispered a boast of their special place in the Prince's affections, their place in society would have been in jeopardy. Hostesses would have crossed their names off guest lists. A careless word in the wrong place and a girl could disappear from the social scene completely.

There was not a great deal of opportunity to indulge in very close relationships. The Prince is rarely alone. Buckingham Palace was totally unsuitable for anything secret to take place. His rooms were in a straight line along a corridor. It would have been impossible for a girl to have spent any time there without a footman or his policeman or me not being aware she was there.

His friends in country houses where he spent many weekends might have turned a blind eye certainly. But those friends had servants, too, with even more brought in, when the Prince was staying the weekend.

Obviously he had a private life, but one managed with amazing discretion. But not such an exciting private life as the media believed. I sometimes thought the limitations on his privacy were part of the reason for his participation in so many energetic sporting activities.

He left practically all his girl friends on good terms. Not that he ever said to me, "Pop up to Wartski's and buy so-and-so a bracelet for a farewell gift." He never bought girls presents, anyway. He would just occasionally send flowers. His romances ended in a slow drift. He was working away so much that it was easy to end a relationship if he wanted to. The girls themselves became fed up waiting for him to call.

It wasn't always easy for him, either. The many tours we made did not help romance. He might have been in the middle of courting somebody only to find himself committed to go off to somewhere like Fiji for a month, a trip that would have been arranged long before he met the girl. And four weeks is a long time when you are fond of someone.

Therefore he rarely courted seriously until Lady Diana came along. His girl friends were just that—girl friends.

There have been those who have given him his marching papers, and I'm pretty sure Georgina Russell was one of them. Georgina is the daughter of Sir John Russell, who was our man in both Rio de Janeiro and Madrid. In both cities she was the toast of the town—lively, pretty, and miniskirted. Her Greek mother—who had been Miss Greece and Miss Europe—had endowed her with an ample figure and the Prince likes curvy girls.

She came to polo and was with him on quite a few occasions. Then she came to Craigowan on a fishing trip as the Prince's companion.

John Maclean and I always used to say that the ones who survived Scotland, Craigowan, and the fishing had a chance of surviving the course to becoming the Princess of Wales.

Georgina was a city girl, and the whole atmosphere of Craigowan appalled her. She was freezing cold and eating scraps—the Prince was on one of his economy drives. I think she thought the week would be rather glamorous—a romantic interlude in the Highlands with the Prince. Nothing of the kind. He was standing with his feet in the water all day while she was bored out of her mind.

"She's not going to last the course," I said. And I was right. She didn't. She went home.

Lady Russell must have been furious—we all felt that she was motivating the whole romance. But Georgina herself realized this type of life was not for her.

There was quite a funny sequel to the Russell affair. We were on a plane and I was flicking through *Harpers* and *Queen* magazines when my eye fell on a picture of Georgina at her wedding to Hugo Boothby.

"Guess who got married?" I said to the Prince.

"Who?" he asked.

"Georgina Russell."

"I know," he said. "I got an invitation to the wedding."

Silently, I handed him the picture and he peered at it.

"Good God!" he said indignantly. "Her hair is black. She's not a blonde at all."

Most of his ex-girl friends have married and he usually gets invited to the wedding. He rarely goes. As he says, "If I accepted every wedding invitation I'd be buying presents morning, noon, and night and never be out of a morning coat."

Another who did not stay the course was Anna Wallace. His staff were all rather disappointed when that ended. She was such a nice girl. We liked her very much.

Anna is the daughter of a wealthy landowner, Hamish Wallace, and she met Prince Charles when he was hunting with the Belvoir—supposed to be Britain's grandest hunt. That was their first link in common. She is as mad about hunting as he is. She began to come to watch him playing polo regularly—a marvelous-looking girl with a sparkling personality and presence, who really turned heads. We could all see that he was enormously attracted to her, and yet he seemed to be more cautious with her than any of his other girls.

The minute any girl appeared in his life, the muckraking press would start to sniff about. It used to anger the Prince, but their revelations did provide a service in a way. The future Queen of England had to be seen to be virtuous.

The first time I met Anna properly was when she

came to the Palace to watch the final rehearsal of the Trooping the Colour. Being Colonel of the Welsh Guards, the Prince was taking the salute.

There had been a lot of speculation that Anna Wallace might get the job. And when I met her I thought what a modest girl she was—not in love with her own publicity as some had been. She watched him from the front windows of Buckingham Palace, while I stood watching with her. I gave her coffee and explained the goings-on in the quadrangle below until at 10:45, as always, they rode off down the Mall for Horse Guard's Parade.

The Prince had said before he went down to the quadrangle, "Look after Miss Wallace while I'm away." So I asked, "Would you like to see around the Palace?"

"I'd love to," she said.

I took her all around. I had my master key and was able to show her the State apartments. She was fascinated; eager to know exactly what the rooms were used for. She had already seen the Prince's private rooms but I wasn't able to show her the Queen's quarters, of course. No one ever goes down that corridor unless sent for.

I wondered at the time if she might be thinking of walking those corridors in a different role one day. There was certainly no one else in his life at the time, and she seemed ideal. A charming girl and one he obviously found very attractive.

She didn't wait for him to come back. She slipped quietly away out of a Palace side door. There were too many people in the Mall watching the rehearsal for her to leave by the front entrance.

But it all went wrong. She and the Prince had a very public quarrel at a dance at Windsor in honor of the Queen Mother's eightieth birthday party. Or rather, she had a quarrel with him. The Prince does not quarrel.

I think she misunderstood the situation. She was invited to the birthday dance as his partner, but forgot that four hundred other people had been invited as well. The Prince had to circulate among them. She became possessive and wanted to be with him all the time.

He left her at the table and went to talk to people he had known for years. When he returned, she was furious. He did try to patch it up, but Anna Wallace is a substantial person in her own right. She was fed up with the secrecy, being hidden, and the press revelations about her private life. She walked out on him.

He never spoke of the end of the friendship, but he was subdued for some time. She'd been important to him. I knew because he was so cheerful and content while she was in his life. It looked like a certainty. She'd been to lunch with the Queen at Windsor, something that never happened unless a relationship looked like it was becoming serious. The Queen was cautious about being introduced to the Prince's girl friends. She did not wish to be used as one of his added attractions.

Anna Wallace married rapidly after the breakup. It wasn't surprising that someone—Johnny Hesketh, the young brother of Lord Hesketh—snapped her up. On the day of the wedding the Prince was in India. And very shortly after her departure, Lady Diana appeared on the scene.

The other girl in his life who would have made a beautiful Princess of Wales and whom he loved was Davina Sheffield. She was delightful, and so pretty, with the sweetest smile. A tall blonde. In fact, rather similar to the Princess Diana, but more grownup.

Davina was a girl friend in 1974, and the romance was still flourishing in 1976 when I first met her at Windsor when she came to lunch with the Queen. She also came to Balmoral that summer of 1974 and stayed the fishing course. She could keep up with him in the countryside. He was more open with her than he was later with Anna Wallace. He took her to polo in a carriage, and the most marvelous pictures were taken. They were obviously a couple in love.

I think he would have married her, but her past was suddenly revealed. She had lived with a young man named James Beard, an old-Harrovian boat designer, in what her ex-lover described as a "rose-covered cottage." He told the story of their romance in great detail—a tacky thing to do, we all thought—and when the story was printed it ruined her chances of marrying the Prince.

They must have spoken of the possibility of marriage because in the middle of the courtship she quite suddenly went to Saigon to look after orphaned Vietnamese children. At the Palace, we interpreted this as a going-away-to-think-about-it period. Princess Diana had the same break from him when she went to Australia before the announcement of their engagement.

He and Davina were together again when she returned after a five-week absence. Then shortly afterwards the story of her love affair was printed, and no engagement announcement was ever spoken of again.

Yet the romance did not end immediately. It went on for some months after James Beard had printed his story. To me this seemed to mean that the Prince was finding it hard to part with Davina.

In the end, the romance had to end. He could not marry anyone who could create any kind of scandal—which is why he waited so long and why he married someone so much younger. His problem was that older attractive girls were bound to have had some sort of past. Yet he did love Davina Sheffield, though he was very good at hiding what he was thinking. He always had his feelings under control.

He was also fond enough of her to try to save her from further embarrassment much later. It just so happened that she was in Australia when he was making one of his tours there. All sorts of stories about them meeting secretly were being printed—so many that he finally issued a statement which said he wished people would leave Miss Sheffield alone and that he wanted it made clear that the stories of her joining him held no credence.

The statement put the record straight, but it was sad for both of them.

Another girl he was fond of, but in quite a different way, was Laura Jo Watkins, an American girl.

Laura Jo was his first "adult" girl friend. The first girl he had taken out who was independent of the family situation. He found her on his own in San Diego, California, when his ship was berthed there. She was his first encounter with America and the Americans. She fascinated him because she was different.

She was an Admiral's daughter, so I imagine that they met at one of those cocktail parties that ships always have when they are in port. The Navy likes glamorous girls about and Laura Jo was definitely glamorous. She was, in fact, the first of the tall blondes. It was 1974 and they were both in their early twenties.

Laura Jo obviously understood there was absolutely no hope of marriage and she had no ambitions in that direction. I got on very well with her because I knew she wasn't going to get the job. I could pull her leg and laugh with her when she'd call him "Prince" in her broad American accent, when she wanted to tease.

Nothing shocked her, though I think she shocked the Prince slightly because she most certainly was not "the English rose" type. She was a very American lady—outward and funny.

She would say, "Oh, damn." Mild, maybe, but the kind of British girls the Prince went around with would never say anything so strong.

Of course, I never met her until she turned up in London. She arrived in the early summer of 1974 and moved into the American Ambassador's home. The wife of the Ambassador, Mrs. Lee Annenberg, threw a very good party for her and the Prince, and it appeared to be accepted she was the Prince's lady for the time she was there.

He made all the arrangements, through his office, for her to be shown London in the greatest possible comfort. Mrs. Annenberg chaperoned her around town.

Laura Jo put a sparkle into the Prince's eyes be-

cause the romance was just fun. There would be no
future in it. She made him laugh. She called him
"sir" but in a very American way, almost as if she
was faintly pulling his leg.

When she came to the Palace I used to slip her into
the building through the basement entrance for reasons of discretion. The basement is rather like the
staff quarters of a big hotel. Linoleum floor, staff tele-
phones, not very smart. After the second time I had
whisked her through this working area and into the
lift, she said to me, "I'm fed up with coming through
the janitorial entrance."

She was summing up what most of his girl friends
felt when they found themselves in the position of always having to be hidden away.

Had she been British, she might have stood a great
chance, but as it was she never formally met any of
the family. She did come to polo when the Queen
happened to be there but even though she said
"Good afternoon" along with about twenty other
people, she could hardly say she had been presented
to the Queen.

But it went on for quite a while with letters going
back and forth. I could always recognize a letter from
her. She used brown ink and had a very distinctive
big, bold handwriting.

He even managed to see her again in the States. An
invitation was accepted to a big charity ball in Miami
for the Variety Club. He was to stay with Titch and
Shortie Green—an American couple who were very
rich, indeed. Shortie's father had invented the vend-
ing machine.

Laura Jo was asked to come as his partner, and she

flew in and was certainly the best-looking girl at the party.

The Prince was still in the Navy and his ship was at Fort Lauderdale. His Private Secretary, David Checketts, his secretary, Rosemary Taylor, and I flew in from London to join him. We were put in guest cottages on the grounds; Laura Jo and the Prince were in the main house.

He had sailing orders after the dance and went back to his ship. Laura Jo stayed and we had a lot of fun, swimming in the Greens' pool, and lying on the beach.

She said to me one day, rather wistfully, "He's a great guy," but she had too much sense to imagine that anything could have come of it.

She was also about at the time when he had done all his slogging in the Navy and was on top of everything. The mid-seventies were the years he really enjoyed as a bachelor Prince.

But new girl friends didn't always put a sparkle in his eye. They were treated as a section of his life. They never dominated him. The only thing that dominates Prince Charles is his work, and then his sporting activities. Girls come third. Prince Andrew, not having the same future, can show much more interest in girls than his elder brother ever could. Prince Charles is basically shy—and extremely cautious.

His response to women is quite unlike that of the old Duke of Windsor. When he was in love with Mrs. Simpson, as she then was, he would keep people waiting for days to see him. People at the Palace still remember and say that the abdication was the best thing that ever happened to the monarchy.

Prince Charles accepts his work load. He knows ministers must not be kept waiting just because he might be in love or have had a late night with a girl friend.

He had enormous opportunities to meet lots of ladies, but most of them were "suitable"—daughters of the Queen's friends. There was speculation he was going to marry Angela Neville, Lord Neville's daughter—but it was totally untrue. The rumor lived by virtue of the fact that she was a young, attractive girl, a dinner party guest—someone who was in the room to balance the numbers. And in Angela Neville's case, she is popular with all the family.

He would never embarrass himself at a dinner asking a girl out until he was sure that she was free—with no current boy friend in the wings—and really amusing to be with. It might take two or three meetings at big parties before he would suggest that they meet alone.

When the suggestion was made, it was usually for a quiet supper. The girl would arrive at the Palace, and I would have given instructions to the policeman at the gate to let her in. I would take her through to his sitting room. She would be given a cold supper, served by the footman. So before she even arrived in his room, two policemen, a footman, and I would all know she was there. It hardly made for intimacy.

If, later, the girl was asked to Balmoral or Sandringham, as both of these are the Queen's home, the Queen allocated the guest rooms. The Queen is a very proper lady, and people were spread well apart. Those who openly lived together but were not married were separated, if invited at all. The house rules

were strict. Princess Margaret was never allowed
to bring Roddy Llewellyn, her young boy friend—
though the Queen Mother often permitted him to
stay at Royal Lodge.

Any courtship by Prince Charles was mostly conducted at friends' homes. When he was invited away
for a shooting or fishing weekend, the current girl
friend was generally invited, too. They were then in
the company of a great many other people. The
Prince's love life was fraught with difficulty.

Interestingly, he has no private telephone line. Any
calls he received had to go through the switchboard at
the Palace. There are two numbers—one general and
another which connects to a separate switchboard for
the family. When a light goes up on that board, the
call is answered immediately. His incoming calls
could never, therefore, be private. And it was only a
couple of years ago that he acquired a self-dial phone
for outgoing calls. This happened when the Palace
switchboard was modernized.

There was, not unnaturally, the occasional girl
friend whom the Royal family would not have considered suitable.

Sabrina Guinness was one—a very pretty girl who
lasted for the summer of 1979. All his romances
seemed to start at polo matches, and as far as I can re-
call, that's where he was introduced to her.

I was surprised he liked her because she was so
thin. He normally preferred his ladies a bit larger.

She interested him, though. Her Chelsea life-style
was so different from his, even though she was a rich
and socially accepted girl. She had been a nanny to
Ryan O'Neal's child in Hollywood and had had lots

of boy friends. The Prince has seen and done more than most people would ever dream of doing, but it's all done from a different angle than a normal person's life. He was finding out about something new to him while he was seeing Sabrina Guinness. He would never have been serious about her. He is a country person and he wanted someone the same. I wonder if she would have survived the fishing at Craigowan. As she was never asked, we never knew.

I liked her. I sometimes see her around London. I've always stayed friendly with his ex-girl friends, and when I would meet them they'd say, "Give my love to the Prince," and I'd say, "Of course, I will."

The next day I'd always say, "Guess who I saw yesterday, sir?"

"Who?" he'd ask.

And when I told him he'd always want to know where and with whom.

Another unlikely girl, though glamorous and pleasant, was the actress Susan George. She's one I bump into who says, "Give my love to the Prince." He liked her. She was rather like Laura Jo—someone there was no hope in the world of marrying, and she knew it, too.

She first met him at a film premiere in 1978. Her family lived down in Berkshire, near Windsor, and she used to come to Windsor to see the Prince. She never stayed at the Castle, because her own home is just down the road. She arrived—she had dinner—and she left.

Her father used to drive her. She was small and pretty, and very pleasant.

I remember one night she popped into the Palace

for a drink at six o'clock in the evening. He used Buckingham Palace as an office, but she was in London, and he had invited her to drop in. He was doing interviews—I believe that day it was with *The Shooting Times*—and the buzzer went to announce that the journalist was coming up in the lift. She had to leave and as she was a famous face, the Prince asked me to take her quietly down the stairs so that she and the writer wouldn't meet. It was a bit of a joke—as one door opened another closed.

She said ruefully, "It's like being in a Whitehall farce," as I saw her out through the side gate.

She never met any of the family. She never came to Sandringham or Balmoral. And he didn't take her out very much.

She did go to his thirtieth birthday party—along with about four hundred other people. It wasn't a very intimate evening. And she did go to "A Night with Dame Edna" with him and he took her on to dinner afterwards at a private house. But most of the time when they went to the theater, he wouldn't have asked her personally. His friends who would be setting up the party and asking him as a guest would say, "Would you like us to invite Susan George, if she's free?"

He'd say, "Splendid," and that was how it was arranged. The Prince didn't really entertain a great deal. Other people did it for him.

The Prince and the Showgirl could never have come to anything, but she has been amazingly discreet about their friendship.

One unfortunate girl was not discreet and lost her job and the house she lived in as a result.

She was a groom with a polo team, an attractive blonde divorcée called Jane Ward. The Prince had seen her about, and I suspect he was short of a dinner companion one Saturday evening because he asked her to dine with him at Windsor, in his rooms.

Something went amiss. She arrived, I took her up in the lift and left her with him. Dinner was served, but, it seemed, rather quickly. The next thing I knew both she and her car had gone.

He never said anything when I went in to see if he needed something before retiring, but the next day the silly girl talked to a reporter. She was all over the papers as a new romance.

He was annoyed, but he realized she was probably unaware of the implications of talking to the press, and how it would be blown out of all proportion. But he was angry enough to have her sent off the polo field the next time he saw her. He wanted to scotch that story once and for all.

There was one girl friend who managed to remain very nearly anonymous. The Prince saw more of her than anyone realized. Her name was Janet Jenkins, and she was a Welsh girl who was living in Canada. He met her in 1975 when he was in Canada on a naval exercise, flying helicopters. An attractive blonde, she must have had some importance in his life because she had been given the Royal telephone number.

I first knew about her when the Buckingham Palace operator asked if I knew a Miss Jenkins. I did not, but said I would speak to her. The girl came on the line, and I could tell by her manner that she must have known the Prince.

"Can you let him know I'm in London?" she asked and gave me a telephone number.

When the Prince came in, I passed on the message. "Thank you—" he said. Nothing more.

But the following day she arrived at Windsor for lunch. The Queen was away, and he was playing polo in the afternoon.

"Can you take Miss Jenkins to the ground in the Range Rover," he asked me quietly before he left. "Just to avoid any interest."

I sat with her on the far side of the playing field while we watched and found her a pleasant enough girl. She was the usual Royal girl friend type. Tall, blonde, pretty, and a bit shy. I had the feeling she wasn't too sure what she had let herself in for, as it was I who finally drove her back to London. Dates with the Prince were intimidating for girls at first—all the policemen, the protection, and the fact that they were looked after by someone else all the time. You could often see what they were feeling by their faces.

That night I put Janet Jenkins on a train for Wales where she was going to see relatives. The Prince, who was still in the Navy, went back to sea.

She arrived again in 1976, and she came up and joined us at Craigowan. As usual, she had to make her own way. It was in May and it rained the whole time, but it didn't put the Prince off his fishing. She just stayed for the weekend. He was commanding HMS *Bronnington*, stationed at Rosythe. He went back to the ship, and she went back to London. Alone.

We saw her once more in Canada. It was Jubilee Year, and he had gone to Calgary for the stampede, and up she turned again. It was hardly worth the effort of her journey from Toronto. She barely saw the Prince, who was busy with all sorts of duties. She couldn't even stay at our hotel—there was no room. They had a drink together and he told me to look after her.

I took her shopping. I couldn't think of anything else to do. She bought him a pullover, which she delivered to him and said "Good-bye." As far as I know it really was "good-bye."

It seems strange now to think just how much speculation there was about his friendship with Lady Sarah Spencer, the Princess' older sister. Personally, I never thought there was anything in it. They were much the same age, and he had known her all through her childhood as the girl next door to Sandringham. Actually, she always got on much better with Prince Edward. They really like each other. No romance, of course—Edward was far too young at the time.

Lady Sarah was popular with everyone, but she disappeared from the scene for a long time when she got anorexia.

She came to Balmoral that summer of 1977, but as a houseguest. She was not there at the Prince's specific request. The following year he went skiing with her. It was reported that they were "in a chalet" together. Quite true, but in the same chalet were the Duke and Duchess of Gloucester and John Maclean. I was in London. I never went on the skiing trips with him.

Eventually Lady Sarah herself issued a statement that she was not in love with the Prince, and she did it to kill the speculation.

It seems strange to think that her sister, now Princess of Wales, was only sixteen at the time.

For many years before he married, the gossip was that the Prince of Wales was strongly influenced in his choice of girl friends by two married women—Lady Tryon, an exuberant Australian, who was known in the Prince's circle as "Kanga," and Mrs. Camilla Parker Bowles, the wife of a cavalry officer.

Both women are the wives of two of his closest friends. And in the case of Kanga, the speculation was that there was more than simple and straightforward friendship involved. This was a dreadfully unfair insinuation. The Prince is simply not the type of man to dally with married women, and most certainly not with women who are married to his friends.

The truth is that only three women until Princess Diana came along had any influence on the Prince: his mother, the Queen; his grandmother, the Queen Mother; and his Nanny, Mabel Anderson. But there was a surprising fourth—Lady Susan Hussey, the Queen's Lady-in-Waiting.

Lady Susan is older—in her forties. She, too, is married—to Marmaduke Hussey, former Vice Chairman at *The Times*. It was to Lady Susan that he talked about his girl friends and problems. She was always at the Palace. Her husband working late hours on his newspaper, she was in no tremendous rush to get off home.

For the same reason, she would always make up numbers in a crisis, and act as chaperone if one were needed. Not surprisingly, she has been chosen as a godmother to the new Royal baby, Prince William.

Lord and Lady Tryon were most certainly close friends until his marriage. The Princess is not so keen on having them around now, perhaps because she has heard and half-believed the rumors about the relationship. Nothing has ever been said, but she must have very much resented the stories that the Prince had a very special relationship with Lady Tryon.

I saw Kanga, as the Prince called Lady Tryon, in spring of 1981 at a wedding and she said, "Stephen—I can't understand why we're never invited. There was never anything to those stories."

It is sad for her because she and the Prince were close. She looked after us very well when he was making a tour of Australia, and I think she is hurt now that she is out of it all.

She came to Buckingham Palace to watch the Queen leaving for the Trooping the Colour in 1981, and I said to Lady Diana, "Lady Tryon is here."

"Oh, is she," she said, her face expressionless. "How nice."

But she did not go and see her. She is still young enough to be slightly anxious that someone might interest him more than she does.

Unfortunately, at the time, I think Lady Tryon herself was slightly flattered by the innuendos and did little to dispel them. But whenever she and the Prince were together, her husband was there, too. They were always part of the yearly fishing trip to Iceland along with other friends, and we did see quite a bit of Kanga when we were in Australia in 1977.

She was rather carried away with the idea that she could represent Australia as far as the Prince was concerned. She was making her annual visit to her par-

PRINCE CHARLES WAS THEIR DARLING

ents' home in Melbourne while we were there, and she took over what was left of his free time on the tour.

There wasn't a great deal to it. He was busy. She only managed to arrange a couple of parties. There was an opera evening and also a very splendid party that must have cost a fortune. Lord and Lady Tryon are careful, and an Australian financier picked up the bill.

The second so-called influence, Mrs. Camilla Parker Bowles, is a hunting friend. She and her husband, Colonel Andrew Parker Bowles (who was at one time tipped as Princess Anne's husband), live near Badminton. He commands the Knightsbridge Barracks. They are in their mid-thirties and the friendship, unlike the Tryons', seems to have survived his marriage.

The Prince is godfather to one of their children, Tom, and when Lady Diana first came to Highgrove, and there was no room for her to sleep, Mrs. Camilla Parker Bowles put her up and encouraged the romance.

Like most of the Prince's friends, they live a low-profile, horsey life. They are part of what I think of as "the house party set."

Someone else who was important in his life was Lucia Santa Cruz. He met her when he was at Cambridge—before my time. They were introduced by the late Lord Butler who was Master of Trinity.

It was a fortuitous introduction. The Prince needed a girl friend for his years at University, and Lucia Santa Cruz was a little older than he, beautiful, intelligent, and a good companion. She was working on a research project, which gave her interests of her own, and he could not have had a more suitable first girl friend.

Lucia was Catholic, which would have been a stumbling block to any serious relationship, but even that did not matter. The Prince, at twenty, was far too young to be thinking of marriage.

They have remained friends. Over the years I have seen her occasionally though she now lives in Chile. She came a couple of times to Balmoral and looked very exotic in the Scottish surroundings, with her dusky skin and huge, dark eyes.

She herself has married—a Chilean diplomat and the word is that he will be President one day.

She is obviously a lady destined to be at the top.

The other strong influence—as a friend—on the Prince's life was Lady Jane Wellesley, daughter of the Duke of Wellington. Lady Jane is lovely; small, dark, friendly, bubbly, liking to tease, and not minding being teased back.

A close friend of the Prince is quoted as saying that Lady Jane was the first girl he ever fell in love with. I don't believe that is true.

She was a friend of the family. She was to be seen at all the Royal houses, but as a member of the house party—not as a special girl friend.

Her father has a splendid home in southern Spain that was given to the first Duke of Wellington as a thank-you from the Spanish for defeating Napoleon.

We went there a couple of times to shoot partridge and it was the traditional English pattern transferred to the dusty, hot, yellow landscape of Spain. The guns would go out in the morning and the Duchess of Wellington and Lady Jane would come out to join us for lunch. Lady Jane was always fussing and anxious that we had enough to eat and drink. She was kind. She speaks very good Spanish and was always teaching the Prince little phrases to say. If he wanted to say thank-you to people on the estate, he'd rehearse it with her and go off beaming, thinking he was speaking Spanish.

The Prince's visits there were semiofficial and the Spanish provided the security. While we were shooting we were always followed around by the Guardia Civil in their funny hats. We'd be dressed in tweeds, trying to blend in with the landscape, and there would be these policemen following. Plus, of course, a regiment of press from all over Europe who were convinced that marriage was imminent between the Prince and Lady Jane.

Lady Jane would never have landed the job of Princess of Wales. She hated the attentions of the press. She got very harrassed and fed-up. She lived in a house in Fulham and finding half a dozen reporters camped on her doorstep when the rumors of a serious romance between her and the Prince were at their height, used to enrage her. She would snap and pull long faces, though normally she was a very good-natured girl. But, of course, as a Duke's daughter she would be used to being treated with considerable respect. Unwanted attention annoyed her.

The press *were* a nuisance, but at the same time very good training for any girl friend the Prince might take up with. The constant attention showed them what to expect and how to cope. This was where Lady Diana scored heavily. She never put a wrong foot forward.

But Lady Jane remained a Royal favorite for years.

She never really went out of his life. If he needed a girl to take out, he would invite her. She was a pal. She isn't married and is probably the only one of his girl friends who is seriously career oriented. Over the years she has held down some tough jobs in the television world. An independent girl, I doubt if the life of Princess of Wales would have suited her at all.

But it really wouldn't have suited a lot of them.

Lord Mountbatten, who saw himself as a king maker, had tremendous influence on Prince Charles, and he was very keen that his great-nephew should marry his granddaughter, Amanda Knatchbull.

Everyone was slightly panicked by this. Had Lord Mountbatten succeeded we would have inherited the entire Brabourne family. Miss Knatchbull herself is a very nice girl, quite pretty, but not really the Prince's type. But encouraged by Lord Mountbatten, who promoted the match tirelessly, they did see quite a lot of each other—usually on holidays at Amanda's parents' home in the Bahamas.

Her sheer proximity might have done the trick, plus the fact that Prince Charles had so much respect for his great-uncle. But it never happened.

If Lord Mountbatten had lived, I do wonder if the course of Royal history might have been changed, and if Diana, Princess of Wales, might still be Lady Diana Spencer.

❧ 14 ❧

Love Match

I FIRST SAW Lady Diana Spencer, as she then was known, on the Royal yacht, *Britannia*, at Cowes in August 1980. She came on with a party of young Royals and their friends, led by Lady Sarah Armstrong Jones, the daughter of Princess Margaret and Lord Snowdon, the most beautifully mannered and generous young lady I've ever encountered.

Lady Diana's presence struck me right away. She was somehow quite different from the other young people in the party, combining a natural maturity with a charming artlessness. In fact, she seemed quite different from any of the other ladies who had ever engaged the Prince's attention.

Commandingly tall, stylish, both shy and confident at the same time, she was obviously very special. She was also wonderfully good-looking, and the Prince has always liked pretty girls. He also likes them tall—most of the ladies in his life have met him eye-to-eye. And the Prince prefers blondes. Lady Diana qualified on all counts.

But beyond her physical attributes she was a friendly and open young woman. The crew of the *Britannia* fell in love with her to a man. The Royal servants liked her. The stewards ran around saying, "Gosh, isn't Lady Di lovely?" Indeed we all thought she was lovely. We all sensed that here was someone different. Someone who might get "the job," as the staff referred to a potential Princess of Wales. She looked couture-made for the part.

Diana was fascinated by the yacht on her first voyage. She explored the ship thoroughly and enjoyed meeting everyone connected with the running of it.

She had, of course, been on the fringes of Prince Charles' life for many years. In fact she was "the girl next door." As a child her family home had been Park House, which sits cheek by jowl with the Royal estate of Sandringham in Norfolk. Her father, the Earl of Spencer, had been a Royal equerry to the Queen in Coronation Year and her grandmother, Lady Fermoy, is still a lady-in-waiting to the Queen Mother, not to mention her sister's earlier involvement with Charles.

However the Prince himself didn't seem to take too much notice of her at the beginning, though *her* eyes followed him everywhere. In September 1980 she came to Balmoral to join one of the Royal house parties. She could have been just another weekend house guest, but having seen her on the *Britannia* just a month earlier, we of the Royal staff felt all our antennae go skywards. We were pretty sure there was something to it. Already the press were starting to sniff around. The spotlight was beginning to focus on her.

It is interesting that Diana has never been concerned with her own publicity—which is more than you could say for some of the girls with whom the Prince had been involved. She didn't rush to see what the papers had said about her, and even when she began to be hassled by the hordes of reporters, she took all their remarks and questioning in her stride. I think that she may have well regarded the pressure that was put on her as good training for "the job."

The Prince, however, was more concerned. He used to say to me, "I wish the bloody press would leave her alone."

But there certainly was no obvious romance that first time she came to Balmoral. The men went out shooting all day and Diana joined the Prince with all the other ladies at an outdoor luncheon, the kind that are normally held at a country house shooting party. The Prince and Diana seemed to like each other but there were no clues to a budding love affair. But still the general conviction that she could be "The One" persisted.

She came up to Scotland for a second time in October 1980, but this time her visit was to Birkhall to stay with the Queen Mother. Her grandmother, Lady Fermoy, was also there, and the sport on that holiday was stalking Highland deer. It was a much smaller house party than the one at Cowes, as Birkhall is not large. Next door to Balmoral, it has been the Queen Mother's Highland home since the Queen came to the throne and is a very familiar place to Prince Charles. He spent his childhood holidays there and loves going back because of what he calls "its cozy atmosphere."

While he was out stalking, Lady Diana stayed at Birkhall and worked on her needlepoint. Still, although they were friendly, there were no signs of the Prince having fallen madly in love. This didn't mean a great deal, however. He used to fall in love regularly, like any young man of his age, but it was never easy to tell just what he was feeling.

But soon thereafter things seemed to be blossoming. In late October after we had returned to Buckingham Palace, the Prince rang for me one morning.

"We are . . ." he often used the Royal "we" . . . going to Highgrove. Lady Diana will also be coming. I want you to drive her down. She'll telephone you later to arrange a rendezvous."

He looked faintly harassed, which was unusual for him. Highgrove was his new home in Gloucestershire, and Lady Diana had never seen it. Although it isn't true to say she turned up her nose, I don't think she was that impressed when we arrived. She didn't say a word, but her face told it all.

The house *was* something of a mess—half decorated, half furnished, and not very comfortable. Indeed, there were only three usable bedrooms at that time: the Prince's, mine, and one for whichever policeman was on duty.

The Prince rather enjoyed this confusion. He liked "roughing it" a little on his time off as an alternative to life at the Palace. And Highgrove was his own home—the first house he had ever owned. Buckingham Palace is, after all, the Queen's home and the other Royals living there usually consider themselves to be her guests.

Highgrove might have been a disappointment at first to Lady Diana as she was used to considerable grandeur at her father's family seat—Althrop in Northamptonshire—and I'm sure that her own flat in London on Old Brompton Road was very comfortable. Now, of course, the Princess has transformed Highgrove into a beautiful and comfortable home for herself, the Prince, and their infant son, Prince William.

When we returned to Highgrove after the Scottish part of the honeymoon, the decorating was finished. The Prince had not seen the house since before the wedding, and the Princess, very excited, led him round, showing him every room.

"Are you pleased?" she kept asking him. You could tell from his expression that he was.

"He likes it," she said to me triumphantly. "And it's my dream house now."

I drove her to Gloucestershire three times that autumn before they became engaged. The Prince was generally out hunting when we arrived, and Lady Diana would walk around the house and gardens waiting for him to return.

They would have tea together alone and generally eat a very simple early dinner, usually egg dishes, which I would cook for them. We'd put a card table and a hot plate up in the sitting room and leave them alone. About 9:30 the Prince would drive her back to

London in his shooting brake—with, of course, a policeman sitting in the back.

He returned to his official duties after the Scottish holiday and she to her job teaching kindergarten at Pimlico.

Courtships are not easy when you are Royal. Still, they were able to snatch some time together. I would frequently collect Lady Diana and whisk her away from the ever-present press who did sentry duty on her door night and day. The Prince would warn me that she would be telephoning to tell me where to pick her up. She would ring, say, "It's Diana" (she never used her title), give me the address where she could be found, and I'd drive her off to meet the Prince. We used all sorts of little schemes to get her away without anyone knowing.

For example, she would take a taxi to her grandmother's house in Eaton Square, and I'd pick her up there. Or she would get to her sister's house at Kensington Palace. Usually once she was in a London taxi she was able to lose her pursuers. On the way back, I'd drop her behind Colherne Court, the block of flats where she lived, and she would go in without the watchers being aware of where she had sprung from.

In the car she would relax in the front passenger seat, her long legs stretched out, chatting cheerfully as I wondered if I had the future Queen of England sitting beside me.

She would chat about all sorts of things: the press interest in her, which she was learning to live with, about children, about clothes. She would look in shop windows as we drove along, saying—"Oh, that's nice!" She loves color and pretty clothes and shopping is an escape from the formality of being a Princess. I think even now she would be more interested in going up to Bond Street for the afternoon than worrying about what the future might bring.

Lady Diana started finding out about the Prince's likes and dislikes from me. She said one day, "Don't you think he's a bit formal, the way he dresses? Perhaps we'll try and change things."

Having dressed him for the past twelve years, I wasn't quite sure what to say.

"Guess what I've bought today?" she said to me one afternoon—and produced a pair of fashionable brown slip-on shoes.

I said, "You'll never get away with those. He's always had his shoes made to order."

She just grinned. That evening I saw the Prince walking around trying to get used to them. He'd never worn slip-on shoes in his life. Now he wears them all the time—and ready-made at that.

Diana wanted to know which colors he preferred to wear. "Blue," I told her. The next week she turned up with a blue pullover sweater for him. She was always buying him little presents—shirts and ties were favorites—and I must admit she spruced up his wardrobe.

She never tried to pick my brains about the Prince's past. Never once did she ask about the other girls in his life. Not that I would have told her anything if she had. I kept careful guard because I didn't know what was going to happen. She could easily have said to him, "Oh, sir . . ." (she always called him sir, in my presence at least) ". . . oh, sir, guess what I heard in the car from Stephen." And he would have been upset with me. So, I was cautious, and we got on well together.

She liked giggling and she loved eating sweets. She always got into the car with her Yorkie bars or bags of toffees. "Have one, Stephen," she'd say. "Go on."

"You'll get fat," I used to warn her. But she undoubtedly burned up all those calories contending with the pressures that were building up.

Before the engagement was announced she had a great deal to contend with. One story in particular upset both of them. The *Sunday Mirror* newspaper ran a front-page splash which said that she had been driven down to the Royal train when it was in a siding at Wiltshire and spent the night there with the Prince. The implications were obvious.

There was absolutely no truth in the story. I myself was on the train with him, plus the two policemen who always travel with him. This is the thing that everyone forgets—where the Prince is, there is also one, if not two, of his personal policemen, usually in the next room. Being Royal means rarely being completely alone.

The Royal train has four carriages and the Prince— or any of the Royal family, come to that—uses it as a convenient way of getting around the countryside for engagements. It means they can leave at nighttime —as late as midnight—if they have something to do, say, in Liverpool, the next morning. We usually pulled into a siding around 2:00 A.M. so that everyone could get some sleep, and the train is then immediately surrounded by local policemen. No one could possibly get near it without being seen, and if the Princess had slipped on board without anyone having spotted her, all I can say is that she must be a female Houdini.

The appearance of the story upset everyone, and the *Sunday Mirror*'s editor, Robert Edwards' absolute refusal to withdraw the statement caused a lot of annoyance at the Palace. At one point people from the Prince's office were even asking me if I was completely certain there was no truth in it. It seemed quite strange that the editor was sticking to his guns.

"We have to issue an absolute denial," the Prince's Secretary said. "You were there. Did anything happen?"

I was able to tell them that there was no truth in it. There had been no sign at all of Lady Diana that night. As I had seen the Prince just before he retired and awakened him early the next morning, I would have known. There had been no lady on his train. Not Lady Diana, nor anyone else.

The Prince himself was furious. "Where do these stories start?" he said to me despairingly. "It's rubbish and it has put Lady Diana in such a bad light." He was also angry because the Royal train is owned by the British public. And he has a very strong sense of not using public-owned things for his own ends.

Of course, the Royal family pays for the use of the train. Every time it is taken out, British Rail presents a bill for mileage. It is not at all cheap, but worth it for the convenience.

Lady Diana was also upset. She had suddenly been given a taste of the type of unpleasantness she could expect as she became more involved with the Prince. She realized she had to learn to face this kind of publicity and she was forced to learn fast.

The weekend of his thirty-second birthday, November 14, 1980, was spent in Norfolk at Wood Farm, the little house on the Sandringham estate. It was a small family gathering consisting of the Queen, Prince Philip, and Prince Charles—and Lady Diana was asked down.

Was this the weekend that the Prince made up his mind? The press thought so. By Sunday they turned up in force at the gates to Wood Farm. The Prince's birthday, Saturday, was spent shooting pheasants on the Sandringham estate, and they had planned to share a four-day weekend from the Friday to late Monday, but with the droves of reporters baying at the gate, all privacy had gone. The Prince and Lady Diana couldn't even go for a walk together.

The Duke of Edinburgh, who has never come to terms with the media's fascination with royalty, was furious because the shooting was ruined. The Prince and Lady Diana were disappointed, and so the weekend was curtailed. It was decided over Sunday lunch that the best thing was for Lady Diana to go back to London.

We made an elaborate plan to spirit her away.

In the hall the Prince said to me, "Where's the Range Rover?"

"Just outside, sir," I said.

"It's become impossible for Lady Diana to stay any longer," he said sadly. "Will you take my Range Rover down the drive and turn left into the fields. I'll take Lady Diana in the farm Land Rover in the other direction."

Very depressed, she went upstairs to pack, and we put her things in the farm Land Rover, which was going to rendezvous with an unmarked police car waiting in the fields a couple of miles away.

Looking thoroughly fed up, she made her exit through the kitchen while I set off fast down the drive, acting as decoy.

It seemed to work. The press was still freezing in Norfolk as Lady Diana was spotted entering her own flat at Colherne Court. The media had got it right, though. There was definitely a romance.

A whirlwind one, too.

The public took to her, and the media interest in her snowballed the romance along. The Duke of Edinburgh was pressuring his son a little—he'd been saying for some time that if Charles didn't hurry up and find a bride there would be no one suitable left. Now I think the Duke was concerned about the Prince leading on a nineteen-year-old girl. Everyone at the Palace, from kitchen maids up, was saying in effect— "What's he waiting for? She's beautiful, she's untarnished, she has no previous lovers." Lady Diana was the stuff that fairy tales are made of, and she was most certainly in love with her Prince. She was always available when he called, and she always fitted in with his plans. She obviously adored being with him, and in January the Prince wrote a memo to his office to tell them to give her a copy of his weekly engagements—just so she would know where he was. I was intrigued. This had never happened before.

They had a very old-fashioned romance—the sort of courtship Barbara Cartland, the Princess' step-grandmother, writes about. We sometimes used to think that she went back home and read the novels and then came back and did everything the author suggested the next day!

I think people might have been faintly put off the scent when both the Prince and Lady Diana spent Christmas with their own families. Then the Royal family moved from Windsor to Sandringham in January, and Lady Diana was amongst the house party one weekend, arriving in her Mini Metro.

Though Sandringham is a large private estate, there are many public roads crossing it, and therefore access is simple—for both the public and, unfortunately for the Royals, the press.

Again the reporters turned up in a pack, disrupting life for the Duke of Edinburgh's shooting party. He was so angry that it was amazing that none of them got shot along with the pheasants.

Poor Lady Diana was practically confined to barracks. She could wander near the house or across to her former home, Park House, which was by now empty, but she could do little else except pop up all over the place. She could often be found drinking coffee with the footmen.

On this visit to Sandringham she met more of the staff, enchanting them as usual, but passed her days waiting for the Prince to come back from the shoot.

A second weekend visit had been planned, but this was abandoned because of the constant attentions of the press. The Prince was becoming concerned.

"We're ruining everyone's holiday," he said to me. "I can't bring her down here any more. Highgrove's full of workmen, but we'll just have to go there."

And once again I was told to wait for a phone call with the time and place of the rendezvous.

I picked her up at her grandmother's house in Eaton Square, and we drove down to the Cotswolds on a very gray day. She slept most of the way while the cassette player boomed out her favorite composer, Tchaikovsky's Piano Concerto. There was no conversation. By then she knew me well enough to relax with me.

The Prince had also left Sandringham and had created a decoy of his own by hunting in Leicester. The gardener at Highgrove had worked out a back route into the house. I followed it, and our arrival went like clockwork. Nobody knew she was there. And the Prince came home late in the afternoon to find her waiting for him. The cat and mouse game had worked. They were both much relieved.

Happily the workmen had disappeared, though the mess still remained. Paul Officer, his policeman, and I made ourselves scarce. I'd brought a picnic from Sandringham and we left them alone to eat it.

Very early the next morning I took her back to London on what we called "a dawn dash" in order to get her back to her teaching job. She was a very happy young woman on that journey to London. Relaxed, smiling—and not chattering.

I don't know for sure, but I'm pretty certain that it was that night at Highgrove when the Prince proposed. There wasn't another occasion when it could have happened. I don't know whether she said yes, right away, but I don't doubt that he said, "Think about it." He always said "think about it" when anyone had to make an important decision.

I didn't see Diana again until the night of the engagement, but on the car trip back from Highgrove in the early dawn, she told me she had planned a three-week trip to Australia with her mother to stay with her step-father, Peter Shand Kydd. He had a farm in New South Wales. It was perhaps fortuitous as it would give her time to think. Meanwhile, the Prince went skiing on his annual holiday in Klosters with the Duke and Duchess of Gloucester.

This gave them the little breathing space the Prince thought necessary, but they spoke constantly but guardedly on the telephone. The Prince rarely says a great deal on the telephone. Generally she called him. His engagements were booked so far in advance she knew where to find him. Her answer had to have been yes, because she cut her holiday short and came home a week early.

It was the greatest compliment I've ever had when the Prince told me himself a full week before the official announcement. It was the most important—and difficult—secret I've ever kept.

He broke the news to me on the weekend of Lady Diana's return from Australia. He had been hunting at Highgrove and he was in great good humor. His staff knew this must be *it*.

When we got back to Buckingham Palace, he rang for me and I went into his study. He looked up from his work and said, "Stephen, I have some very good news."

"Oh, yes, sir," I said, keeping my expression blank but pretty sure what was coming.

"Lady Diana and I are to announce our engagement."

I tried to look as if I hadn't guessed, and said, "That's marvelous news, sir. May I congratulate her when I see her?"

I asked because sometimes he would tell me things that he hadn't mentioned to her, and I wanted to be sure it was all right.

"Of course," he said.

I would like to have shaken his hand, just as there had been times when I had wished over the past weeks I could have asked if Lady Diana was going to be his wife. But then that would have been presumptuous. I always had to remember that he was the future King of England and I was his valet. The servant/master relationship must never slip.

However, I couldn't resist asking teasingly, "Was it on both knees, sir?"

"Neither," he said, and grinned.

Back home Lady Diana dined at Windsor with the Queen on Sunday night and then on the eve of the engagement, Monday, February 23, came to the Palace with her sister, Jane. Jane is married to Robert Fellowes, the Queen's Assistant Private Secretary. The Prince was not back from his day's engagements and she waited in Fellowes' office. I was told she was there, and when the Prince came back I rang down and asked for her to be sent up. She knew her way by then, but I met her at the lift. She was very tanned from her Australian trip and looked very happy.

"How nice to see you again," she said.

"You must be exhausted from all that traveling," I said.

"I'll survive!" she said chirpily.

I showed her into his rooms, and I was just leaving

when the Prince said, "Stephen, I believe you have something to say to Lady Diana." There was a big smile on his face.

"Congratulations, Lady Diana," I said.

"Thank you." She, too, was smiling broadly, standing at his side.

"Do you have the ring?" I asked her.

"Not yet," she said with a little wail. "But it will come soon. It's gone to be adjusted."

Later that evening she told me she had chosen the engagement ring the night before at Windsor, after dining with the Queen.

"There was a whole tray of rings waiting for me from Garrards [the Royal jewelers]," she said. "The Queen's eyes popped when I picked out the largest one. It's a beautiful sapphire with diamonds. I love it."

After choosing the ring, she had come back to London that night and gone back to the kindergarten the next morning. She was, of course, bursting with excitement but had to try to act as if nothing had happened.

I left them alone in his rooms and he rang a little later. "Lord and Lady Spencer will be coming for a drink at half-past seven," he said. "Will you bring them up?"

They arrived right on time. She looked very glamorous in mink and pearls, he looked slightly strained from the stroke he had suffered and walked very slowly. I showed them into the Prince's sitting room where the Earl's daughter was waiting with her future husband. As far as I knew, it was the first time the Spencers had met the Prince since the courtship began, and I believe that he must have asked the Earl for Lady Diana's hand by telephone!

It was a very quiet engagement party. None of the group really drinks so there were no corks flying and the Spencers only stayed half an hour. Lady Diana left about twenty minutes later and went off to stay with her sister, Jane, in Kensington Palace. The Prince then joined the Queen for dinner. Afterwards, I found him in his study busily telephoning relatives. "Oh—" he said. "Getting engaged is hard work! Now have I forgotten to tell anybody?"

We went through various names as I jogged his memory and at 10:30 I left him.

That was the pre-engagement night, and knowing the Princess I don't doubt she was in bed and asleep by 10:00 P.M. She most certainly is not a night owl. Supper at seven and bed by ten is her idea of bliss.

The rest of us, it must be said, had a much jollier time when the engagement was announced the next day. The atmosphere in the Palace was electric. Everyone from the kitchens to the Household knew that something was up. Cases of pink champagne were being chilled and we felt as if an explosion was about to happen.

The Palace and the people who live and work there always come together on occasions, whether they be sad or happy ones. And a happy occasion like an engagement ripples right through the house.

On the morning of February 24, 1981, the Prince's Household was called together in the Private Secretary's office on the ground floor at 10:30 and I knew exactly why.

We were waiting impatiently when he and Lady Diana came in. It was about 10:40.

"Good morning, everyone," the Prince said. "I'd like to introduce you to my future wife."

A buzz ran around the fifteen or so people gathered in the big room, followed by a discreet cheer. Everyone began to talk at once and try to offer their own personal congratulations. The girls who had never met her before all clustered around Lady Diana, asking to see the ring, happily back from the jewelers.

Someone opened champagne, and the Princess had literally just a teaspoonful, apologizing that she had a long day in front of her. The Prince stood at her side, holding her hand, beaming broadly.

"When did *you* know?" the girls from the office were asking me.

"Oh, only just this minute," I said, not wanting to breach the Prince's confidence even at this stage, but very relieved that the secret was now out without any leaks.

At 11:00 A.M. the news was official. The Queen beamed as the Lord Chamberlain announced the engagement at her weekly investiture. In seconds, everyone in the Palace knew. The pages told the footmen, the footmen told the chefs, the chefs told the kitchen maids; the Palace grapevine was working overtime. Champagne was the order of the day at lunch. Everyone from the Lord Chamberlain to the youngest housemaid was given a glass. The atmosphere was incredible.

Lady Diana and the Prince went off to lunch with the Queen and by then flowers started arriving from all over the world. It must have been a great day for

Interflora. I had difficulty finding space to put them all. The Prince's apartment looked like the Chelsea Flower Show. I put some in the corridors, sent some to the other apartments and finally sent a mass of blooms over to Clarence House where I had been informed that the Princess would be staying for a day or two.

Telegrams arrived—three thousand of them. The switchboard was jammed; the operators were going mad; and outside in the gardens for most of the afternoon, the Prince and Lady Diana posed for the press photographers who could at last really get their teeth into the story.

As my own sitting room overlooks the garden, I couldn't resist peeking out of the window, watching the photographers at work, hiding behind the curtain and trying not to be seen. Everyone, photographers, the Prince, and his fiancée seemed to be having a lovely time.

When the Prince came back up to his own apartment, and I went in to see if there was anything he needed, he said, mock accusingly, "I saw you looking out of the window."

"Oh, sir," I said, "I am sorry. I was trying not to be seen."

He laughed. "It's all right," he said, "the Queen was looking out of her window, too, and she was trying not to be seen. Whenever the photographers looked up at the Palace you both shot back like cuckoos in a cuckoo clock."

At 6:30 that evening, with the Palace full of flowers and excitement, Lady Diana left to take up temporary residence at Clarence House with the Queen Mother.

I couldn't help thinking how Lady Diana's circumstances had changed overnight. The evening before she had left the Palace with her sister and had to dodge the hordes of press outside her home.

Today, she was leaving with two plainclothesmen in attendance and all the protection she could possibly need.

Her new life had begun.

~ 15 ~

Engagement Days

FOR SOME unknown reason everyone seemed to think that Lady Diana remained at Clarence House as the Queen Mother's guest right up until the time of the wedding. This was not the case. After two days she came to live at Buckingham Palace, where a small suite of rooms had been prepared for her. A maid and a footman were assigned to her. She was beginning to learn the job and learn what it was to lose her privacy.

Not that she will give up her privacy easily. She still fights for it. She insists on going to the same hairdresser she has always used—Headlines in Kensington. She has to get out of bed early to go, but she prefers the outing to having a hairdresser call at the Palace as the other Royals do. She uses any excuse to leave the gilded cage.

The suite she was given had been that of Miss Peebles, the Royal Governess, for many a long year. Afterwards Mabel Anderson, the Nanny, had used it once Prince Edward and Prince Andrew had grown up. The rooms were rather smaller than is usual in the Palace. We made them as comfortable as possible, putting in a TV set and cheerful furniture and flowers that were still fresh from the engagement day. As the Prince still had to carry out his duties, this meant that Lady Diana was alone for much of the time.

She had a sitting room, bedroom, and bathroom, but she used the old nursery kitchen. The Nursery Footman (there is no nursery now, but there is still a Nursery Footman) looked after her. He was a pleasant young man named Mark, who said to me, puzzled, "What shall I do? Lady Diana never seems to ask for anything."

"Maybe she's shy to ask in case anyone thinks she's getting grand," I suggested.

I had the same problem. I'd pop in and see her when the Prince was out. "Are you sure you don't want anything?" I'd ask.

"No, I'll be all right," she'd say.

She would give little lunches in her sitting room for the girls she had shared the flat with in Old Brompton Road and invited her mother, Mrs. Peter Shand Kydd, and Jane, her sister, along as often as they could come. I once asked her if she minded being alone so much.

"Oh, no," she said. "Not in the least."

Which is just as well. All Royals spend a lot of time alone when they are not on holiday with the family.

She also took up tap dancing to pass the time. A

236

woman came in to accompany her on the piano and to the horror of the Department of Environment who look after the floors at the Palace, the Princess quite ruined the Music Room parquet.

She was instantly popular at the Palace and was always trotting to the kitchens. A footman had to show her the way the first couple of times until she could find them for herself.

Lady Diana never ate properly then. She picked like a bird at chocolate, yogurts, and cereal. She never drinks but eats lots of fruit, and in those days she was always running down to ask the chefs for an apple or any sweet leftovers made by the pastry cooks. It seemed funny to us—she wasn't adjusting to being Royal. The Prince hasn't been to the kitchens for years. They are right at the back of the Palace and miles from anywhere. It seemed a long way to go for an apple, but I suspect it was yet another way of showing her independence, and one, incidentally, that made her terribly popular with the kitchen staff!

"Keep an eye on Lady Diana for me, will you?" the Prince had said. All I did was make sure she was all right. I was afraid of overkill—she was so friendly that I was a little worried that some of the footmen would take advantage and try to get too familiar with her. The Master's office at the Palace asked me to let them know if this happened, but it never did. The Princess is friendly, true—but she has a natural dignity that would prevent over-familiarity.

But whenever the Prince came back from engagements his first question was, "Is Lady Diana all right?"

So, in this waiting period, she seemed happy

enough in her rooms. We filled the nursery refrigerator with yogurts and foods she liked. She'd sew, read, and watch TV. She particularly loved "Crossroads," an English soap opera. And when the Prince returned, I'd go to her rooms. "He's back," I'd tell her.

"Hurray!" she'd say and would come hurrying along the corridor to see him.

She was the only person whose presence I did not announce to him. She just knocked on his door and entered. "Is he free, Stephen?" she'd say first. "Is it all right to go in?" She didn't want to burst in if he had a visitor. Another thing that amused us was her attempt not to call him *anything* at this stage. She was obviously too shy to say "Charles" in front of anyone else, and "Sir" must have seemed very formal now that they were engaged to be married. At that time he always called her Diana.

Today they call each other "darling." The word reverberates around Highgrove as they shout up the stairs for each other.

The six-month waiting period for the wedding probably passed quickly for her. She had a lot to do. The Prince had very little.

I did not need to buy him anything to wear for his wedding. He was going to be married in his naval uniform. He planned to wear his favorite gray pinstripe suit to go off on the honeymoon. He didn't need even so much as a new pair of socks.

Diana, on the other hand, was very busy shopping, which was no problem to her. Choosing and fitting the wedding dress took a lot of time, particularly as she steadily lost weight throughout the engagement period. The Emmanuels, who made the dress, were forever taking it in, and I reckon she must have lost about fourteen pounds, coping with all the pressures.

By this time she was recognized by everyone. Wherever she went heads turned. But then she would turn heads anyway.

Her mother shopped with her most of the time, and Lady Diana had a splendid time buying a great many new clothes.

She bought them with her own money. No bills arrived at the Palace office, and she must have spent a considerable sum, although many of the clothes she wore for photographs were loaned by *Vogue* magazine, which was good for them and good for Diana's pocketbook.

Clothes are a passion with her, just like most young women of her age, and most of the time she showed very good taste. Sometimes she'd buy things that I felt were too old for her, but of course *the* dress that caused such a sensation was the black off-the-shoulder one that was so revealing.

When I saw it all I could say was, "Gosh!"

"Don't you like it?" she said defensively.

"It'll certainly catch everyone's attention," I said. Which it did, and I had to admit she looked stunning in it when she wore it to the musical gala—her first public appearance. The late Princess Grace was there as well and they were photographed side by side.

The Prince and Lady Diana's routine during the engagement period before going out was that she would dress in her rooms and then come along to see if he was ready. Invariably he wasn't because an appointment had run late. All dressed up, she'd wait for him

239

until he came through to the sitting room from his bedroom. She was more organized than he was.

For the first months of her marriage, her appearance was constantly changing—a metamorphosis from the see-through Indian cotton dress that caused such a fuss when she was photographed wearing it with two of her pupils. She kept up with most of the people she dealt with before she became Royal. The only ones she cut off have been the Emmanuels, who made her wedding dress. They got carried away and talked too much to too many people. "We'll see about *them*," said the Princess, which meant that she didn't see them again.

During the engagement, she started to redecorate Highgrove, driving down in her Mini Metro with Graham, her newly acquired police officer, crammed in the passenger seat. Set in 347 acres of beautiful hunting country in Gloucestershire, Highgrove is a Georgian house consisting of eighteen principal rooms, plus several bathrooms and a kitchen. Although it was already decorated, it was fairly run down when Prince Charles purchased it in 1980. The Prince decided that the easiest thing would be to repaint the entire house white and think about a color scheme and furnishings later. Then, of course, he became engaged, and things started to move with Lady Diana firmly in charge.

She hired an interior designer—Dudley Poplak—whose work she knew as he had decorated her mother's apartment in London. For several weeks Highgrove was a mass of paint swatches and fabric samples. The main colors Princess Diana chose were coral for the halls and staircases, yellow for her sitting room, green for the dining room, and a very pale green for the drawing room. Their bedroom was done in a very pale pink with green and pink-flowered drapes on the four-poster bed and windows. Old master oil paintings from the Royal collection hung through the house and both old and new furniture were added to the wedding presents. Princess Diana loves cushions and makes them herself, so there are a lot of them around the place—sometimes used for throwing at the Prince when he teases her. In sum, she and her decorator had managed to create a beautiful, cheerful home by the time they returned from Scotland after their honeymoon.

All her own furniture from the flat is now in the staff's quarters at Highgrove. Her very pretty flowered living room curtains have been lengthened to fit the Highgrove windows, and her two rather good sofas are in use. Also the cane chairs and typical bachelor girl's odds and ends have gone into the rooms. Nothing has been wasted.

And, of course, there were all those wedding presents to find a place for. There seemed to be thousands of them, and as the wedding day drew nearer, the Palace theater where we stored them temporarily began to look like Harrod's warehouse.

I spent an enormous amount of time in the Prince's office at the Palace, watching the wedding presents come in. People sent things from all over the world, and extra staff had to be taken on to cope with the unpacking, the categorizing, and the thank-you letters. There were so many to send out that they had to be coded.

There were gifts from the family, official bodies,

241

governments, foreign royalty, and just well-wishers from all over the country. Every day I'd take in a list of what had been sent, and the Prince would go through it carefully, muttering to himself, "How generous, how kind."

Very often he'd ask if he could look at a particular present, and I'd bring it up to his sitting room. He was particularly keen to see any drawings and paintings that arrived, and he was absolutely delighted with a Munnings picture of horses that the American oilman, Dr. Armand Hammer, gave him. Good glass interests him, too, and I would carefully carry any of that upstairs for his personal inspection.

There were, like at any other wedding, some very strange presents. The Prince's word for the worst of them was "frightful!" Then he'd add, "They can go in the staff rooms."

The staff rooms are now pretty cluttered—mostly with dreadful pictures painted by people who think they're Picasso.

There were an awful lot of silver toast racks. "Can you believe—" he said, "all these toast racks and no one's given us a toaster! Ours must be the only wedding that didn't receive one."

He and Lady Diana used to go down to the theater to have a look at the gifts and also to thank the staff for their help with all of the additional work that the influx of gifts created.

I suppose the most exotic present was from the late King Faisal of Saudi Arabia. It was a beautiful sapphire set—a bracelet, a watch, necklace, and earrings, made from enormous sapphires all set in gold and designed by a Parisian jeweler. I thought Lady Diana's eyes would pop out of her head when she saw it. "Gosh," she said, "I'm becoming a very rich lady." King Faisal gave the Prince a large, gold box. Prince Charles must have more gold boxes than anyone else in the world. It seems to be the only present that people ever think about when they have to buy him something. But then—what do you buy a man who has everything?

We in his Household subscribed together to give him some silver menu holders, engraved with the Prince's feathers on the front and our names on the back.

A lot of jewelry came from other rulers, but nothing was as spectacular as the sapphires from Faisal. The poor Princess hadn't had a chance to wear any of it by the time I left their service. The wedding presents were "touring" for the public to view, and I assume that the sapphires were sent with everything else.

The Queen, as far as I know, has not yet given the couple anything. Some family jewelry was passed to the Princess, but the Queen, who is a very practical lady, undoubtedly waited to see what they really needed after all the other gifts had arrived. And I don't doubt that her present will be something extremely useful that no one else has thought of.

The weeks ticked by, and the wedding day drew closer and closer. Then with just five days to "W Day" they both went to stay with Lord Romsey at Broadlands—which was proving to be one of Lady Diana's favorite places. The Romseys are a young couple and they all get on well together.

It was on the afternoon that the Prince was playing polo at Tidworth in Hampshire that Lady Diana cracked. The cameras flashing in her face, the constant pestering finally got through. She burst into tears.

I was back at Broadlands, and the first I knew of the incident was when Lady Romsey and Lady Diana came back early. Lady Diana's face was puffy and she had obviously been crying. She went straight upstairs to lie down.

"She's a little upset and doesn't feel well," Lady Romsey said. That was obvious.

The Prince came back as soon as he could and comforted her, but it was easy to see that he was worried. Was she going to fail to cope with all that being Royal demands, right at the last minute, five days before the wedding? It was very much on his mind. But the young lady is very resilient, and she soon perked up again.

The wedding rehearsals at St. Paul's started. Lady Diana quietly went to several, but the Prince, more used to State occasions, only went twice. Once to the final one, and once to hear the music he had chosen. He had asked for Kiri Te Kanawa, the New Zealand opera singer, to sing at the wedding. He'd first heard her in 1970 when we were in Duddinen, the South Island of New Zealand, and had been an admirer ever since.

Though the wedding preparations were hectic, the Prince and Lady Diana did manage to find time to give a very private and special party for his staff, on July 16. Everyone on his payroll—about twenty of us—plus wives and girl friends, received an invitation, the only joint invitation ever issued before Lady Diana became the Princess of Wales.

The party was held at the exclusive Mark's Club, which was closed to everyone else for the evening.

Lady Diana wore a very full-skirted red dress and looked just like Scarlett O'Hara. She came and spoke to us all. We all sat down at separate little tables for a buffet dinner, and table by table, the Royal couple joined us all.

After dinner a disco was set up and we all danced, with Lady Diana leading. She moves very well and enjoys dancing.

The sad thing was that at midnight the Prince had to leave to catch the Royal train for an engagement in the morning. But Lady Diana stayed on.

His last instructions to me were, "Look after her, please."

In fact she left fairly soon afterwards. As I said, she is not a night owl, but the rest of us were still there until the early hours.

The final rehearsal was held the night before the wedding—and the night of the fireworks. After the rehearsal, the Royals had an early supper at Buckingham Palace while we, the staff, went to Hyde Park. There was a stand for us where we had a superb view.

Lady Diana was faintly grumpy as the only one of the family not allowed to see the fireworks. She went back to Clarence House. She wanted very much to go, but the prewedding night tradition ruled it out.

"Isn't it silly," she said. "I'll have to watch them from the window while everyone else is there."

And she did miss a jolly good evening.

∾ 16 ∾

Honeymoon Afloat

IT WAS DAWN on the Saturday when Mervin, the chef, John, the policeman, and I drove down to Eastleigh Airport where the Andover of the Queen's Flight was waiting to fly us all to Gibraltar, where we were to join the Royal yacht for the Royal honeymoon.

We waited at the airfield for the Prince and Princess to arrive from Broadlands before we got on board, but we didn't see much of them on the flight. They stayed at the back of the plane in their own compartment while the staff, still in the wedding mood, enjoyed ourselves up front.

We were all looking forward to two weeks of absolute relaxation—because that's what the trip would be for us. Nothing more than a magnificent holiday.

The reception at Gibraltar after we landed was incredible. The Prince and Princess drove from the airport through the town to the yacht, which was anchored in the harbor, in a converted, open-topped Triumph Stag. The Gibraltarians seem to be Royalists to a man, and I think the Prince and Princess were both stunned by the enthusiasm of the reception.

They drove the scenic route through the cheering crowds, and we went a back route to get to the yacht first. I wanted to check and be sure that all the Prince's clothing had arrived and was put in the order I wanted it. He'd left England in what he was dressed in, without taking a thing. I'd packed weeks before for the private fortnight, putting together swimming things and casual clothes, and sent the Prince's luggage on ahead. The yacht had sailed well before the wedding, so everything was already on board. It had been necessary to do this as the Andover is really too small to take a lot of suitcases. I always liked to send things ahead and just grab the personal things like toothbrushes, hair brushes, etc., at the last minute.

I must admit that as we sailed majestically through the Mediterranean, I occasionally had to pinch myself. Here I was, sharing the Royal honeymoon. Sometimes it didn't seem possible.

They were an enchanted fourteen days. I had little work to do. I didn't have to call the Prince in the mornings. For the first time in years he slept as long as he wanted. I merely had to wait for his bell to ring and then ask the steward to take in a cold breakfast and leave the trolley for them to serve themselves.

I did not have to wait for him to retire. He and the

Princess spent most of their evenings alone on the Royal deck, and we never knew at what time they went to bed.

Their quarters were very simple but comfortable and charming. Everything on the Royal deck is white with red upholstery and gray carpets. The Royal quarters consist of two bedrooms and a dressing room—the Princess used the Queen's bedroom as her dressing room for the trip. There is a large formal drawing room on the main deck, but they preferred to use the smaller, glassed-in sitting room above. This leads out to a verandah where they spent much of their time in the sunshine by day or in the cool air by evening.

The corridor joining the rooms is lined with drawings of previous Royal yachts. There is a lot of cane furniture that is heavy so it doesn't shift in a storm. They rarely used the main dining room, which also does duty as a mobile movie theater. They preferred intimate meals in their sitting room where they could serve themselves and not be overwhelmed by the size of a room that can seat forty people.

An escort vessel followed us some miles back and would catch up occasionally to deliver mail and private papers to the Prince. Other than that, we were alone on a wide, wide sea.

The Assistant Private Secretary, Francis Cornish, also came and went. We took him aboard from shore at various points. His role was to make sure that there would be no problems in the host countries we were passing, and he observed the formalities and courtesies to the other heads of state on behalf of the Prince.

We hugged the North African coast with its endless

deserted beaches and yellow mountains rising behind and never saw a soul. Every day the Admiral (there is always an Admiral aboard the Royal yacht) would visit the Prince and Princess in their quarters and show them on the charts exactly where we were. He would then make suggestions as to the best beaches—or islands, once we reached Greece—that would be pleasant and private enough on which to picnic.

Then a small boat would be sent out to make sure that the chosen spot was deserted, and if all was well, Charles and Diana would picnic ashore. The Prince loves to sunbathe and the Princess loves to swim, so they were both content. We all sunbathed and one day the Prince said to me, "You're getting browner than me." "Of course not, sir," I said. I was *never* browner than he! It wasn't politic.

We sailed past Morocco, Algeria, Tunisia, Italy, Greece, and on to the Suez Canal without seeing one native of those countries. The odd helicopter, completely ignored by the Prince, flew over trying to get pictures, but nobody succeeded. No one on board, except the official yacht photographer, and the Prince and Princess, had cameras. They had been banned. Everyone had been instructed to leave any photographic equipment at home.

The Princess spent a lot of time snapping away— mostly views and pictures of the Prince. Back in Scotland at the end of the honeymoon, she showed me the results.

"I'll never be a Lord Snowdon, will I?" she said.

Reluctantly I had to agree.

On board the Prince rarely came down from his

deck, but the Princess used to roam the boat, and we had a lot of fun. Sometimes in the evening we had barbecues ashore, but again, we never saw any of the locals. It seemed the world was deserted.

Sometimes at sea, the sailors would lower the steps and barges so we could all swim. The Princess would be swimming by herself in her bikini at one end of the yacht, while the crew swam at the other. The Prince didn't bother to go in. He was quite happy stretched out on the sundeck acquiring a splendid tan.

Of course, they were hardly alone. There were two hundred odd sailors aboard, plus naval officers, and when they did go ashore in the little boat to picnic, the policemen were always with them trying to keep a discreet distance.

The Princess enjoyed her honeymoon enormously, considering she had the crew of the yacht to contend with. She was in great form, giggling, running around in simple little sundresses over her bikinis.

One day she and the Prince made a formal tour of the entire yacht and showed themselves to everyone, but they did try to retain some privacy. They usually dined alone, and she always put on a pretty dress at night, then occasionally they would show a film after dinner and invite some of us to that.

They also watched videotapes of their wedding while they were on board. Both were fascinated with them.

"It's so marvelous to see all the bits you missed," the Prince said, and there were giggles over her gaffe where she got the Prince's names in the wrong order in the ceremony.

In Greece the Ward Room gave a barbecue for them

one night on a moonlit beach while the *Britannia* rode at anchor in the bay. The naval officers did all the preparation—getting the fires going, cooking the food. They had invited Mervin, the Royal chef, but he did not lift a finger. Like the rest of us, he was a guest.

They all swam, but the Princess noticed I was a bit slow getting into the water.

"You're still dry, Stephen," she said accusingly.

I was about to have my first Pimm's, but as if by Royal command two of the officers picked me up and chucked me in to peals of laughter from the Princess. She did have the grace to wade in and rescue my glass.

After we had eaten, a barge from the yacht came ashore and landed the accordionist from the Royal Marine Band. The officers then dished out song sheets and we all sat around the fire on the sand in the warm night for an impromptu singsong. It was mostly the old sing-along boy scout songs, and the Princess seemed to know the words and proved to have a very good voice, loud and clear. She and Evelyn, her dresser, were the only two women there, and they took the soprano roles, their voices ringing out into the blackness around us.

There were a lot of similar parties, and one lunchtime toward the end of the tour we, the Royal Staff, decided to give a Pimm's party for some of the crew. I was in the kitchen with Mervin, preparing lots of fruit for the punch when the Princess popped her head around the door.

"What's going on?" she asked.

"We're having a Pimm's party," I told her. "We've been so well looked after by all the different messes.

We're going to ask representatives from all of them to join us."

"Oh," she said, "that sounds like fun. Can I come?"

We let it be known that that was fine, but in a gentle way we made it clear we didn't think it would be a good idea if the Prince came, too. The party would have immediately taken on a formal tone, and his presence would have changed the atmosphere completely. Everyone would have had to be on his best behavior. "Oh, all right," she said and came on her own. I have no doubt that the Prince knew what she was up to, but he wouldn't have minded in the least as long as she was happy.

I must say she helped to make our party a great success. Without telling anyone exactly what we were doing, we'd invited a mixed bag of crew from the Admiral down to representatives from the stokers' mess; I think the Admiral was a bit surprised to find the stokers there. The stokers were even more surprised to see the Admiral. The Navy has as much protocol in its own way as the Royals, so that someone might have gotten stuffy, but the Princess saved the day. When officers and ratings arrived and found her there they were all thrilled, if somewhat surprised. But everyone immediately relaxed. She has the gift of making people relax and no one felt he had to be on his best behavior. She was great fun—in fact "fun" is one of her favorite words.

"I'm going to talk to the stokers," she said, grabbing a jug of Pimm's. The stokers drank the Pimm's as she was the one pouring it but kept sidling up and asking if there were any beer or lager. Interestingly,

the Princess seemed to be more at ease with the ratings who were more or less her own age.

John Maclean, Graham Smith, the Princess' policeman, and I were going to the crew's quarters one day,
just to say hello, when we bumped into her. She had
been to see the chef to arrange the day's meals.
"Where are you three off to?" she asked, obviously
looking for something to do. When we told her she
said, "That sounds like fun. I'll come, too."

The sailors went mad when they saw her. A great
cheer went up, and she dived into the crowd and was
chatting away. Everyone had politely gotten to their
feet.

"Oh, do sit down," she said. While standing, the
crush of bodies had hidden the mess piano. "A piano!" she said. "You've got a piano. Who plays?"

No one volunteered, but some brave soul shouted,
"Give us a tune."

"All right," she said, grinned, sat down, and gave
a near faultless rendering of "Greensleeves," accompanied by the none-too-sweet voices of thirty or so
ratings. Everyone was having a great time, but the
Petty Officers got wind of her being there, appeared,
and gently guided her upstairs again.

"Oh, all right," she said, but went quietly.

Her disappearance was a great disappointment to
the sailors. While she had been in their mess, the bar
had been kept open in her honor.

Though she loved company and enjoyed exploring
the yacht, she was also very happy to be alone with
the Prince. There is a good stereo system on the
yacht, and I'd packed all their favorite tapes to take
along as the ones kept on board are mostly military

music. She loves Elton John and Supertramp and the Beach Boys. He likes Donna Summer and Barbra Streisand, as well as classical music.

She busied herself in the morning discussing menus with the chef at the Royal galley where their meals were prepared. As the weather was so glorious, most of the food they ate was cold. They served themselves from trolleys and the stewards cleared away afterwards. Ice cream was always on the menu. They both loved it and the Royal deep-freeze looked like the freezer of an ice cream shop.

The voyage truly was a rest for all of us. The only official engagement that they had was dinner with President Sadat and his wife in Egypt. The Sadats came on board at Port Said and the Prince got yet another box as a wedding present. There was more jewelry for the Princess. It was a very private dinner—just the four of them in the big dining room of the yacht —at which they achieved a real rapport, which made Charles and Diana's grief three months later that much more poignant.

On the last night at sea we had the ship's concert on the fo'c'sle. For days rehearsals had been going on all over the yacht, curtains put up and lighting arranged. The cruise was nearly all over. But it was going to end in style.

There were at least fourteen acts—from stand-up comics to impersonations of two famous English comedians.

One large sailor was dressed up as Lady Diana, in her kindergarten teacher days, and made rather salty jokes. She thought it all rather funny. Graham, John, and I, plus two members of the household who had

arrived aboard, did a routine to "We Are Sailing."
We changed the words to "We Are Loafing"—
around the Med for two weeks and thank you very
much. We were dressed in swimming trunks, T-
shirts, and flippers, and were a total surprise as we
weren't on the program.

Evelyn, the only other woman on board, came on in
her bikini, carrying a large cue card for our invented
words to Rod Stewart's song. The board covered her
from chin to thigh, effectively making her look naked.
We needn't have bothered rehearsing. As soon as the
sailors saw her legs the uproar drowned anything we
were singing.

Afterwards at a party in the wardroom, the Prince
said to me, "How long were you rehearsing? I noticed
you were out of step."

We finished up after a tour of the messes in the
Equerry's quarters where we'd retreated for an un-
needed nightcap. The Princess came by, peeerd in
and said, "My God! You're all high as kites," and
went off giggling.

Well, it was the last night.

The next morning we left the ship and said good-
bye at Hurghada in Egypt near the Red Sea. The sailors lined the decks, saluted, and gave three cheers as
we all came down the gangplank. From there we flew
back to Lossiemouth in Scotland on a VC 10 while the
yacht sailed on to Australia, where she was to meet
the Queen who was going there to attend a Commonwealth Conference.

The entire Royal party was on the same plane, but
we did not see much of the Prince and Princess. They

stayed in their section and we were in ours. No one was invited to join him for meals as had often happened before the wedding. It was the first sign of changes to come.

I went off on a private holiday to the south of France while the Prince and Princess spent the next few weeks at Balmoral. Then I returned to work and Scotland. It all seemed very tame. By then they were staying at Craigowan, where the Prince spent most of the time stalking or walking with the Princess.

He and the Princess gave a very special barbecue for his staff at the end of the honeymoon in October 1981. We were at Craigowan, and we drove about ten miles to a log cabin on the Balmoral estate. We took a big barbecue in the Duke's specially designed trailer.

The Prince set up the barbecue and got it going. We weren't allowed to do anything. The Princess, who doesn't drink, dispensed lethal cocktails quite unaware of their strength.

There was just a rough table and long benches in the cabin, and the Princess set the table and we all sat around after the meal discussing my future. It was common knowledge by then that I was leaving.

Someone suggested I go into show business.

"I don't want to work too hard," I said.

"I know that," the Princess said, and giggled. "Why don't you read the weather? It only takes two minutes a day."

It was a very special evening. Outside night had fallen, and it was freezing cold. The heat from the burning charcoal kept us warm, and we sat talking

257

and laughing until after midnight. Before we left in three Land Rovers, the Prince thanked us all for helping make the Scottish part of his honeymoon so successful.

∽ 17 ∽

Lady of the House

THE PRINCESS was happier at Craigowan as she was out of the Royal system and could run the house. I didn't seem to have anything to do until their honeymoon was interrupted with the sad news of President Sadat's assassination.

There was a brief flurry of activity while he and I came and went to the funeral in the space of two days, and it was when we returned that I decided to give my six-months' notice.

I never had a qualm about the decision. During that six months I realized more and more that I had done the right thing. Nothing was ever going to be quite the same again.

Now Kensington Palace is the Prince's base, but most of the time he lives at Highgrove. He and she have become country people and it's understandable. There is no privacy in London, whereas in the country they can open their own door and go out into the sunshine on their own grounds.

Highgrove is not an enormous house. There is no parkland—just a few fields around—but the house itself is big enough for a nanny and a baby. In fact, the old nursery quarters were ready and waiting for their first child. The Prince had left them as a nursery as it was inevitable they would be used again one day.

And undoubtedly she will have more children. The Princess seemed to like being pregnant—unlike Princess Anne, who finds it a great bore because it restricts her activities. As the Princess of Wales doesn't hunt or ride, pregnancy makes no restrictions on her life-style.

She is very much her own person. She doesn't like horses, nor a lot of the people associated with them. Show jumping and hunting simply don't interest her. I remember one Monday at Highgrove, they'd just sat down to lunch and the Beaufort hunt came through the garden, literally in front of the dining room windows. In a flash the Prince was out of his chair and through the front door to watch them. I was upstairs in his room, making sure everything was tidy when I spotted him on the lawn chatting to Mrs. Gerald Ward, an old friend and one whom the gossip columnists suggested had a lot of influence on him. When I got back downstairs the Princess had come through the kitchen to ask for the food to be kept warm and she seemed very irritated.

The Prince wasn't mad about hunting, but now it is his dominant passion. Maybe she'll learn to like hunting and horses, too. I can remember when we used to go to Royal Ascot and the Prince hated every moment of it. In the Royal Box there is a little sitting room and he'd spend his afternoon in there with the Duke of Edinburgh, who still dislikes racing. I used to take the Prince's briefcase and he'd pass the time writing his letters. Today you can't drag him from a race course.

Another thing the Princess doesn't care for is the opera. She's mad about ballet. He loves opera, but he's not mad about ballet.

She came to a couple of the opera parties that he likes to give in the Royal Box for his friends in the early days when they met but she was bored stiff.

The Prince's opera guests tend to be on the intellectual side. I remember the Princess said to me once when she heard how many O levels (university examinations) her dresser, Evelyn, had passed—eight altogether—"How many do you think I've got?"

"I've no idea," I said.

"Two," she said, pulling a schoolgirl face.

"You've done very well on two O levels, marrying the Prince of Wales," I told her.

The Prince did try to go to the ballet with her a couple of times, but he spent more time nodding off in the Royal Box than watching.

She doesn't mind shooting, but she was absolutely furious about the story that she had shot a deer, not killed it properly, and fainted. She had merely been out for the day with a ghillie, and as a country girl she is quite used to blood sports.

The story came out on a Saturday, and it ruined the Prince's Sunday. He spent the day on the phone, taking advice from his Press Office on how to handle it. In the end he decided not to deny the story. It was thought best just to let it fade away.

I still believe the Princess is trying to retain some of her own identity, which is not simple if you marry a Royal. It's very easy to be submerged and become thoroughly miserable. So I think she is quite right to refuse to do things she dislikes while leaving the Prince his own freedom of movement. He still does what he wishes and goes where he likes. For example, he loves Barry Humphries (an Australian female impersonator) and I said to her one day, "Are you going to see Barry Humphries as Dame Edna with the Prince?"

"Dame Edna," she said, "is an acquired taste. No, I am not going."

The Prince does like older people. Many of his friends are considerably older than he is; he finds them interesting because he is always interested in learning, and he is also fascinated by success and ability.

In January 1982, just before I left his service, we went down to Althorpe, the Princess' family house. We were to stay with her father, the Earl of Spencer, just for two nights so that the estate workers and tenant farmers could hand over their wedding gift. The presentation was taking place a little belatedly as the Princess hadn't had time to get to Althorpe until then.

Althorpe was something of a surprise; it was so much grander than its royal neighbor, Sandringham, which is a very simple home. We stayed in the Prince of Wales suite, where other Princes of Wales have stayed down through the years. We arrived on a Friday and went straight to the candlelit picture gallery, where the Princess' ancestors line the walls. It was full of tenant farmers and estate workers, and a check from the estate was handed over to go toward the swimming pool that was being built at Highgrove. While the speeches were being made, the sound of hammering could be heard outside. Alas, the wedding cake, made six months earlier, was now rock hard. The butler's attempts with a knife failed, and he took stronger action with a rolling pin.

I went into their bedroom mid-morning to find the curtains blowing wildly. As the windows were sealed I was a bit surprised until I realized there was a broken window.

"There's a broken pane," I said to the Princess.

"Yes," she said, her face very innocent. "It was an accident. There was no air in here."

I just laughed.

It was a very interesting weekend. The house is very splendid and the Countess a remarkable lady. There is not a great deal of love lost between the Princess and her stepmother—their relationship is a mutual toleration. But the Prince liked the Countess of Spencer. She is a very clever woman, who looks, lives, and loves the role. She is probably unpopular for being so good at being a countess. In the end I could see the Princess getting very uneasy as Prince Charles was enjoying her stepmother's conversation, and eventually she made an excuse to get him away.

That weekend it seemed that the Spencers live in far grander style than the Royals. A pianist had been brought from the Savoy for the occasion (poor man came on the wrong night and had to come again).

They dined with silver and candles (the Countess enjoys using candles) and they all dressed. The Countess is well groomed from the crack of dawn to late at night with never a hair out of place, and I wonder if the Princess tolerates her because she did nurse the Earl through a very bad stroke and virtually brought him back to life. She adores her father and therefore has respect for his choice of wife.

But I doubt if she and the Prince will be spending very much time at Althorpe.

~ 18 ~

A Difficult Decision

WE HAD RETURNED from the honeymoon after fourteen glorious days on the Royal yacht, *Britannia*, cruising the Mediterranean. Then we went to Scotland for the remainder of the honeymoon, and it seemed to me that we were there for weeks. I just sat and thought, "I'm not really interested in the job anymore."

It was beginning to dawn on me that now the Prince was married there was so much less for me to do. Many of my tasks were being taken over by the Princess' staff and because the Prince's household was expanding there were more people employed. Also, it was most natural that the Princess of Wales had herself taken over many of the small duties that I used to perform for her husband in his bachelor days.

I no longer had to call him in the mornings and bring in his breakfast. I no longer arranged the menus for the day. I no longer chose the suit, shirt, tie, shoes to put out before he dressed for the day's engagements.

There were many small things that were no longer my responsibility, and I was beginning to feel superfluous. Where once I had always been on call, now I saw him only midmornings when I took in his mail and sometimes briefly in the evenings when he was changing to go out.

The chief reason for my resignation was that circumstances had changed, and I must make it clear that I was leaving the Royal household on the best of terms. People found this hard to believe and it seemed as if everyone I knew had said, agog, "Did you have a row with her?"

I did not have a row with Princess Diana. Nothing of the kind happened. In fact we weren't close enough to quarrel, although when she first met the Prince I had been very much on the scene. I would nod to her approvingly if she were doing the right thing; cough gently if it looked as if she were about to put a wrong foot forward. And she picked up my signals amazingly quickly. She never made a mistake.

But then she had an instinctive understanding of Prince Charles. The only time that I perhaps needed to slightly raise an eyebrow was when she wanted to giggle and he wanted to be quiet. The Prince needs periods of silence. Then Diana would quickly pick up a book or the tapestry work she loves to do and sit silent herself. Right from the very beginning it was obvious that she cared about him deeply, so I had made it my duty to help her.

I handed in my resignation as valet to Prince Charles in the middle of October 1981, just after I had accompanied the Prince to President Sadat's funeral in Cairo. The reason that I had given the Prince, to whom I had been valet for twelve absorbing years, was that I did not want to travel any more, having traveled many, many thousands of miles with him.

Although this was quite true, there were other reasons as well. Some of these reasons I felt I could not discuss with him without sounding disloyal, although we had shared a remarkably uncomplicated master and servant relationship for so long.

The Prince and Princess wanted to live most of the time at Highgrove, their country home. I love life in the city and enjoyed my rooms in Buckingham Palace, where I looked out onto the forty acres of Royal gardens.

I knew I couldn't face spending nearly all my time at Highgrove so it seemed the appropriate moment to say farewell. I would never had resigned while the Prince was single—there would have been no reason to do so. But now he was a married man, and with less need of someone like me around, it seemed a good idea to go. In addition, I felt that I was still young enough to learn to do something else but a few more years in Royal service could have made it difficult for me to find other employment.

Therefore I decided to resign.

I went to see the Prince in his sitting room at Craigowan House in Balmoral one evening in October when the Princess had gone to London. I could tell by his face that he knew exactly what I was going to say. After so long, he knew me as well as I knew him.

We'd both gone through tremendous changes. He was giving up his bachelorhood, and I was finding it difficult to work for a married man. He certainly would have sensed my restlessness.

"Sit down, Stephen," he said. "Would you like a drink?"

"No, thank you, sir," I said, but sat down and with some difficulty started to tell him that I was leaving. He listened, his face serious, and then said, "Are you absolutely sure?"

"Yes, Your Royal Highness," I said, deliberately being formal.

He looked at me questioningly and then said, "Why don't you go away and think about it?"

Well, I went away and I thought. But I didn't change my mind.

Twelve years of chasing around the world had been enough. Sometimes the circumstances had been dangerous and uncomfortable; more often we traveled in great luxury and style. The pressures had always been great. In the year just past there had been the excitement of the buildup to the wedding and finally the honeymoon itself. There was no way that any of those experiences could ever be bettered. Because of the Prince, my life had been one long treat.

We were both the same age. We almost grew up together, though always as master and servant, so resigning was not easy. I had been in such a privileged position with enormous access to the man who will one day be King. I had been with him for so long that I almost knew what he was thinking. I often knew what he wanted even before he asked for it. But then that was what I was paid to do.

I felt that I should tell the Princess of my decision myself. The opportunity came on the following Saturday when the Prince was out stalking and the Princess and I were in the kitchen having some lunch. At Craigowan, lunch was always informal. Unless there were guests we helped ourselves to food, usually straight from the fridge.

The Princess was standing leaning against the kitchen table, eating one of her favorite yogurts. I had made a bacon sandwich for myself.

"Has the Prince mentioned that I'm leaving his service?" I asked.

She grinned and said, "Y-e-s" rather doubtfully, then added, "People will say we've had a terrible row!"

"As long as we know we haven't, that's all right, isn't it?" I said.

She nodded and took a spoonful of yogurt.

"When do you plan to leave?" she asked.

"Not until April," I said. "That should allow plenty of time."

"Right," she said, ending the conversation by putting down the container of yogurt. "Well, I'm off for my walk."

I think that perhaps she was a little relieved. Others who had been with the Prince for years were going; his staff was changing. It's quite reasonable and not surprising that anyone as young as Princess Diana would want to be surrounded by people of her own choice. Understandably she would not wish to have around herself and her husband those who had known him at earlier times when there were other girl friends, long before she came into his life.

The realities of being Royal don't seem to hold any fears for her. But what will she make of the drudgery of a Royal tour, I wonder? That experience planned for the spring of 1982 in New Zealand was postponed because of the baby, a postponement that caused much consternation in the Prince's office at the Palace as all the arrangements had been made and had to be canceled.

It was this sudden alteration of plans that made all of us who were close to the Prince believe that the Royal couple had not planned to have a baby so quickly. Prince Charles is far too considerate to have given his staff so much work if he had intended to start a family right away. And the tour itself would have had so much more impact if they had arrived as newlyweds rather than a young married couple.

But none of us were particularly surprised. Almost the most positive character trait that the Princess of Wales has is her love of children.

The day the Princess of Wales announced that she was pregnant Prince Charles said to me, "Well, you won't have to rush off now, will you? You can stay on for a bit."

We were in his sitting room at Buckingham Palace. I had gone in to congratulate him on the news and standing in front of him, I hesitated only momentarily.

"No," I said. "I think I'll stick to my six-months' notice, sir, if you don't mind."

He half-shrugged, looked as if he might have said something more and then said, "Whatever you want to do, Stephen."

I left the Prince's sitting room in BP (as we always call Buckingham Palace) and met the Princess outside in the corridor. There are some extra wardrobes there for his clothes, and she was selecting a dress to wear for the Guildhall lunch that day.

"Congratulations, Ma'am," I said, and she beamed at me, patted her midriff and said, "Isn't it lovely! I want lots of babies."

She was rightly very pleased.

⤎ *19* ⤏

Good-byes

AFTER I RESIGNED from the Prince's service in October 1981, I stayed on working with him for my full six-months' notice period for very valid reasons—I wanted to train my successor properly, and if I had left immediately it would only have added fuel to the rumors that I had been fired.

However, I discovered that long good-byes are not really a good idea. People kept asking me, "When are you going?" or "Are you *really* going?" and the new staff naturally wanted to plant their feet solidly under the table. It was all a bit uncomfortable.

The Prince was marvelous through my last six months. He was concerned about my future, and our relationship subtly changed. With my successor taking over most of my duties I had more free time, and some mornings after breakfast he'd call me into the study and ask me to sit for a while. Then he'd talk. This was unusual. In the past it had been rare to sit in his presence.

He needed to get quite a lot of information from me. For years I had looked after his private papers, cataloged his photograph collection, and turned his books into a library. He had come to depend on me to find him anything he needed. I knew where everything was. Whilst I was handing over his clothes and possessions to my successors, I was handing him back his more personal things.

Always cautious, he would not have wanted me to pass these on to someone he really didn't yet know.

It was intended that I would leave on April 1. When the significance of the date sank in, he laughed and said, "Better not go on April Fool's Day. Leave on the second." And I did.

Saying good-bye to my lovely rooms at Buckingham Palace, which I'd furnished with my own things and where I'd lived for fourteen years, could have been a wrench. But there was a reason why leaving was nowhere near as painful as it might have been. Over the years, at my request, the Prince had always given me a small picture for a Christmas present. The Christmas of 1978 he said to me, "Where are you hanging all these pictures?"

"By now, in the cupboard," I said.

He laughed, "In that case I'll have to build you another wall."

The wall, in fact, turned out to be the lease of a beautiful two-bedroom flat on the Duchy of Cornwall's estate in Kensington, London S.E. I've been using this as often as I can ever since. Therefore packing up my rooms at the Palace was painless because I had a home to go to, just a short drive away.

Had I stayed in his service, I wouldn't have kept my Buckingham Palace rooms anyway. The Prince and Princess were moving to their new apartments at Kensington Palace—and coping with a much larger packing problem than mine!

During those last months life was quiet. The Princess was at a difficult stage of her pregnancy, and we spent most of the time in the country at Highgrove. The Prince cut down on his hunting activities to be with her. She had morning sickness very badly—and not only in the mornings. She often felt low and he was very caring of her.

She had completely lost her enthusiasm for shopping, and so I purchased all the Christmas presents for the Prince as usual. The Princess was very efficient about getting the presents for her own family and the Royal children, but feeling unwell she shopped from glossy catalogs. She bought lots of woolly garments for the children, and I spent cheerful days wrapping endless presents for them both.

That last Christmas with him was a good one. Every year he takes his staff for a special Christmas lunch somewhere unusual. We'd been to the Tower of London, the Bank of England, the House of Lords, down the river on a barge, to his own bank, Coutts, and once to Scotland Yard. After the meal we would be taken on a tour to see how everything worked.

He decided on this first Christmas after his marriage, that as so many of his staff were intrigued to see what his new home at Kensington Palace was like, he would give a "Bare-Rooms" Party in the half-decorated apartment.

By the time we arrived, the rooms didn't look bare at all. Lyons had waved their catering wand and transformed the place. We had a buffet meal, and afterwards some of the girls from his office asked me to show them around as I knew the rooms.

We were going one way, and we met the Prince coming the other way with his own group.

"Your tour first," he said, letting us go past.

At that time, the walls only had an undercoat of paint and the L-shaped apartments had no furniture. Now everything is beautifully decorated with wallpaper with the Prince of Wales feathers woven into the fabric.

I had Christmas off, but I joined the Prince and Princess in Sandringham for New Year's. All the usual Royals were there, but with the Princess as an added member of the family. She wasn't well and spent most of the time resting. She certainly wasn't feeling up to going out on the shoots. It was a quiet New Year's Eve for everyone.

One evening wasn't so tranquil. Sandringham is built on different levels and sound seemingly travels down chimneys. One morning just after New Year's, the Princess said to me,

"Were you upstairs last night?"

"Yes," I said.

"I thought I heard your laughter," she said cryptically. She didn't seem annoyed, but I thought I should explain.

"I'd been with the pages," I said. "We were having a nightcap and a gossip."

276

"I see," she said.

Later in the morning, I saw the Prince in his bedroom. He was sitting at his desk, and I thought I'd sort things out.

"Sir, I gather from the Princess that you could hear us last night. I hope we didn't disturb you too much."

He looked up and said, "It's all right. It was just that the Princess couldn't get to sleep so we had to come in here. It was too cold, so we went back to her room."

"Oh, dear," I said. "I hope we didn't ruin your night."

"No," he said. "It's all right. It wasn't that lute."

I was making sure his rooms were in order during the afternoon when I spotted something on the bedside table.

"What are those?" I asked the maid.

She roared with laughter.

"Earplugs," she told me.

We spent the rest of the Sandringham visit whispering when we had a nightcap. The difference was that nothing ever woke the Prince, but Princess Diana is a very light sleeper.

The day finally dawned when I was actually leaving. We had returned to the Palace and everything carried on as normal. I knew the Prince was leaving that night on the Royal train for Liverpool so I wouldn't see him in the morning. Then at 7:00 in the evening he rang for me. I went into his study and I found him standing in the middle of the room.

"Close the door," he said. I did. "Do sit down," he

indicated the sofa, and I sat while he settled down in his own yellow armchair.

"I suddenly remembered you're going tomorrow," he said.

"That's right, sir," I said, nodding.

I felt strange. I'd seen other people say good-bye to him, and now it was my turn. I knew how they must have felt. It was curious to think I was in his company for probably the last time when I had spent so much of my life in his presence. I had known him better than anyone else at the Palace. For me his character, his mannerisms, his likes and dislikes were more familiar than those of some of my own family.

Yet because the concept of Royalty is unique, and still shrouded in a certain kind of mystery, he is unique. Therefore, though I had had insight into the mind of the man, even after all those years there was still a barrier between us—a barrier of respect.

He asked, "Is everything sorted out about your future?"

"I hope so, sir," I said. "I'm off to learn public relations at Turnbull and Asser."

"I'll come to buy lots of shirts off you," he said. There was a silence, then he said, "It's been a long time, hasn't it?"

"It seems to have gone very quickly," I told him. Then I was silent. There was so much to thank him for—all the travels, which were an education in themselves. The exposure to beautiful things—music, pictures, fine furniture, learning about the countryside, food, and wines.

Working for the Prince had been the best possible

finishing school in the world. I knew how fortunate I had been. But I didn't know how to tell him.

"How many Independencies did you do with me?" he asked.

"Four, sir," I said.

"And funerals?"

"Four."

"Haven't I spent a lot of time in planes?" he said thoughtfully.

"A lot indeed," I half-smiled.

"And all those uniforms. It doesn't seem to have left you careworn."

He knew the thought of getting something wrong on the uniforms always put the fear of God into me.

"I was never happy until you got back and everything was still in place and no one had complained," I said.

He laughed Then he said, his face turning serious, "Is everything all right? You will keep the flat, won't you?"

"Oh, yes," I said and thanked him with real sincerity for what was a truly generous gesture.

He waved away my thanks and then took two boxes from a small table.

"Just a little memento," he said, handing me the smaller of the two. I opened the suede leather box while he watched. Inside was a piece of silver that he had had specially made at Wartski's. It was a paper knife with the Prince of Wales feathers engraved in gold and set into the handle.

"And this is from both of us," he said, giving me the second present. It was my favorite photograph of him and the Princess—the one that had been taken on

279

their honeymoon in Scotland. It was placed in a green leather frame with the Prince of Wales feathers in gold at the top. Both of them had signed it.

I thanked him then, feeling more than a little choked up. By this time we were both standing and the audience, so to speak, was over, and suddenly, the formality disappeared. We were both back in our normal routine.

"What time do I leave?" he asked, looking at his watch.

"Ten o'clock, sir," I told him, bowed and left the room.

I saw him once more that evening. He and the Princess were leaving for the station. As I was escorting them out of the Palace, he turned around and said, "Stephen, take care of yourself and don't hesitate to get in touch if you need anything."

"Thank you, Your Royal Highness," I said.

"Good-night," he said. She gave me a little nod, and they climbed into the car and left.

I haven't seen him since.

I made my own departure the next afternoon. Royal staff have a saying that you arrive at Buckingham Palace in your school blazer, minus the badge, with your best Sunday suit on a wire hanger, and you leave with trunksful of clothes and possessions.

Mine had been shifted gradually over the past six months, so after a staff party and the presentation of a beautiful tray, I slipped out of the side door quietly for the last time. I drove off in the Prince's estate car that he had loaned me to tide me over until I got one of my own. Royal service was all over.

Epilogue

Do I miss the life, people ask me.

The short answer is both yes and no.

I miss being looked after. I looked after the Prince, but others looked after me. Maids cleaned my room, laundry was sent and delivered back twice a week, the garage looked after the car I used.

I miss the private Post Office where one never had to queue, and the banking facilities that were provided for twenty-four hours a day. I miss the food. Our senior staff dining room was like a St. James club, a room lined with paintings of horses, and a staff bar with subsidized drinks. We could use this as an off license, too. If I wanted a bottle of gin or wine in my rooms I sent down for it.

What I don't miss is the constant, relentless travel, and the living out of suitcases all the time.

We were always on the move.

The work, too, was not easy. A lot harder than it might seem to people outside. I worked what a trade union would call unsociable hours and lived in so many different places. I missed my friends a lot.

Naturally enough, the truth is, I miss the perks of the job, but not the duties.

I did have to adjust to the outside world. I've discovered about banking hours. I know where the supermarket is and how McDonald's hamburgers taste. It is so easy to be trapped in the Royal life-style. There are older people at the Palace who had come to depend on it totally.

One changes as one gets older, and I did want to settle down. But nevertheless, twelve years of Royal service with Prince Charles was an extraordinary privilege and gave me enormous opportunities in every imaginable way.

I consider I have been a very lucky man.